Unleashed

Unleashed

Lois Greiman

This is a work of fiction. Names, characters, places, and incidents are either products of the writer's imagination or are used fictitiously and are not to be construed as real. Any resemblance to actual events, locales, organizations, or persons, living or dead, is entirely coincidental.

ISBN: 9781535258265

NYLA Publishing
350 7th Avenue, Suite 2003, NY 10001, New York.
http://www.nyliterary.com

Praise for Lois Greiman

"Dangerously funny stuff."

Janet Evanovich

"Simple sexy sport may be just what the doctor ordered."

Publishers Weekly

"Lois Greiman is a modern day Dorothy Sayers. Witty as hell, yet talented enough to write like an angel with a broken wing."

Kinky Friedman, author of Ten Little New Yorkers

"What a marvelous book! A delightful romp, a laugh on every page."

MaryJanice Davidson, NYT bestselling author of the Undead series.

"Amazingly good." (Top Pick!)

Romantic Times

"L.A. psychologist, Chrissy McMullen is back to prove that boobs, brass, and brains make for one heck of a good time ... laugh out loud funny ... sassy ... clever."

Mystery Scene

"Excellent!"

Library Journal

"Sexy, sassy, suspenseful, sensational!! Lois Greiman delivers with incomparable style."

Bestselling author of To the Edge, Cindy Gerard

"Move over Stephanie Plum and Bubbles Yablonsky to make way for Christina McMullen, the newest blue collar sexy professional woman who finds herself in hair raising predicaments that almost get her murdered. The chemistry between the psychologist and the police lieutenant is so hot that readers will see sparks fly off the pages. Lois Greiman, who has written over fifteen delightful romance books, appears to have a great career as a mystery writer also."

thebestreviews.com

"Ms. Greiman makes a giant leap from historical fiction to this sexy and funny mystery. Bravo! Well done!"

Rendevous

"A fun mystery that will keep you interested and rooting for the characters until the last page is turned."

Fresh Fiction

"Fast and fun with twists and turns that will keep you guessing. Enjoy the ride!"

Suzanne Enoch, USA Today best-selling author of Flirting with Danger

"Lucy Ricardo meets Dr. Frasier Crane in Lois Greiman's humorous, suspenseful series. The result is a highly successful tongue-in-cheek, comical suspense guaranteed to entice and entertain."

Book Loons

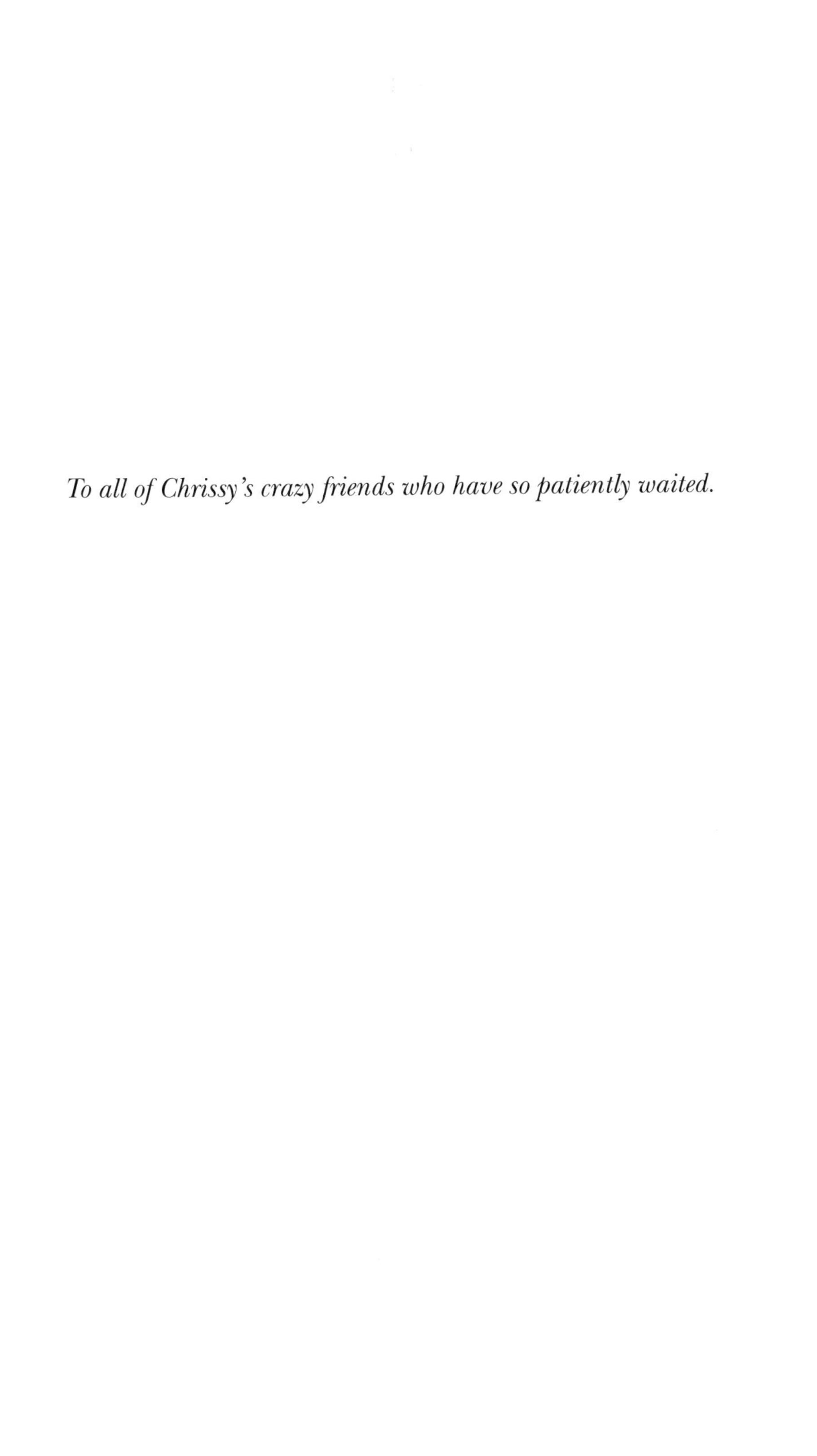

To all of Chrissy's crazy friends who have so patiently waited.

CHAPTER 1

You're pretty, you're skinny, and you're nice. But I think we can still be friends.

—Christina McMullen, following a flare-up of teenage angst and a buttload of chocolate mousse

"How's the unborn?" I asked. My best friend since fifth grade, Brainy Laney Butterfield, was due to give birth to a baby girl in a matter of weeks. In fact, months ago, she'd named the adorable little zygote Tina, after *moi.*

"What's wrong?" Laney's voice was terse, steady, and take-no-prisoners focused, though we hadn't, as of yet, exchanged more than the vaguest of cell phone pleasantries.

"What? Nothing. I was just calling to see—"

"Are you okay?"

I laughed. "Of course I'm okay. I'm better than okay. In fact, my life's fantastic."

Silence.

"If things were any better it would be forbidden by California statute 3021–2304 to be Christina McMullen. PhD," I added, just to make sure she remembered that I was, in fact, well educated and hopelessly euphoric.

"What's going on?" Judging by her tone, she wasn't buying the euphoria segment of my proclamation, but it's not as if Elaine Butterfield, better known to the television-viewing masses as Hippolyta, Amazon queen, was psychic or anything. She could probably just guess at my current state because we've been bonding over dreamy guys and hokey movies since time out of mind.

"I have a date." My voice was chipper as hell, like a Laker Girl on a helium high.

"A date?" She'd gone from terse to suspicious. In the big scheme of things, I preferred the former. "With Rivera, right?"

I turned off the 170 and zipped onto Riverside Drive. My car has about ten million miles on it, but it still runs like a champ... or like a seriously outdated Saturn, kind of bumpy and a little whiny but still moving. At my seasoned-but-unsullied age, I've realized that it does no good to allow your expectations to become too lofty.

Speaking of expectations, I was wearing a silky lavender skirt topped with an ivory cap-sleeve blouse. Manolo sling-backs adorned my feet. They were a sassy little pair, even if they were secondhand. The ensemble hinted of class and whispered of sexy. Or maybe it screamed that I was holding on to hope by my well-manicured fingernails. *"Who?"* I asked.

"Rivera," she repeated dryly. "Is your date with Rivera?"

Jack Rivera and I had been running hot and cold and crazy all over for a couple of lifetimes. He's a cop. I'm a psychologist. He lives in Simi, where the neighborhood kids play ball on manicured lawns. I live in Sunland with a lone cactus and neighbors who probably wish I would move to Tibet... or at least install a sprinkler system. But irrigation systems are environmentally detrimental... and expensive.

"You mean that relatively attractive police officer I socialized with for a short while?" I asked.

"Yes," she said, then spoke quietly to someone nearby. He was probably male, ungodly handsome, and wonderfully obsequious. Laney attracts that kind of guy like masochists draw sadists. And I should know. I'm a psychologist, remember?

"We had a long-overdue colloquy," I said.

"Holy moly. A *colloquy*?" Suspicion had morphed into an arid sort of what-the-hell-are-you-yammering-about tone, but Laney had been swearing off swearing for a long time. Now, with mommyhood impending, her phraseology had become increasingly G-rated. If I weren't so fucking sophisticated, I would have enjoyed the shit out of mocking her.

"Yes. It was all extremely civilized.

There was a stunted silence. I would say it was fraught with disbelief, but I've never been entirely sure what *fraught* means, despite my aforementioned education.

"We're still discussing Rivera, right?"

I smiled with genteel tranquility. "Yes."

"And you," she added.

The jacaranda trees were beginning to bloom, thrusting out their purple trumpet flowers with Seuss-like surrealism. I used the calming beauty of nature to nurture my inner Zen. "Listen, Laney, I'll admit that in the past I may have acted somewhat..." I considered, then subsequently discarded, several terms, one of which might have been *batshit crazy*, and continued on. "Irrationally where the dark lieutenant is concerned, but—"

"Irrationally? I believe Captain Kindred was called in to mediate on more than one occasion."

It was true that I had a somewhat fractious relationship with Rivera's commanding officer, but I didn't see a need to address that just then. "As I was saying...things have changed."

"So I don't have to notify the paramedics?"

I held on to the smile. "I can't tell you how relieved I am to know you haven't lost your stellar sense of humor."

She ignored my sarcasm with well-practiced aplomb. "Tell me now if I have to call an ambulance; I'm due on set in five minutes. We're shooting..." She gasped softly, as if struck by a terrifying thought. "I don't have to call the morgue, do I, Mac?"

"You just get funnier and funnier."

"Must be the clean air out here."

Due to Laney's delicate condition, the powers that be had moved the production from New Zealand to Idaho, so as to continue the queen's questionable adventures practically up to the moment of parturition. I worried that she was working too hard, but at least she wouldn't have to board a plane to return to L.A. for the birth.

Personally, I think anyone who intentionally brings another squalling Homo sapiens into the world must be a couple rungs short of a full ladder. But diplomacy suggested I keep that information to myself.

"I can assure you that not a single drop of blood was shed."

"Strangulation, then?" she asked.

"You're hilarious."

"You didn't poison him, did you?" Then, to Mr. Handsome, who I could picture perfectly with my extremely fertile imagination, she said, "I'll be right there."

"This may surprise you, Laney," I said, breaking out the terminally snooty tone I had been holding in reserve, "but we didn't even raise our voices."

"That *does* surprise me." She sounded impressed and, I thought, more than a little dubious.

"We came to a mutually agreeable decision." My hands tightened on the steering wheel, but I convinced myself to relax, employing one of the many techniques I learned at a recent symposium given by Dr. Bram Dirkx, a genius in the field of schizophrenia. I was operating on the theory that if his methods were effective with psychopaths they would probably work for me.

"You're certain you were talking to the right Rivera?" she asked.

I pursed my lips and a couple other sphincters. "Yes," I said. "And we decided it would be best for all parties concerned if we discontinued our..." I thought hard, trying to disavow a hundred lewd memories that involved a scantily clad Rivera. Those lean-muscled hips, those dark, do-me eyes. My fingers were beginning to hurt, convincing me to loosen my grip. "Our romantic relationship. That doesn't, of course, preclude the possibility of us remaining platonic friends."

The phone went silent for several beats. "You and Rivera," she said again. Dubious may have stretched into the land of are-you-nucking-futs.

I narrowed my eyes and tapped an index finger against the Saturn's unoffending steering wheel as I turned sedately onto Camarillo Street. "Yes," I said, voice rising just a little. "We're—"

"I'm sorry to bother you, Ms. Ruocco," Mr. Handsome said, cooing her stage name. "Frank says they need you right away. You're shooting the male-harem scene today," he added, but she still didn't speak.

"Laney?" I was beginning to worry that my news had caused shock-induced heart failure. But that was ridiculous. Jack Rivera and I were two perfectly mature individuals.

There was no reason to believe our relationship couldn't come to an amiable conclusion. "Laney?"

"Ms.—"

"Please extend my apologies and inform them I'm going to be a little late," she said to Mr. Handsome.

"But—"

"Tell them now." Her voice was firm. Almost borderline ... brusque. I held my breath. Brainy Laney and I had attended Holy Name Catholic School together, where we'd bonded over preteen ugliness and shared ice cream. (She shared. I didn't. Let it be said in my defense that growing up in a household with three idiot brothers, it was eat or be eaten.) And in all the years since, I have never known her to venture near the unfriendly border of brusque.

Apparently, Mr. Handsome was just as shocked as I, because in a moment I heard a murmured apology and handsomely retreating footsteps.

"Laney," I said. "Are you okay?"

"What happened?"

"What?" I was within three blocks of Le Petit Château, a lovely little restaurant resembling a French castle, where I was to meet my date, one Tyler Simonson. I slowed the Saturn down despite the fact that my stomach was growling carnivorous obscenities at my mouth, demanding that it be fed. In the past, food and I have had what some might refer to as a confrontational relationship. But I'm classy now and had gained control over my baser corporal impulses. I hardly ever have wet dreams about lobster manicotti anymore.

"Tell me what's going on," Laney ordered. "And start at the beginning."

"There's nothing to tell," I assured her. "We mutually agreed to go our separate ways. We're too ..." I shrugged. My throat felt kind of tight. Maybe I was coming down with a cold. "The unfortunate truth is, I've simply outgrown him."

"Mac—"

"You know it's true." My voice was absolutely level, perfectly logical. I've never been more proud. "He's a police officer. Not that there's anything wrong with his chosen profession. It's a commendable career choice, and I'm sure he's excellent at his job. But his work calls for a certain degree of..." I remembered him in cop mode...all hard lines and dark intent, head lowered as he sauntered toward me. I cleared my throat and tried to do the same with my memories. "Base physicality. My chosen path is more... cerebral. More cultured. A therapist requires a certain amount of tranquility if she hopes to assist her patients in achieving the same. And with Rivera out of my life..." My voice cracked. I cleared my throat again. "Listen, Laney, I'm afraid I'm going to have to call you back. I think I'm having an asthma attack."

"You don't have asthma."

"I can if I want to," I snapped, then closed my eyes and found the inner peace that Dr. Dirkx had written of so eloquently in chapter seventeen. "I'm sorry, Laney, I guess I'm a little stressed. But it is six fifty-seven, and I don't like to be late."

"Since when?"

I gritted my teeth and wondered why I loved her so much. "Perhaps you're unaware of this, but the last several months have been a time of introspection and growth for me. I feel I've become a better human being, more stable, more empathetic. More..." I paused, thinking. "Outward-looking, if you will."

"I won't."

"Excuse me?"

"Talk to me, Mac," she said, and there was something in her softening tone that made me want to curl into the fetal position and blubber like a baby, but I fought back the infantile urges.

"I would love to," I said. "But I've made a commitment to Mr. Simonson and I really must go. We'll talk again as soon as I get a spare—"

"If you hang up on me, I'm taking the first flight home."

I laughed, confident in her inability to shake the truth from me. "Don't be ridiculous. You're due on set in about three—"

"Jean-Claude," she said, voice muffled slightly. Apparently, there had been two ungodly handsome, obsequious men in the room. "Please get me on the first available flight to LAX."

I was a little less amused now. "You're not flying anywhere, Laney," I said. "I'm fine. I'm great. *Everything's* great."

"Any available seat will be fine," she added to Mr. Handsome II.

"Laney," I said, tone a little less dulcet, "you have a show to do. What would the unwashed masses do without their queen?"

She ignored me. "Tell Frank we'll have to wrap up the harem scene next week."

Panic was setting in. I understood, of course, that the delay was not going to cause the crash of civilization as we knew it, but a bazillion rabid fans were dying to find out if Queen Hippolyta and her swarthy but oh-so-sensitive man-slave were ever going to be free to "share their love." Not me, of course, I was far too busy rereading Dr. Dirkx's chapter thirty-one, succinctly titled "The Hidden Agenda Behind Every Seemingly Logical Decision: A Therapist's Guide to Delving Into the Truth Behind Falsehoods." It was absolutely gripping and couldn't possibly be considered competition for over-the-counter sleep aids. Neither had I, on several occasions, set it aside to read novels with scantily clad men on the covers. That would be wrong.

"You're not going to wrap anything up next week," I said.

"You might be right," she agreed, returning her attention to me. "My midwife thinks the baby might come early."

My stomach twisted into a double knot. I wanted to see her more than I wanted a fudge-brownie sundae supreme. But even I was not so selfish as to risk her well-being for my crisis du jour. "Laney, you can't fly when you're eight months pregnant. It's not—"

"Have Britta pack me an overnight bag, will you, Jean-Claude?"

"Okay!" I snapped, cracking like an Easter egg in a pressure cooker. "Our parting wasn't perfectly cordial."

"What happened?" Her voice was low and quiet, filled with gut-level caring and a bottomless well of friendship. My eyes watered, blurring my vision; I pulled into a McDonald's parking lot and turned off the engine. Nearby, a thousand hopeful roses bloomed in wild profusion. The air smelled heavenly... I felt like I was doing an extended stint in purgatory. "I'm a therapist," I whimpered.

"So you've mentioned."

"A licensed psychologist."

"And a very good one."

Was I? I wondered, but shoved aside the doubts and glanced out my passenger window. At the top of a steep concrete incline, three teenagers were arguing over a dented shopping cart that looked like it, too, had spent a considerable amount of time in the underworld. "My career, my chosen path, dictates that my life be relatively sedate... you know, so that I might better serve the clientele that comes to me with their troubles."

"So you've said," she agreed cautiously.

"But Rivera makes me..." I paused, clenching one fist as I searched for the proper phraseology. "He disturbs my tranquility."

"Are you serious?"

"Yes, I'm serious. He makes me...less than perfectly rational," I said, and rubbed my eyes with my fingertips. When I withdrew my hand, one of the teenagers was scrambling into the shopping cart. I wondered distractedly if he had won or lost the argument.

"Have you ever considered the fact that that might be your gift, Mac?" Laney asked.

"What's that?" I asked, tearing my attention from the adolescents and wondering vaguely how our species had ever clambered out of the primordial ooze.

"Maybe your particular personality type is the reason you're so successful?"

"I'm successful?" I asked, feeling my aching insecurities clatter like wind chimes.

"Now's not the time for false modesty," she said.

"If not now—"

"Maybe the reason your clients appreciate you so much is because you can relate to them on their level."

"Are you saying I'm deranged?"

"I'm doing my utmost to avoid that," she said, and I almost laughed despite everything. "When did this talk take place?"

"Talk?" I said, hedging carefully.

"Don't mess with me, Mac. I've got a tankard of toxic hormones swimming around in my system."

"You mean the talk with Rivera?"

"Yes." Her tone suggested that I was testing her patience. I was used to hearing that tone since before I was able to breathe without the aid of an umbilicus.

"Oh. Monday."

There was a pause that suggested repercussions to come. Repercussions from Laney usually consisted of hurt feelings. I'd rather be boiled in castor oil. "And you didn't tell me before this?" she asked. I tensed against the guilt.

It was Wednesday. I had spoken to her twice since Monday and had failed to broach the subject on both occasions. "It's no big deal," I said. "It's not as if I haven't broken up with guys before."

"Eighty-three times, if my math is correct."

"It's not." I tried to sound indignant. Eighty-three failed relationships might suggest a certain lack of... something. But for the life of me, I couldn't figure out what that something was, despite the damned PhD.

"I might have missed a few guys," she said, then steered back onto the verbal track. "Listen, Mac, I know you and Rivera are ..." She paused, possibly still searching for a euphemism for *weirder than shit*. "Fractious. But I don't think that's necessarily a bad thing. I mean, people fight. Everyone—"

"Do you?"

"What?"

"Do you and ..." I drew a deep breath, searching for the proper term. J.D. Solberg, her husband of nearly a full, mind-numbing year, was the dweebiest, most obnoxious man on the planet, a fact that I had voiced on more than one occasion. The new and classier me, however, would no longer lower myself by mentioning that fact to the woman who honest-to-God loved him. "Do you and ... your spouse ..." I winced a little as I admitted their union. "Fight?"

"Of course. Jeen and I fight all the time."

"Really?" Atop the concrete incline, a second teenager was scrambling disjointedly into the shopping cart. "When was the last time?"

"What?"

"When was your last big blow out, Laney?"

"Well, I wouldn't call it a blow out exactly."

I felt tired and strangely... dusty. "What *would* you call it... exactly?"

"It was more like a... a disagreement."

"A disagreement."

"Yes."

I nodded. Laney *would* have disagreements. Rivera and I had what might better be referred to as street brawls. But that was the old me. "When was it?"

"Just..." I could almost hear her shake her head. Maybe it was her hair crackling against her cell phone. The Amazon queen's on-set stylists liked to starch her coiffure to magnificent heights. "Just last week we had an argument."

"What was it regarding?"

"I don't think that's the point, Mac."

"Was it about who loves whom the most?"

There was a pause.

"Are you fucking kidding me?" I might have momentarily lost my fabulous composure, but seriously..."That was your argument?"

"I didn't say that."

"Excuse me," I said, and turned away from the phone to produce gagging noises possibly loud enough to be heard without a cellular device. I know it was infantile, but honest to God, the thought of the sweetest, most beautiful woman in the world consorting with the dweebiest man on the planet always makes me queasy.

She laughed. "Listen, if anyone gets to barf, it's me."

I pushed my phone back to my ear. "What do you mean? Are you sick?"

"I'm fine," she said. "Just a little nauseated sometimes. And tired. And I don't know. Kind of lonely, I guess."

"Lonely?" I scowled at the squabbling teenagers. One of them—the sanest of the trio, I suspected—was still outside the cart. The other two were hanging onto the corner of the nearby building, keeping their soon-to-be vehicle immobile. I could see the muscles in their scrawny, spider monkey arms stretched taut. "I thought Solberg was there with you?"

"He is, and it's great to have him here. But I just..."

"What?" Memories of death threats and hostage situations jolted through me. Laney's life had been endangered on more than one occasion. The disappearance of the dweebster had nearly killed us both when my misbegotten attempt to find him took us to Vegas, the only place on earth with more oddballs per capita than L.A.

"I miss you, Mac."

My heart ached, my vision went blurry, and my stomach twisted. Three sure signs of love. Or gastric irregularities. "I kind of miss you, too," I said.

She sighed. "Maybe when I get home we should buy a horse ranch together."

"Sure," I said, and fondly remembered our requisite horse-crazy years, when she and I had haunted every equestrian stable within a ten-mile radius of Schaumburg, Illinois. "Because I've got so much money and you've got so much time."

She sighed at my sarcasm. "I think you should give Rivera another chance."

But he made me crazy, and I so very much wanted to be sane.

"Maybe sane's overrated," she said, making me wonder for the hundredth time if she was just a little more psychic than I cared to believe.

I glanced at the teenagers. The one I had tagged as "most sane" was climbing laboriously into the cart/suicide vehicle, knobby limbs folding like a praying mantis's. "I don't think so."

"What'd he do wrong?"

"Listen, Laney..." My eyes stung. I blinked repeatedly. "You know I love you, but my date's waiting and I—"

"I can still catch that flight."

"I doubt it," I said. Despite my flirty skirt and classy top, I felt hot and wilted. "I have to assume Jean-Claude has passed out by now from waiting with bated breath for your next command."

"Who?"

"Jean—" I began, then narrowed my eyes. "There is no Jean-Claude dying to buy you airline tickets, is there?"

She laughed a little. "Tell me what happened. Please."

I sighed and ignored the teenagers, who were now frozen in anticipatory pre-death. "Nothing happened, Laney." I fought the urge to unload my pathetic troubles onto her unreasonably capable shoulders, but I was weak. "All month," I added. "Nothing happened all month."

"You haven't seen him for a month?"

"Except for the *talk*, I haven't even spoken to him."

"Well..." She seemed to be searching for some sort of platitude. "He's a busy man, Mac."

"Too busy to push a button on his phone?"

"I don't mean to worry you, honey, but he *is* in law enforcement. I mean, you both work with troubled individuals, but his clientele tends to try to kill people with more frequency."

"I don't know. It might be about par," I said. The laundry list of guys who had recently tried to off me was deplorably long.

"The point is he's probably been working on something really important. Pretty soon, he'll solve the case and the two of you won't be heard from for three days and four nights ... except for ... you know, the complaints from your neighbors."

I remembered the last night we'd spent together; my neighbor, Mr. Al Sadr, *had,* in fact, alerted the authorities about an animal in distress. Apparently, achieving sexual satisfaction after what some might refer to as a dearth can sound something like a hyena in the throes of torture.

I sighed, then pulled on my big-girl panties and moved on. "But that's the thing, Laney. I'm almost thirty-five years old."

"In your dreams."

I ignored her. "And a licensed therapist, a PhD, a respected member of my community and ..."

"Respected?" she began, but I powered through.

"I don't want to disturb the neighbors anymore!"

"Are you sure? Usually—"

"I'm tired of the highs and lows. I want normal."

She exhaled softly, as if about to divulge a hard truth. Generally speaking, I like my truths in small doses and laced with copious amounts of chocolate. "I don't think normal's for the likes of you, Mac," she said.

A door squeaked in the background. "Ms. Ruocco?" The voice sounded as timid as a mouse, as smitten as a kitten. "Frank says we're going to miss the sunset if you don't come soon."

"I'm sorry, Andy. Can you convince him that I need just a couple more minutes?"

I could hear his backbone stiffen from nine hundred miles away. Maybe other anatomical parts were stiffening, too. Laney's boobs had been pretty impressive pre-gestation; I could only imagine her proportions now. "I can and I shall," he said. The door closed resolutely behind him.

"You should go before Andy finds a cross and hangs himself on it for you," I said.

"He's a nice kid."

"Kid?"

"Twenty-six in a couple of weeks."

"Ah, yes, barely out of swaddling. How many times?"

"How many times what?"

"How often has he proposed?"

"I'm already married. Not to mention pregnant. Remember?"

"Did he just ask you to run away with him, then?"

She sighed. Hunky men throwing themselves at her feet seemed to make her weary. I don't have that problem. "Listen, Mac. Don't do anything drastic. Eventually, Rivera might get tired of you breaking up with him."

"That's what I'm talking about, Laney, I'm tired of it, too. I don't want any more drama."

"Are you sure? Because your extremities tend to go numb when you get bored."

"Not anymore," I said. "I've changed. Grown up." Outside my little Saturn, the trio of teenagers loosened their simian grip on the building and screamed toward the bottom of the incline. "Boring is the new orgasmic."

Chapter 2

While in a romantic relationship, women generally endeavor to be well-dressed, sophisticated, and articulate. If men manage coherency, they are well ahead of the curve.

—Regina Stromburg, professor of Women's Studies 101, bitter but not entirely inaccurate

Holy hell, he was boring, I thought, and nodded at yet another of my date's endless anecdotes.

Don't get me wrong. I wasn't reconsidering my statement to Laney: Boring is good. So what if I had long ago lost feeling in my right foot? I had a spare. And Tyler was really quite attractive... in an industrial sort of way. He had blue eyes and a square jaw. Generally, I'm not fond of facial hair, particularly my own, but the carefully cropped beard looked good on him. As an added bonus, he seemed willing to pay for my meal, which, if you're wondering, can be pretty spendy at a French castle.

So I nodded for the fifty-first time and refused to let my eyeballs roll back in my head like a drunken monkey's. "Uh huh," I said with enough enthusiasm to suggest that I not only remained conscious... I was still listening. But I seemed to be experiencing a loss of sensation in my shins.

"That's when I decided to become an engineer," he said.

I smiled again. My teeth felt tired. "Do you get to wear one of those cute little hickory-stripe hats?"

"What?" Not a dollop of humor showed on his face. I stifled a sigh as I felt my right butt cheek surrender to the inevitable. My left, however, was holding up like a real trooper.

"I've always wanted to blow the whistle."

He watched me in silence for a few endless seconds. "I'm not a train engineer."

"I thought maybe," I said, and noticed that he hadn't eaten his fair share of the shrimp appetizer. The waiter, fabulously pretentious, had informed us that they had been lovingly sautéed in garlic and brandy.

"You were making a joke?"

"I thought so," I admitted, and tried to quit staring at his remaining hors d'oeuvres. The new Christina was only interested in food on the basis of its nutritional value. "What kind of engineer are you?"

"Electrical," he said, and I felt my entire rear end go dead.

When the date whimpered to a merciful finale, I slumped into my Saturn and headed toward home. Two blocks from the restaurant, a shopping cart lay on its side at the bottom of a concrete ramp. In a fit of altruism mixed with entrepreneurial genius, I had given a business card to each of the still-conscious teenagers, who, I hoped, would hand them off to their parents before their next longevity-shortening adventure.

It was clear that there would always be the need for a good shrink in the greater metropolitan area. Still, I felt dejected. I turned on the radio. Bach's Mass in B Minor soared from the speakers. I winced, remembered Classy Chrissy had outgrown Mick Jagger, and turned off the sound.

Harlequin greeted me at the door with a tail whap and a wiggle. When he reared up on his hind legs, his face was level with mine. He put his saucer-sized paws on my shoulders, laid his snout against my neck, and sighed. I closed my eyes and kissed his ear. He's a gigantic pest and a flatulent coward who shows an ounce of bravery only when scouting the kitchen for nose-pinching aluminum cans and scraps of burnt bacon. But I couldn't love him more if I'd given birth to him. Such is true devotion. In actuality, our rapport had lasted far longer than ninety percent of the relationships I shared with my fellow Homo sapiens.

Two minutes after my arrival, we were snuggled up on the couch, sharing a bowl of Velvet Vanilla ice cream and watching *The Princess Bride* for the umpteenth time. Classy Chrissy generally didn't participate in such self-indulgent behavior, but it seemed wrong to force abstinence on my innocent canine friend.

Thirty minutes and a full pint later, we were both asleep, while my sweet Westley rode through my dreams on a pearl-white stallion.

By the time I awoke from my post-consumption coma, it was 7:42 in the morning. I had a 9:00 client and a fifty-minute drive to my practice in Eagle Rock. After letting Harley out to relieve himself and terrorize the avian community, I rushed through a shower. With no time left for breakfast, I jumped into my trusty Saturn and raced off to work. The freeway gods were in a frolicsome mood. Nevertheless, I managed to careen to a halt in front of Hope Counseling by 8:54.

Still feeling groggy and out of sorts, I eyed Sunrise Coffee across the parking lot. I'm not a caffeine addict, but the old Chrissy appreciated any drink that wasn't too self-important to incorporate massive amounts of sugar and a buttload of whipped cream, while the new Chrissy didn't wish to deprive any small business of its ... business. So, after a quick glance at my humble office, I hurried across the pavement and ordered a Caramel Carnival. The guy behind the counter was new ... and cute ... with surfer-dude hair and eyelashes that would make any member of the camelid family green with envy. Fortunately, Classy Chrissy cared naught about physical appearances and kept the transaction strictly business.

The damages came to more than you'd dish out for your mortgage payment in most parts of the world, but I shuffled rapidly through my wallet, handed over a couple crumpled bills, and hightailed it out of there without waiting for change.

My secretary/receptionist met me at the door. "You skipped breakfast again, didn't you?" Shirley Templeton was not the most beautiful woman on the planet. I appreciated that almost as much as I did her light-years-above-pay-scale efficiency, especially since the stunning Brainy Laney had held the position before becoming Amazonian royalty.

"Not to worry," I said, speed-walking toward my office in the back. "I ate a small hamlet last night."

Shirley remained at her station but raised her voice so as to be heard. "There ain't no substitute for breakfast. I told my nephew the same thing when he called about that sticky window of—"

"Good morning, Mr. Nettleton," she said, switching to what she called her "show me the money" voice. "Ms. McMullen is currently updating records, but she'll be with you momentarily."

By two o'clock, my stomach was rumbling like a hungry volcano. I had counseled an insomniac, an egomaniac, and a boobiac, my own term for guys who spend their session staring at my fairly unimpressive chest.

With an hour's break before my next client, I shambled up to the reception area just as the front door opened.

"Hi." The guy from the coffee shop stepped inside and smiled. He was carrying a brown paper bag. "You overpaid," he said, and stretched out his arm. "So I brought you a turkey sandwich."

"I…" I scowled at him, suspicions firing up like smoke signals in my underfed psyche. If you're at all familiar with my history, you're probably aware that people tend to try to kill me. Hard to say why, but no new attempts had been made for several weeks and I was hoping to continue that fortuitous trend. So I tightened my fingers around a freshly sharpened pencil just retrieved from Shirley's desk and faced him head-on. "How did you know where I work?"

"I, ummm…" He stepped back a pace, as one might when facing a rabid dog or really ugly shoes. "I saw you cross the parking lot."

"I could have been a client," I said.

His brows dipped cautiously. "Not unless you're *really* disturbed."

I could feel Shirley's attention darting from me to him and back, like a spectator at an overactive tennis tournament.

"You come in every day," he explained. "And don't leave until late."

"You've been watching me?"

"My window faces this direction."

"But—"

"It was awfully nice of you to stop by," Shirley said, and rose to her feet.

The silence that followed ticked like a time bomb.

"Wasn't it nice of him to stop by?" she asked. Her tone was the kind one generally reserves for fractious two-year-olds and guys with plastic explosives strapped to their chests. "And bring lunch."

I cleared my throat and loosened my grip on the pencil. "Yes. My apologies." I tried a smile. *Charming* was probably not the adjective most would have used to describe the expression. *Ghoulish* might be a little too complimentary. "Working in this field can make one rather suspicious, I'm afraid." I didn't bother to mention that a couple dozen attempts on a girl's life can kind of mess with her head, too. I thrust out a well-manicured hand. "I'm Christina McMullen."

"Tony Amato. So you're a psychiatrist?"

"Psychologist."

We shook hands. His fingers were long and tapered, his grip firm. His eyes were summer blue and pretty as a picnic.

I introduced Shirley, who said her salutations, then hustled into my office in the back. The room was the approximate size of a thumbtack, which made her sojourn there a little suspect. But I wasn't complaining. Tony did have nice eyes... not as seductive as the scents emanating from the brown paper bag, but nice.

"The extra money was a tip," I said, indicating the bag.

"I can't take tips."

"Really?" I enjoyed being a therapist more than schlepping drinks at the Warthog, as I had in my former life, but I still mourned the lack of gratuities. "Allergic to making a profit, are you?"

He grinned, flashing teeth as white as last night's ice cream orgy. Twin dimples winked in his cheeks. "I'm the owner of the establishment."

"Are you sure?"

"Pretty sure."

"I didn't even know it had been for sale." A man named Igor Kuchuk, known as Icky Igor by some of his employees (one of whom was his wife), used to own it. He had been, by all accounts, icky.

"I was a regular for years," he explained. "When I heard Kuchuk was thinking about retiring..." He shrugged. He was dressed in a lime-green tee and cargo shorts. The lean muscles in his forearms flexed pleasantly as he mimicked a lunging motion. "I pounced."

"I see," I said, and tugged my gaze from his forearms. In my experience, men with nice forearms were usually serial killers. "Well... it really was nice of you to stop by. But I don't feel right about accepting gifts from anyone I don't know well." Besides, the way my luck had been running, he'd probably peppered the turkey with arsenic for as-yet-to-be-determined reasons. "But I really appreciate—"

"You're not vegan, are you?"

Vegan? Hardly. The old Chrissy had been one baby step from cannibalism. But the classy new Chrissy kept that fact strictly to herself. "No, but I'm afraid I overindulged a bit yesterday evening." I remembered the beef Wellington with lascivious joy, but managed to refrain from drooling. "So I'm going to have to be more judicious today."

He rocked back on his heels. The water shoes he wore were made of eye-popping orange neoprene, as if he were prepared, at any given moment, to dive into the surf and wanted to be seen beneath the waves. "Overindulged? Are you kidding me? You're perfect."

I blinked, regrouped, and realized with some surprise that I'd always had a soft spot for serial killers.

"But if you're seriously worried about your caloric intake, I'll leave off the bacon next time," he said, and lifted the bag a little.

"There's bacon in it?" My voice sounded a little weak. I don't mean to put too fine a point on this, but bacon to a McMullen is like catnip to a ... McMullen. Seriously, my brother James got high on catnip on more than one occasion.

"Apple-smoked," he said, giving the contents a little shake. "I hate to throw it out."

I forced my gaze from the gift with some effort. "That *wouldn't* be very environmentally responsible."

"And I'm trying to cut down on my carbon footprint."

I realized at that moment that I might be in love. Some practical portion of me suggested I could simply be hungry. But how was a woman to tell the difference? Love and hunger ... they both suck.

"Once we run out of our current inventory, all our cups will be corn-based and compostable."

"Well, then ..." I said, and reached for the bag. "I can hardly turn it down." There was no tingle as our fingers brushed, but my stomach did rumble a little. "Thank you."

"My pleasure," he said, then shuffled back a step. "Hey, would you ..." He shrugged, a nervous lift of substantial shoulders. "Are you busy Saturday?"

"This Saturday?" Surprise snagged me.

"Sure. Why not? We could catch Baker's Marionette Show or something."

My eyebrows zipped toward the ceiling. Marionettes? As in, puppets? How old was this guy?

He laughed. "Or go to a movie."

"I'm sorry ..." Thoughts of my latest ass-numbing date were spinning in my mind, making the myriad attempts on my life rather appealing by comparison. "But I have an appointment with my..." I thought fast. "Accountant that day."

"On a Saturday evening?"

"Tax season." I shrugged, feeling guilty. If my olfactory system was correct—and it had a 97.2 percent accuracy where high-caloric treats were involved—the turkey and bacon were being lovingly cradled by a toasted croissant. I love toasted croissants. They're classy... and buttery. "She's very busy. I was lucky to get—"

"Which is why she canceled," Shirley said.

I glanced to the left. She was just zeroing in on us from the back.

I scowled at her. She raised her brows in tacit challenge. "Said she had another appointment she'd forgotten about."

"Oh," I said, while my mind scrambled for another excuse. "Darn. I'm afraid I forgot another appointment, too."

"With whom?" she asked, giving her head a sassy tilt.

I gritted a smile in her direction. "I promised Micky a consultation."

"Mr. Goldenstone canceled too," Shirley said.

"I just spoke to him this morning," I lied.

"He called while I was in back," she parried.

"I didn't hear the phone ring."

"He called my cell."

"Micky Goldenstone has your cell number?"

"On speed dial," she said, and propped capable hands on ample hips, ready to do battle.

I opened my mouth to object, but just then the door jangled.

We turned toward it. A young woman stepped tentatively inside. She darted her gaze from me to the others.

"Is this the psychiatrist's office?"

"Psychologist," I corrected, then smiled, hoping to soften the mood from someone's-gonna-die to confrontational. "Can I help you?"

"Saturday, then?" Tony asked, taking advantage of the cease-fire.

"Seven o'clock. At The Blvd," Shirley answered, sashaying behind her desk. "I'm Mrs. Templeton," she said to the newcomer. "And this is Ms. McMullen, PhD. Can we help you?"

"I don't know." She fiddled nervously with the strap of her Prada knockoff. "My boyfriend doesn't think anyone can."

Dumb-ass boyfriends, I thought, *a starving psychologist's best friend.*

Chapter 3

Blind dates, proof positive that our species is, as a whole, eternally optimistic... and somewhat stupid.

—Christina McMullen after her date with Vigo Wilshire, who did not, as his online bio suggested, have a BMW, washboard abs, or an IQ higher than that of your average nail file

The remainder of my week was filled with hypochondriacs, flashers, and your garden-variety nut jobs. I didn't hear a word from Rivera. But that didn't bother me. Why should it? I was the one who'd called it quits. I made myself feel really good about that as I dressed for my Saturday night date.

Shirley had been extremely pushy about arranging it, but I had generously agreed. The fact that The Blvd was a chic little restaurant on Rodeo Drive that served melt-in-your-mouth filet mignon had almost nothing to do with my decision.

I dressed conservatively in a plum-colored sheath with dangling silver earrings. I had once dined at The Blvd with Senator Rivera, the lieutenant's illustrious sire, and bolstered myself with the knowledge that it was highly unlikely that I'd run into my ex-lover/nemesis, since he studiously avoided his father's haunts.

Tony was already sitting at the bar when I arrived. He stood when he saw me. Good manners and twin dimples. If this guy didn't try to kill me soon, I'd consider taking him home to Harlequin.

"Thanks for coming," he said.

"Thanks for inviting me," I said, though, in actuality, it was Shirley who had issued the invitation. Tony was dressed in a blue button-down shirt and pinstripe vest casually overlooking a pair of rust-colored skinny jeans. His shoes were retro and his autumn-gold hair charmingly tousled. We were seated in moments, after which he ordered a twelve-year-old bottle of Château d'Yquem. I didn't bother to tell him I wouldn't be able to differentiate it from grape Kool-Aid. We were painfully quiet. I was the one to start the proverbial ball rolling.

"So..." I refrained from fiddling with the silver fork, which weighed, I was pretty sure, more than my handbag. "Have you always wanted to be a barista?"

He glanced at me through charmingly long lashes. Maybelline might have paid him big bucks to do a commercial had they not been such female chauvinists. "I suppose that sounds boring to you," he said. His tone suggested mild embarrassment.

"Actually..." I did fiddle now. First dates are like the plague. Horrible and potentially deadly. "I'm a big fan of boring."

He raised his brows a little, looking hopeful. "Really?"

"It's the new exciting."

"I didn't know that." He thanked the woman who brought our wine and barely gave her a second glance after she'd poured. I added another tally to his ongoing score; she was obnoxiously pretty, probably an Oklahoma-farm-girl-turned-Hollywood-extra-turned-waitress.

"How about you?" he asked. "Have you always wanted to be a psychologist?"

I couldn't help but be impressed that he had actually gotten my occupation right. My own father was still pretty sure I was a psychiatrist. Or maybe a psychopath. Glen McMullen didn't like to become overly involved in his kids' lives. It was one of my favorite things about him. "Anyone would if they'd grown up with my family."

He took a sip of the lovely tawny beverage. "If family is the determining factor I'd be a therapist too." He pulled a thoughtful expression. "Or a hit man."

"You must have brothers," I guessed.

"Four."

God save me. "And nary a hit man in sight?" I said it like a question, since one couldn't be too sure.

He chuckled, making me wonder if he might be in possession of a sense of humor. Dimples and a funny bone ... the idea was almost too much to hope for. "I do own a bar, though, in case I feel the need to self-medicate."

"Your family must be close by, then."

"Too close, yes."

"In L.A.?"

"On planet Earth. How about you?"

I laughed, relaxing a little. "Chicago area. What do you do when you're not self-medicating or hopping up others with java beans?"

"I like to cook."

"You're a chef?" I loved chefs. Or more correctly, I loved the fruits of their labors.

"Not really. I just help out when someone can't make it in."

"Make it in where?"

He looked kind of embarrassed again. "I have a couple of restaurants."

"A couple?"

"Well, three."

"But you wanted a coffee shop, too?"

"The Sunrise was on my way to work, and I was spending so much on caffeine, so I thought..." He shrugged.

"You bought a shop so you wouldn't have to buy coffee?"

He grinned a little and changed the subject. "Aubry said you've had your practice for a couple years now."

I braced myself, mind screaming with possibilities. Aubry—his mother, with whom he cohabitated and shared a collection of human entrails? His ex-girlfriend, who he still loved "like a sister"? The pet hamster that had taught him everything he knew about world politics? "Aubry?" I kept my tone neutral on the off chance that he wasn't as weird as the last eighty or so men I had dated.

"An employee. She's got three brothers, too, and I thought—"

"Four."

"What?"

I felt as if all the blood had drained to my feet. I tightened a fist around the substantial weight of my butter knife. "You said you had four brothers."

"*You* have three." He explained it so easily that for a moment I almost accepted it, but the truth dawned on me in an instant.

"I never told you how many I have."

"Well..." He paused for an instant, smiling. "You moved all the way from Chicago. So I figured it was more than two but less than—"

"How did you know?" My voice was a little reminiscent of Darth Vader's now... raspy and kind of scary.

"I just—"

I raised the cutlery.

He lifted a palm in mild self-defense. "I just wanted to know a little bit more about you, so I…I checked you out." He paused again, perhaps noticing my expression, my tone, my weapon of choice. "I didn't really consider becoming a hit man, Christina. I'm pretty normal, considering."

"Considering what?"

"Listen, if you're not comfortable with this, I understand."

"This?"

He indicated the restaurant with an open hand. "This date. I just…honestly, I don't know how women do it."

I gave him a head tilt.

"Go out with unknown men," he explained. "I'd never have the nerve, knowing what I know."

"What do you know?"

"That people are crazy."

I nodded a little. "Are *you*?"

"I don't think so."

"Not exactly a ringing endorsement, Tony."

"It seems to me the most reliable sign of instability is the absolute certainty of sanity."

The man had a point.

He was watching me, suntanned brow wrinkled with concern. "I'll leave if you want."

I remained as I was, mind spinning.

"Dinner's on me. Order anything you like." He shoved his chair back. "I'll just take off."

My heart was thumping in my chest, but I forced myself to shake my head and put down my impromptu weapon. "No. I'm sorry. I've just…" I glanced at my drink, wishing I could blame it for my neuroses, but I hadn't yet taken so much as a sip and it probably hadn't inebriated me through the ether. I exhaled heavily. "Maybe I should quit watching the nine o'clock news. Scary... scary stuff... you know?" Or, better yet, maybe people could quit trying to kill me. That'd be a dandy idea, too. "Please stay."

"Are you sure?" he asked.

No. "Yes," I said. "Forgive me."

Conversation was a little bumpy after that, but it smoothed out over appetizers and was flowing pretty effortlessly by the time the entrees arrived.

"So you have a restaurant in the valley?" I asked. I had ordered the bream with braised artichokes. It had been seasoned to perfection and drizzled with something that resembled ambrosia. Still, I had refrained from licking the plate. Go, Chrissy.

"The Florence," he said. "Paulie makes a pretty good seafood manicotti."

"With lobster?"

He took a sip of wine and nodded. "And shrimp."

"That sounds..." Orgasmic. "Quite good."

His gaze met mine. "Maybe you'd like to try it sometime... once... you know... you're certain I'm not planning to..."

"Kill me?" I suggested. I'd finished my first glass of wine, and although I hadn't yet slipped under the table, the alcohol had certainly eased the knot in my stomach. The thought that Tony might bear me ill will seemed ridiculous now. Probably those past few murder attempts had been nothing more than a bout of bad luck.

He gave me a look of confusion. "Why would I want to kill you?"

I laughed at his expression, jolly as an elf. "I'm sorry I was so suspicious. What are your restaurants' other specialties?"

He shrugged. "Tommy's gnocchi is a favorite. And the fettuccine is always popular. But I like the chicken piccata the best."

"Chicken—" I began enthusiastically, but something across the room caught my attention. I glanced to the right and felt my brain freeze.

It hardly seemed possible, and it certainly wasn't fair, but Lieutenant Jack Rivera was standing not twenty feet from us. I had to look twice to make sure he wasn't some sort of apparition, but sure enough, he was there. As dark and intense and damnably magnetic as I remembered. Our gazes met with a sparking clash. The air rushed out of my lungs like a cyclone leaving a collapsing building, but in a second I had caught myself. Swallowing hard, I dragged my gaze back to Tony's affable expression.

"Piccata," I said, remembering the topic.

He was silent for a second. My teeth ached. I eased them apart, drawing my lips into a smile that might have resembled something rather lupine.

"Do you know that guy?" he asked finally.

"What?"

"The man who's staring at us like he might eat you," Tony said. "Do you know him?"

"Oh ..." A couple dozen likely lies rushed through my brain, but at the last moment I reminded myself there was no reason for fabrications. "Yes." I cleared my throat and loosened my fingers around the stem of my wine glass. "We, um ... we dated a few times." The memory of the other things we had done *a few times* made my hormones fire up like the flames of Mount Doom.

"Is he the guy who made you so nervous about men?"

I tore my mind from the libidinous memories. "What?"

"Did he hurt you?" he asked. His voice was low and level now, his attention entirely focused on my face, and in that moment I thought I could really like him.

"No," I said, and managed to heave a fairly normal exhalation. "No. We just weren't...we just weren't right for one another."

He nodded but kept his gaze riveted on me, as if he could read my thoughts. As if he cared enough to try. "He's still watching you."

"Oh?" My heart did a quick little jig in my chest, but I stifled the sophomoric thrill and shuffled my gaze to Rivera's. Something snapped between us, almost yanking me to my feet, but I kept my lustful Manolos firmly planted on the floor, my plum sheath wrapped demurely around my thighs, and in a moment I managed to wrangle my gaze back to my date's. "He's, umm..." I did my best to keep from wriggling, though my bra felt too tight, my dress too long, my lungs too full. "He's a cop. A..." I gazed intently at my plate. I had devoured every morsel of fish and the accompanying sauce but left the frilly edge of a kale leaf. I'm not an idiot. "A police officer. He's probably just scouting for evildoers."

"Evildoers?"

The muscles in my quads were starting to jump a little. "He's very intense," I said. "Very involved with his work."

"Is that why you broke up with him?"

I could feel Rivera's gaze burning into my solar plexus, but I ignored him as best I could. It was like trying to disregard a tsunami. "Let's not worry about him," I said. "I want to hear more about you."

Tony pulled his gaze from Rivera with as much effort as I had exerted. "What would you like to know?"

"Is he still there?"

"What?"

I almost closed my eyes to my own neurotic obsessions. "Your um...your chef. At..." Holy fuck, was Rivera still there? Was he watching me? Was he remembering the night at his house, or in the office supply store, or on my kitchen table? "At the Florence ... what was his name?"

"Paulie?" He sounded dubious at best.

"Yes. Paulie, is he working right now?" I had no idea what I was talking about.

"He's got the night off."

"Oh, well ..." Was he on a date? Was she someone I knew? Was it that skank I had caught him with, who he swore was nothing more than a cover, when I knew—

"Are you okay?" Tony asked.

"What?" The strain of keeping my gaze front and center was starting to make my eyeballs quiver. "Of course. Yes, I'm fine. Why wouldn't I be? Why wouldn't I be fine?"

"He's pretty good-looking."

"You think so?" I kept my attention glued to Tony's face and wondered dismally if that was weird. Under normal circumstances, which I couldn't even imagine, would I glance at Rivera now? Would I skim his lean jaw, his take-me eyes, his hotter-than-hell body? Would I give a little shrug and move on? Was that even a possibility?

"Don't *you*?" he asked.

My hair, recently colored a becoming cocoa cinnamon, was beginning to sweat. "Don't I what?"

"Don't you think he's attractive?"

"Oh. He's, um ... he's all right," I said, and almost winced. Sister Celeste, one of Holy Name's more terrifying nuns, had often alluded to the fact that God could strike you dead for lying. Since He or She had not yet seen fit to knock me flat with a divine lightning bolt, I rather doubted the validity of the statement, but perhaps the sheer size of the lie was the determining factor. I braced myself for impact.

"She's pretty, too."

"She?" My eyeballs jerked toward the lobby. Rivera had his head bent to listen to his date, but his gaze was still locked on me like a heat-seeking missile. It took me several seconds to drag mine to the woman who stood beside him.

"But that makes sense," Tony said.

She was facing away from me, but I could see enough. She was small and curvaceous, with glossy black tresses that tumbled halfway down her shapely back. I could have spanned her waist (or her throat) with my fingers. She wore a red print dress and a pair of kick-ass stilettos. I felt the hair rise at the back of my neck. Felt a growl roll up my throat.

"... family," Tony said, but I had no time to decipher what he was talking about. I was rising to my feet... slowly, body unbending one stiff muscle at a time. My attention was glued on Rivera's latest skank. My hands had curled unconsciously around the neck of the bottle of twelve-year-old grape.

And then she turned.

Her gaze swept the restaurant and settled on me. Rivera spoke to her again. She scowled... and recognition dawned on me. Rosita. She was gorgeous, confident and powerful. She was also the dark lieutenant's mother. I felt my body wilt like a tired leaf of kale.

"You still okay?" Tony asked.

I pulled my gaze from Rosita's and sank back into my chair. "What?" Embarrassment flooded me. "Yes. Of course. Sorry. I was just going to ..." What? What exactly had I been planning to do ... with the prepubescent bottle of Château d'Yquem clutched in my trembling hand? I released it with an effort, uncurling my fingers one creaking digit at a time. "What were you saying?"

"Do you know her?"

"Who?"

He stared at me as if he wasn't entirely certain I was still human. "The woman with your ex."

"Oh her...Yes." I laughed a little. Ha ha ha. Good God, I was nuts. "She's, um...she's his mother," I said. Reaching for the just-surrendered bottle of vino, I sloshed half a cup into my glass and polished it off in one quick quaff before glancing to the right again. Rivera's expression was as hard as Italian granite. His mother's dark brows were drawn low over snapping jalapeno eyes. I chiseled my gaze away. Rivera could be scary as hell. But Rosita had been married to Senator Miguel, and being the wife of a cheating politician was bound to put a little power in a girl's punch. Add that to the fact that she adored her only son with a Spanish woman's zealous devotion and you had a recipe for a rumble. Not that I hadn't had very good reason for breaking up with her baby boy, but still..."What are your other chefs' names?" I asked.

"What?"

"The cooks at your other restaurants...what are their names?"

"Why?"

"We should go there!"

"Now?"

"Right now."

He didn't move. "Are you afraid of him?"

I would have had to be blind not to notice the spark of protectiveness in my date's eyes. For a moment I was almost tempted to fan that enticing little ember and watch the fireworks. But that was the old Chrissy. The new Chrissy didn't get a feral rush when men brawled like slavering wolves for her attentions. "No," I said. "Not of him."

"Of her, then?"

"Of course not," I said, and wondered if I could take her if it came to fisticuffs. I had the advantage of size and comparative youth, but she was Latino and, if the stories were to be believed, the A seared into her cheating ex-husband's left buttock was not from a branding accident. Rosita, it was said, had grown up in cattle country south of the border and still retained some relics from her *vaquera* days. "It's just..." I refrained from squirming, though I could still feel her hot-metal gaze on the side of my face. "It's simply a bit... uncomfortable."

"I can get rid of them."

I felt my attention being dragged toward the couple by the bar again, but Tony's words sunk into my mind like a poisoned dart. I snapped my gaze to his. "What?"

"You won't have to worry about them anymore."

"I don't want them *dead*!"

"Dead!" He looked at me as if the last marble had just dropped out of my cranium and rolled under his feet.

"Isn't that...?" My stomach roiled. Classy seemed light years away suddenly. In fact, it looked as if normal was well out of reach. "That's not what you meant, is it?"

"I thought asking them to leave might be a little aggressive."

"Oh. Oh. Well..." I laughed. Sweating, I glanced toward the bar again. The Riveras were gone. My heart dropped. But I'm sure it wasn't disappointment that curdled in my gut. Rallying, I cut off a tiny piece of kale and nibbled it to death. It tasted like bedbugs. "That won't be necessary."

Not much was said for a while. Funny how suggesting your date is a murderer will slow down idle conversation.

Complimentary desserts arrived. Orange sherbet flanked by spunky-looking spearmint leaves. I felt my sphincters relax marginally and turned my attention to the last course, but honestly, sherbet doesn't get me too riled up. The old Chrissy has been known to say that it's not dessert if you can lift it with one hand.

"Is she the reason you two broke up?" Tony asked.

"I beg your pardon?" I raised my attention from my pseudo dessert.

"Families can make outside relationships pretty tough."

"That's true," I said, and remembered the time my brother Pete had glued my thumb and index finger to my forehead while I was asleep. The accosted digits didn't form the perfect L he had hoped for, but turns out anytime your fingers are adhered to your forehead you look like kind of a loser.

"Didn't his mother approve of your line of work?"

"What?"

"I suppose it's just *my* family that doesn't think you should choose your own career."

"Do they disapprove of food in general or just chicken piccata?"

He shrugged, looking sheepish. "They assumed I would join them in the family business."

"Oh." I was devilishly tempted to search the restaurant for the Riveras again, but I resisted. Maybe they had chosen a table outside. "Families are a pain in the ..." I paused, finding my classy inner self with some difficulty. "Families can be problematic."

"Tell me about your parents," he said.

I sampled another miniscule bite of sherbet and called my progenitors neither Neanderthals nor cretins ... classiness achieved yet again. "I think one might call them blue-collar."

He nodded, watching me. "What does your father do?"

"He's retired now," I said.

"But he still pressures you? Still worries that you're about to spill trade secrets and tilt the known universe into chaos?"

I raised my brows at him. "You have trade secrets?"

"No. Believe me. My family are the worst business people, possibly the worst *people* in the world. If they had secrets no one would want them." His tone was rife with frustration, making me wonder if his family might be even worse than mine. But then I remembered the running feud that had existed between Dad and the Carusos, who lived in the little bungalow on the corner of Thorwood Street. Their Chihuahua, Fritzy, had spent most of his surprisingly long life barking at anything that moved and most things that didn't. Dad, who liked to relax with a beer and the Bears of a Sunday, had taken to shooting bottle rockets in Fritzy's general direction, escalating the feud and setting a number of inanimate objects ablaze. So, unless Mr. Amato had been raised by rabid badgers, chances were good I still had him beat.

"Generally, I don't think Dad is aware of my existence," I said.

"I'm sorry."

"The greater regret is that I can't say the same about Mom." I took another bite of orange-flavored nothing.

"What does *she* do?"

"Pries, spies, denies." I laughed and chanced a glance to the right. The Riveras were still out of my line of vision. I felt a muscle between my shoulder blades relax marginally.

"And your brothers?"

"The idiot three." Who always managed to seem like three dozen.

"I got you beat there."

"Not in psychological damage, I'm sure."

"I hear it's therapeutic to talk about it."

"You'd have to have a comfy couch and a few hundred billable hours to clear up that mess," I admitted.

He smiled. It wasn't knock-your-socks-off charming, but it could certainly cause a girl to throw a shoe every now and again. "They've got to be better than mine."

"Are you a wagering man, Mr. Amato?"

He chuckled. "What'd they do?"

I took a sip of wine and considered remaining discerningly reticent, but griping about my family had been a favored form of entertainment ever since the Stupids had put catnip in my diaper and sent me out to play with our neighbor's overly aggressive Siamese. "I divide their sins into three categories: food, friends, and farm animals."

"Food?"

I fiddled with the stem of my glass. "They were especially fond of placing items in my meals that were not necessarily meant for human consumption."

He stared at me. "Friends?"

I squirmed a little, then drank. Memories of my brothers' fucktard shenanigans still made me uncomfortable, which, in McMullen speak meant I often wanted to remove someone's spleen with a spoon. "When I was in tenth grade, Gilbert Finley asked me to the prom. He was the quarterback for the Fighting Saxons. I was ecstatic. I didn't think he even knew my name."

"And?"

"And he didn't. Turns out, all drunken Irishmen sound alike."

He thought for a second, then shook his head. "It was your brother? Pretending to be Finley?"

"One of Michael's many clever jokes," I said, and drank again.

"Do they still live in the Chicago area?"

"Nowhere else will have them."

"Thus your move halfway across the country." His voice was thoughtful.

I stared at him. "Where does *your* family live?" I asked.

His eyes were very steady. "Boston."

"Not bad," I said.

"Shanghai would be better."

"To distance ..." I said, and raised my glass.

"And pretending we were orphaned at a young age," he added, and we drank in companionable unison.

Chapter 4

Confucius say, Do unto others before they fully conscious.

—Michael McMullen, advice he took to heart with eye-jabbing regularity

By the time we had finished off the Château d'Yquem, I liked Tony quite a lot. He was quiet and thoughtful and intelligent. True, he didn't make my hands shake and my endocrine system fire up like roman candles, but wasn't that just what I was looking for? A man who was attractive but not mind-boggling. A man who had a job but didn't take it home with him. A man who was self-aware enough to realize he didn't have all the answers.

Distracted by this Renaissance man, I had almost forgotten about Rivera by the time I made a beeline for the ladies' room. Maybe I straightened my spine a notch and skimmed the tables hidden behind the pillars, and perhaps I fluffed my hair a little at my reflection as I passed the windows that lined the hallway to the restroom. But anyone with a droplet of estrogen would have responded similarly when a former beau was in the vicinity. It didn't mean a thing. And anyway, the Riveras were nowhere in sight. I might have surreptitiously checked again. And again. Still nothing. Good. Excellent, I thought. They were long gone. Angrily grateful,

I turned into the posh powder room, chose a marble-sided stall, and relieved myself.

It took me a second to wrestle my sheath back into position. One snazzy slingback torqued a little as I approached the sinks, making me question the wisdom of heels. The old Chrissy preferred to be barefoot. Shoes, after all, are a pain in the ass, but so are men, and thus far they haven't gone the way of the dodo bird. I was still mulling over that little truism as I turned on the water and soaped up my hands.

"What's his name?"

I squawked at the sound of the low-timbred voice and jerked my gaze to the mirror above the sink.

Lieutenant Jack Rivera stood not four feet behind me. He was casually resting one lean shoulder against the wall beside the wooden door. But he still looked dark, sinister, and as sexy as hell. If... you know... hell was sexy.

"Did I...? Is this...?" I glanced to the left, suspicious of my surroundings. It wouldn't be the first time I had stumbled into the wrong restroom after imbibing a teaspoon of alcohol. But there was nary a urinal in sight. I narrowed my eyes but managed to conjure up my classiest tone. "To what do I owe this pleasure, Mr. Riddler?" Mispronouncing his name had been a favorite hobby of the old Chrissy. Even New Chrissy enjoyed it more than can be understood by those whose fingers have not been superglued to their foreheads.

"He's not your usual rebound type."

I straightened, hands dripping. "I don't believe I need to inform you that it's against the law in the state of California for a man to enter a woman's restroom."

"He probably graduated from high school three or four years ago already."

I wasn't sure what he was referring to. Possibly the fact that I had once, after a particularly turbulent breakup, dated a gentleman who was not technically old enough to order a beer. "Los Angeles County executive order C-27–12." I was making shit up, but the sight of him standing there cocky and know-it-all pushed all my crazy buttons. "You should leave before I call law enforcement."

A corner of his mouth quirked up. "You must be more desperate than I realized."

"Well..." I returned to my hand washing. My expression, I was thrilled to see, was calm, but my knees felt a little noodly, and I was entirely unsure what the hell I was going to do after I'd scrubbed the skin from my knuckles. "Curfew comes so early for my usual type, and there was a special on college kids." I shrugged. "They eat a lot, but they've got such excellent endurance."

He watched me like a hound on a hamburger. Fire burned in his eyes...an out-of-control inferno that threatened to consume my self-constraint like dry kindling. "And?"

I shut the water off and picked up one of the small terrycloth hand towels. "And I thought I had better get him some sustenance before we began round five."

He smiled, or made a carnivorous facsimile of the same, then straightened from the wall. "If you wanted a cheap all-nighter, sweetheart, all you had to do was call."

My stomach clenched. "I *did* call."

A range of hot emotions flashed in his eyes. "You should have told me you were desperate enough to fuck someone who was still drooling into his bib. I would have considered it an emergency."

A dozen nasty rejoinders zipped through my head, but I kept my tone above reproach. "It's fortunate, then, that you were otherwise occupied."

He shrugged. The motion was stiff, almost indiscernible. "Just investigating a couple pesky murders."

I ignored the niggle of guilt that swam through me. After all, he was here, wasn't he? If he had time for his mother, he probably could have spared a few minutes for me.

"Well ... at least it wasn't anything important," I said, turning toward the door, but he caught my arm.

Rage ripped through me in a trembling arc, but I refrained from killing him ... like a civilized human being.

He, on the other hand, looked about as domesticated as a panther.

"Who is that asshole?" he growled.

I raised my brows, surprised and maybe just a little bit thrilled by the barely controlled anger in his tone. It made my own rage subside into the periphery with a girlish titter.

"Do you want the truth?" I asked. My voice was impressively mature.

He snorted, maybe remembering there had been a time or two when I had been less than forthcoming. But seriously, at the beginning of our relationship, the lieutenant had accused me of murdering a guy whose intentions had been less than honorable. In fact, judging by the size of the corpse's woody, *rape* had been Andrew Bomstad's intention. How honest did he expect me to be?

"Why not give it a try?" he asked.

I stared into his eyes, held them steady. "His name is Tony," I said. "And we're talking. Just talking. Did you ever consider that?"

"With you?" He scorched my ventral region. Swear to God, it felt like he was going to singe the boobs right off my body. "No."

I held myself steady, ignored the insult, disregarded the compliment, and forced myself to speak with lugubrious lucidity. "Well, maybe you should have," I said, and eased my arm out of his grip.

He released me, then took an abbreviated step backward and shook his head, as if trying to convince himself of the wisdom of letting me go. "You'll be bored out of your mind in a week."

I glanced over my shoulder at him, making sure I was looking up through my well-groomed and dutifully enhanced lashes. "Maybe that's exactly what I want."

"To be out of your mind?"

I kept my chin tilted down at that sexier-than-thou angle. "This may surprise you, Lieutenant Ridiculous, but the fact that an individual isn't willing to accost an innocent in a public restroom doesn't make him boring."

His lips twisted a little higher. "You haven't accosted me... yet."

Maybe it was his cocky grin that made me snap. Or maybe it was the fact that I wanted to eat him whole. "You're an ass," I snarled. My boobs heaved as I leaned forward to deliver that denunciation. His gaze dipped to my cleavage, and in that second I felt my sexual allure like a poorly controlled superpower.

But after a hard-won struggle for maturity, I straightened. Settling my breasts back into their kryptonite case, I reminded myself that with great power comes great responsibility.

"I'm glad you noticed my ass," he said, and pulling his gaze from my chest, lasered it into my eyes.

"Well, on that note..." I gritted a smile and turned smugly away. "I believe I will return to my boyfriend."

"He is a boy and he may be a friend," he said, "but that's not what trips your trigger, McMullen."

I turned back, teeth clenched, eyes narrowed. "You don't know anything about my trigger, Mr. Regurgitate. Not what it is, how it works, or where to find it."

"That's not what you said the other night when you were screaming my name and—"

"The other night?" My voice may have vaguely resembled the growl of a Tasmanian devil.

Still, he remained as he was.

"The other night!"

His brows had lowered a little and he was watching me closely, as if it might be prudent to make the sign of the cross and back away, but he remained unmoving. Leave it to Rivera to choose the path of the unwise.

I drew a deep breath through my nostrils, causing my boobs to swell above my relatively modest neckline. His gaze dipped, then rose more slowly.

"At Office Depot," he said.

I pursed my lips, remembering our time together in the office-supply store. Jack Rivera can be a first rate douche. Sometimes he's overbearing. Generally, he's irritating, but in all my dating years I've never found anyone who can match him in an out-and-out sex-a-thon.

I'd rather be skinned with a potato peeler and sautéed in coconut oil than admit that to his face.

"I have no idea what you're talking about," I said.

"On Foothill and Ramsdell."

I raised a dubious brow. "Dr. Dirkx believes that anyone can become delusional if he has a sufficiently weak psyche," I said.

"In the electronics section," he added.

I cleared my throat and tried to do the same with my mind. But the memory of being crammed between the all-in-one printers and the laptop accessories made my cheeks flush. All of them. Nevertheless, I remained suitably haughty.

"For your edification, I haven't seen you for twenty-seven days," I said.

"So you're pissed that we haven't visited office supplies for a few weeks?"

To be honest, the old Chrissy used to find staplers pretty alluring, but even in my currently turbulent state I wasn't deluded enough to admit that little factoid.

"I was referring to the luncheon we shared at Casa Bonita."

He stared at me, expression unreadable.

"You had the carnitas with rice; I, a lovely taco salad."

He watched me for another several seconds, then huffed a snort. "How the hell much have you had to drink?"

I scowled, tried to think of the answer, and gave up. After a shot and a half of anything, I'm pretty much incoherent. To say I'm a lightweight is an insult to light. "How much I imbibe is no longer any of your concern, Lieutenant Riveter."

The smile dropped from his lips. He straightened from the wall. "You didn't let that dippy surfer dude pick you up, did you?"

"Tony happens to be a perfect gentleman."

"A perfect gentleman who knows where you live?" he asked, and took a glowering step toward me.

"No!" I held up a hand as if to ward him off with magical powers and managed to refrain from telling him that he was one of a very few whom I had invited to my house. "I met him here."

The flames banked a little in his dark-brew eyes. "Good to know you haven't become a complete moron," he said. "Come on. I'll drive you home."

I stepped back. The motion wasn't quite as graceful as I had envisioned. I may have ricocheted off the vanity and upset the basket of used washcloths. "*Now* you want to take me home?"

"I would have offered sooner, but I thought Mr. Cool Dude out there might be insulted," he said, and reached for my elbow.

I jerked away, though he never actually made contact. "Leave me alone," I snarled.

"What's wrong now?" he asked.

"Now? Now!" I stared at him. He stared back, as uncomprehending as a turnip ... or your average man. "Now you're suddenly interested in me. Now that I have a date. Now that I—"

"Is that what you think?" he asked, and prowled a step closer. It was like being stalked by a grizzly. A tight-assed, hotter-than-Tijuana grizzly. My heart jumped to my throat. Man, I love the ursine family, but I managed to raise my chin and glare at him.

"That's what I *know*," I growled. "I don't even exist for you until there's someone else in my life."

"You're the one who called it off." He made some kind of slashing motion with the edge of his palm, sweeping it through the air that sizzled between us.

"Am I? Really?" I asked. "Because if I remember correctly, I haven't heard a word from you since—"

"The best sex of your life?"

I licked my lips. "You're ..." I had already used several of my favorite insults and took that moment to return to one of my adolescent favorites. "Stupid!"

"You're horny," he said, and stalked closer.

My palm smacked against his cheek like a clap of thunder.

He stared at me to the count of three. My chest was rising and falling madly. A dozen rational thoughts whizzed through my brain: He wasn't right for me. It was time to grow up. I needed to...

Jump him.

And that's what I did.

Chapter 5

Is it premarital sex even if you're never gonna get married?

—Sixteen-year-old Christina McMullen, who, prior to this question, had believed herself too old to be spanked

Rivera caught me in midair. I wrapped my legs around him. He growled something, then smashed my lips against his. His hands were squeezing my ass, already diving up under my dress.

I grappled with his belt. He was rough and ready. I was rougher and readier and—

"I shall make certain no one enters," someone rasped.

I jerked my bruised lips from Rivera's, slamming my attention to the right. His mother stood in the doorway, eyes bright, expression determined.

My jaw plummeted in concert with my libido.

She winked and backed out of sight, letting the door swing closed behind her.

Rivera and I remained exactly as we were, frozen in place, staring at the exit in shocked silence.

"I—" Couldn't think of anything to say.

"We—" he began and subsequently seemed to run out of words.

I cleared my throat, failed to meet his eyes, and released my leg lock. His hands, caught under my sheath, lifted the fabric almost to my waist before my Manolos touched tile. I swatted the dress down, cleared my throat again, and backed up against the comparative safety of the sink.

Looking for a place for my gaze to land, I inadvertently scanned across his face. He was glaring at nothing in particular. "Is she—" I could barely force out the words. In fact, my voice was no more than a pained whisper. "Is she really standing guard?"

Lifting one hand that had very recently been caressing my nether parts, he ran his fingers through his hair. It might have been my imagination, but I think they trembled a little. "I don't think..." He shook his head, then nodded economically, though he winced a bit. "Yeah. Yeah, she is."

I gazed morosely into middle space, trying, with no success whatsoever, to figure out how a respected psychologist had arrived at this ignominious situation. "You know, it's funny." I laughed a little. Ha ha ha. "I thought *my* family was weird."

"Your family *is* weird," he said, but his voice lacked conviction.

Maybe that's why I didn't argue with him. Or maybe it was because it was absolutely true. Either way, I had the good sense to remain silent on that front. Go, crazy-ass Chrissy.

"Well..." I clenched my fists against my thighs. "Listen, I'm sorry I called you..." My gaze slipped toward the appropriate body part, but it was obscured by other, more active parts of his anatomy. "An ass."

He drew a deep breath and glanced toward the door, as if having his mother nearly witness our ill-advised coitus changed everything. "Maybe I shouldn't have..." He shook his head once and jerked up one lean shoulder. "He looks like an okay guy."

"Yeah. Yes." I was only vaguely aware of whom he was speaking. "I think he is."

He nodded, but his teeth were gritted. He unclenched them with an obvious effort. "You were right."

I was holding my breath. This might have been the first time Rivera had ever suggested such an unlikely possibility to anyone. Certainly, he had never mentioned it to me. I waited impatiently to learn in what way I might have strayed into the land of rightness.

"We shouldn't..." He glanced away. "You deserve someone..." His eyes looked old, suddenly, and tired beyond reason. "Different."

For a moment, I almost argued, almost said it didn't matter. It was okay if he didn't always call me back. We were together now. But then I remembered where we were and what we had been about to do in a classy public restroom...with his mother standing guard at the door, for God's sake!

The thought made my cheeks want to disassociate themselves from the rest of my face.

"Well... I'd better..." I motioned toward the door.

He reached out. I told myself I should back away before I was scalded, but I failed. His hand, large and warm, skimmed my arm, scaring up goose bumps before falling to my hip. I was holding my breath. Our gazes clashed and my breath hitched, but he only smoothed a wrinkle from my dress and pulled his smoldering gaze from mine.

I gave him a stuttering nod and stumbled back half a stride.

"Well...it's been...It's been good knowing you, Lieutenant." Those might have been the weirdest words I had ever uttered in my life. And that's saying something. But they were also true. Yes, okay, knowing him had also been crazy and disorienting and scary as hell. But it had been good. For a while.

"Yeah," he said. The world froze as we stared at each other, and then he reached for me again.

I wasn't as strong this time and leaned toward him as though there were a hard wind at my back, but he just pulled the door open beside me.

It only took me a couple of lifetimes to come to my senses, an eternity to stomp out the fire in my underduds. Then I turned like a poorly programmed automaton and goose-stepped out the door.

His mother glanced at me, wide-eyed, then raised her dark gaze accusingly to her son.

"Geraldo!" she scolded, sotto voce. "What are you thinking? You will never have the woman of your dreams if you are done so quick."

Chapter 6

> Death is nothing but a vague rumor to the young ... until someone tries to off you with a poker. Then it gets pretty damn real.
>
> —*Christina McMullen, PhD*

"So, Jeremy..." I glanced down at the handwritten record on my little desk and swiveled my cushy chair toward the comfy client couch. I was sitting in my modest office in a modest part of town across from the modest coffee shop I could no longer bear to look at after the debacle with its owner two nights before. Even though Tony had said nothing about my extended visit to the restroom, I was pretty sure my electrocuted hair and steam-wrinkled sheath must have made him guess that something had gone down in the ladies' room. And I use the word *ladies'* quite loosely here. "How's school going?"

He shrugged. This was only my second session with Jeremy Jones, but I was getting pretty tired of his indolent shrugs already. He was one of those kids who thought his life too hard to bear ... one of those kids, coincidently, who'd had everything handed to him on a silver salver. Salver ... ah, my erstwhile classiness had returned.

"Have you had any more trouble with Mr. Fowler?"

Another shrug

"He's your chemistry teacher, isn't—"

"Just..." He turned toward me, disdain written across his arrogant features like a road map to teenage angst. He had very pale skin, very dark hair, and enough attitude to suggest he might actually be a vampire. I considered that possibility for a second before remembering, with some ambiguity, that vampires didn't actually exist. Which gave Sookie Stackhouse a whole lot less to worry about. The old Chrissy had loved the *True Blood* series and the books that inspired them. I mean, seriously, the men were sexy as hell and didn't feel a burning need to wear a lot of superfluous clothes. But the new, improved Chrissy didn't have time for such tripe. She simply felt it was important to stay abreast of my clients' literary choices. "Just give it up!" He paused and narrowed his eyes. "'They certified that I am sane, but I know I am a madman.'"

I stared at him.

"That's Tolstoy. Maybe you've heard of him."

Ah, an intellectual. I smiled benignly.

"You can't help me. Nobody can," he added.

"Bullshit." I said the word calmly and with very little inflection, just to see what would happen.

His eyes opened wide. My smile amped up a little.

"That's Tony Stark. Perhaps you've heard of *him*."

He lowered his brows. Despite his considerable height and obvious anger, I was pretty sure I could take him down if I had to. He weighed about as much as a hangnail. And in my present mood, I rather liked the idea of a tussle.

"Human beings are trash," he said. "That's Freud."

"Yes, I recognized the reference."

"He also—"

"Freud was an ass," I said.

He stopped short, mouth agape.

I watched him blandly, waiting for his next gambit.

"My last therapist thought he was a genius."

"Maybe he was an ass, too."

"She!" He spat the word, as if the gender difference explained everything.

I watched his expression, read the hostility, and tried to guess at its roots. His parents seemed to believe it was caused by "sexual confusion," aka his homosexuality...which they completely condoned; they just wanted to see him happy. Or so they told me in no uncertain terms. Perhaps it was the absoluteness that made me question their sincerity. "I didn't mean to imply that women can't be asses, too." A particularly poignant moment in a restroom barely thirty-six hours ago was living proof.

He struggled through that with narrowed eyes.

"Which one hurt you?" I asked.

He stared at me, all hot rage and cold bravado, but underneath that fragile patina was a frightened little boy. If only I could find him amongst all the bullshit.

"I just want to be left alone," he rasped finally.

"Why? What's the problem?"

"I told you last week, I don't have any problems. My life is perfect. You said so yourself."

I hadn't said that exactly, but it has been proven time and again that facts are some of the easiest things in the world to ignore. "Are you concerned about your sexual orientation?"

He looked surprised for the briefest of seconds, then locked it away, going for his default expression: boredom with a touch of I'm-the-shit and a big-ass dose of you-*are*-shit. "Being queer's all the rage these days. Didn't you know that?"

"I didn't. Tell me about it."

"Everybody wants to have a gay friend. It's not a party without a pansy."

"Wow. And here I am without so much as a daffodil. So you go to a lot of parties?"

"Everybody needs a mascot."

"When was the last one?"

That shrug again. I considered slapping him upside the head just to provoke a different response, but sometimes parents get a little uptight about physical abuse.

"Do boys and girls want mascots in equal measure?"

I could see the fragile beginnings of his desire to talk, to unburden. It was that burning need to share that made my job possible. I waited.

"The jocks are jealous of us."

"Of the gays?"

He shrugged. "Fags are the ones hanging with their girlfriends."

I ignored the crude terminology. I had to guess that despite the fact that he attended Harvard Westlake, a school that probably cost more than my humble little abode in Sunland, he'd heard worse. "Why?"

"Because we don't waste our time on sports and crap."

"That seems like a generalization," I said. "I've known gay men who play football, wrestle, run track."

"That's not my thing."

"What is?"

He shrugged, struggled to remain silent, then spoke. "I sing."

"Really?" I felt a little like singing myself. Maybe he was finally ready to open up. "You any good?"

Another shrug.

Or not.

"I sing, too," I said. "Make a little money on the side."

Interest flickered in his eyes. "You got a band?"

"No. Actually, people pay me to *quit* singing."

He stared at me, snorted derisively. It wasn't a vast improvement on the I'm-so-bored-I'm barely-breathing shrug, but I'd take what I could get.

"What kind of music do you like?" I asked.

He glowered. I probed.

"Rock? Soul? P—"

"Fucking ad execs!"

His outburst came out of nowhere. From which, coincidently, the most pertinent information often appears. "You don't like ad executives?"

"Corporate stooges, selling worthless shit to worthless people."

I took a wild leap, knowing something about his familial situation. "Do your parents want you to follow them into the family business?"

He ground his teeth.

"Dad wanted me to be a plumber," I said. "Mom's goals weren't quite so lofty, but she thought I could be an okay hairstylist if I really applied myself."

He stared at me, probably sure I was kidding. I wasn't.

"I told her I'd rather die."

The following silence was heavy. I spoke softly into it. "Why do you want to die, Jeremy?"

He glowered, but the effect was somewhat ruined by the tears that flooded his eyes. "I never said I did."

"Not to me."

His lips trembled. His face contorted. I had seen that expression on a hundred other lovelorn souls.

"What's his name?"

"Who?"

"Whoever you think is worth dying for."

He didn't respond.

"Listen, Jeremy, I know you think this is the end of the world as you know it, but—"

He jerked to his feet, grabbed the armrests on my roller chair and yanked me close. "I'm not the one who's going to die!" he snarled.

I didn't move. Couldn't. The raw rage on his face held me immobile, and before I could articulate an appropriate response, he pivoted away and stalked from the room.

I remained as I was, waiting for my heart to quit trying to jump from my chest. Had he just threated my life? Or was someone else in danger? And if so, did I call the school? His parents? The cops?

Uncertain of everything and tired beyond reason, I swiveled shakily to the right and dropped my forehead onto the desktop as I tried to remember why I had ever become a therapist.

Holy hell, I was a loser. What did I think I was doing, counseling others while my own life was a joke? A joke in very bad taste. Maybe my father had been right. Plumbers hardly even have to talk to people, and, as an added bonus, they get to wear those low pants that show their butt cracks while—

Hearing Shirley's footfalls coming down the hallway, I lifted my head, straightened my spine, and fiddled heroically with Jeremy's file.

"How'd it go?" she asked.

"Okay," I said, and silently wondered if I was losing my lying edge.

"Yeah?" She squinted at me. "He looked kind of angry when he left."

"Who? Jeremy?" I waved a dismissive hand. Shirley was a single mother of about 117 kids. Admittedly, the majority of them were grown, but she still had a passel of people to care for and I didn't want her to worry that her employer was stupid enough to get her pants sued or possibly worse... get herself killed. "It's just the eye makeup that makes him look that way."

"So you're all right?"

"Yes. Sure. Of course. Why do you ask?"

"You don't hardly ever have paperclips stuck to your forehead 'less you're a little down."

"Oh." I put my hand to my brow and, sure enough, paperclip. I cleared my throat as I tugged it away.

"What's up, Ms. McMullen?"

I considered lying, but she seemed to have inherited Laney's psychic powers with the job. I felt my shoulders slump. "I should have listened to my dad."

She considered that for an instant before shaking her head. "Plumbing wouldn't be any easier than this job."

"You sure?"

"My uncle was a plumber. Threw his back out installing a sink in a fourth-floor walkup."

But you get to wear those low-rise pants."

"It wouldn't be no good fashion statement for you. And look on the bright side... no one's tried to kill you today." She gave me an appraising glance, followed by a scowl that probably kept all 117 of her kids shaking in their Nikes. "Have they?"

"Not that I know of."

"Well, if you don't know about it, it don't hardly matter," she said, then, "Andrews is still in jail, right?"

Just the thought of the man who had once kidnapped Laney made me feel a little shaky, but I kept my chin up. "So far as I know."

"And that dirty cop what tried to kill you and Lavonn, he still dead?"

I swallowed my bile, remembering the showdown on 6th Street. "Probably."

"And the old dude with the poker—"

"Shirley!" I snapped, then calmed myself. "You've got to quit trying to make me feel better."

She grinned a little, teeth shark-white against her ebony skin. "I'm out of time anyhow. Your next client is on his way."

I winced, but resisted clonking my head back onto the desktop. "Is it the cross-dresser or the narcissist?"

"It's the cross-dressing narcissist," she said, and left my office just as the front bell rang.

By the time the day was over, I felt like my mind had been weed-whacked to within an inch of its life. It was seven o'clock on a Monday evening and I wanted nothing more than to eat my weight in fried foods while watching *The Princess Bride* for the thousandth time from the relative comfort of my ratty couch. But when I had traipsed across the parking lot, I saw my gym bag sitting on the passenger seat of my little Saturn. I glowered at it as I slid behind the wheel. It glowered back. Usually, I'm a runner. And by that I mean that if I roll out of bed in time, and if it's not too hot or too cold or too windy...and if it's the right cycle of the moon with the proper degree of humidity, I will drag my sorry ass up and down the streets of Sunland twice a week. But the cycle of the moon had been off lately and my sorry ass was getting sorrier by the day. So I had paid actual money to work out. To me, it has always seemed counterintuitive to pay for something you don't want, but upon further consideration, I realized that if I invested real money for the right to exercise, I would, by dint of being truly cheap, exercise.

I glared at the gym bag again, still dreaming of my sweet Westley ... and my sweet couch ... but as I snugged up my seat belt, I noticed that my belly was making inroads over the webbing.

Angry at the seat belt, my belly, and the world at large, I cranked up the Saturn and puttered toward Foothills Athletic Club in La Crescenta.

The sun was just slipping behind the Santa Monica Mountains when I reached my destination. Leery about getting too much exercise before I began to exercise, I cruised around the parking lot twice in an effort to find the slot closest to the door. Spotting a nifty space not twenty feet from the handicap parking, I gunned the motor, but a silver Lexus was closer. Seeing me coming, however, the driver waved congenially and sailed on past.

Huh ... a Good Samaritan ... in L.A. Feeling marginally better about life in general and the human condition in particular, I parked the Saturn and marched into the gym.

Fifteen minutes later, I was climbing fictional stairs and staring at the well-toned derriere of the guy in front of me. Which led me to the secondary advantage of having a gym membership. If the fact that I was paying money didn't get me in the door, heavily exercised glutes should do the trick. These glutes in particular sauntered up to a well-muscled back and arms massive enough to dead lift a pachyderm. I could imagine him lifting *me* in those well-toned arms. Could almost feel his—

"You ready to have some fun?"

Jerking my gaze to the right, I realized Adonis was standing next to me. His bare chest glistened with sweat. His biceps were bulging and the overhead lights glistened off a smile with enough wattage to intimidate Tujunga Electric.

"I…" I glanced around, wondering if I had entered an alternate universe, but two overweight women were still pumping iron on the benches against the wall, while a balding fellow in a T-shirt that read *Beefcake* was using the butterfly machine. His man boobs jiggled in an unbecoming but familiar manner. I shifted my gaze back to Adonis. I knew I should act affronted. Perhaps a truly dignified individual would even slap his face. But I didn't want to be rude…or alone. "What do you have in mind?" I asked.

His smile dimmed by a couple dozen watts. "I…asked if you were done," he said.

I blinked.

"With the Stairmaster," he explained. "You quit moving a couple of minutes ago."

Chapter 7

Tomorrow *is* another day. And isn't that just the shits.

—Christina McMullen, deep in a Cool Ranch Doritos binge and not quite ready to be cheered up

My trip to the Saturn followed quickly on the heels of the humiliating interaction with Adonis. I didn't bother to take a shower or change out of my gym clothes, but I did buy an ultra-nutritious, uber-expensive yogurt, which I stuck into the pocket of my less-than-classy hoodie before hustling, red faced, out the door.

It was dark by the time I reached the parking lot, and even though the area was relatively well lit, I felt the hair on the back of my neck stand at attention. Maybe it was the dip in my self-esteem that made me jumpy, maybe it was my frequent interactions with folks who had a few quackers out of order, or maybe it was Shirley's earlier attempt to cheer me up.

But whatever the reason, I was on the alert as I quick-stepped across the asphalt to my car. Footfalls echoed in my wake. I jerked around, scanning the area, but there was only a little old lady slipping into her Mercedes. She was eighty years old if she was a day, but she was lean and upright, and by the look of her could still take me down if it came to blows. Such is L.A.'s fitness-obsessed populace. Such, also, is my frame of mind that I continually consider whether or not I can best octogenarians.

Trying to calm my heart, I turned back to my car. It was then that a body lurched at me, arm raised. I screamed and jerked away.

From my right, someone yelled. My attacker lurched back, giving me time to catch my breath and realize, rather belatedly, that the knife I was certain he'd been holding looked a little more like a cell phone than a deadly weapon. His brow furrowed nervously as he clutched it to his chest.

"I'm... I'm sorry," he sputtered. "I didn't—"

"You okay?" A second man, presumably the one who had yelled, came trotting around the cars that remained between us. "What's going on?"

"It's my fault," Guy One said. I scanned him again for a knife, but he seemed to be bereft of bloody stilettos. Neither did he have a hatchet, AK-47, or nuclear bomb. "I didn't mean to scare you." He spread his hands out to his sides. He was Hispanic and wore a faded green T-shirt over black sweatpants. His demeanor was apologetic. "I just wanted to tell you..." He glanced at my face, which, even on normal days, is as pale as rice flour. Right about then, it was probably translucent. He backed away another half a step, as if he feared I might pass out should he venture within ten feet of my personal body bubble. "Your tire's bad."

It took all my rapidly depleting reserves to jerk my attention to the Saturn's left front tire. It was as flat as Adonis's belly. I blinked at it, mind tripping along in slow motion.

The men stared at me in tandem silence.

"Well... Sorry again about scaring you," Guy One said, and scurried away as if escaping the plague.

I might have nodded. I might have recited the Pledge of Allegiance. Who knows? My mind was numb.

The other fellow was still staring at me. He wore a dark windbreaker, jeans, and a red baseball cap over summer-blond hair. "Do you have someone to help you with that?" he asked.

"What?" My thinking cells were tumbling around like loose dice in my cranium, but I tried to shake them back into some semblance of order. "What?"

"An auto club or a ... a husband or something who could change your tire?"

I didn't have either of those things. AAA was too expensive, and husbands, so I had been told, could be just as costly. I shook my head again. The numbness in my hands had obviously spread to my brain. The parking lot was silent except for cars zipping by on the 210. "How 'bout a jack, you got one of those?"

I cleared my throat, trying to bring my mind back into focus. "I think so."

"You want help?"

"No." I did. I really did, but not if he was going to try to kill me, and judging by the number of attempts on my life thus far, the odds were pretty high. "I'll be fine."

"You sure?" he asked, but he was already backing away, looking relieved as hell.

"I'm ... Yes. I'm sure," I said, finding my equilibrium slowly. "But thank you."

Half an hour later, as I struggled with nuts and jacks—neither the kind I secretly wished to be struggling with—I knew for certain that I was crazy. No sane person would turn down a Good Samaritan. At least not in Los Angeles, where angels go to die.

Still, by the time I reached home, I was feeling better about myself. I had, after all, defeated the flat tire without any testosterone intervention.

When I punched in my security code and shambled into the house, Harlequin greeted me with the ebullience usually reserved for long-lost lovers and good news from Powerball. After resting his broad muzzle on my shoulder for a moment, he dropped to his platter-sized paws, trotted to his empty food dish, and gazed at it in mournful longing. He looked hungry enough to cry. Apparently, I had, for once, been successful in hiding all my empty soup cans and candy stashes. And a good thing, too, because the cans tended to get caught on his oversized snout, while chocolate more often than not precipitated flatulence reminiscent of a backfiring Fiat and emergency visits to Dr. Kemah.

Still, the fact that I had neglected to buy kibble caused curse words to swarm through my head. But I try not to corrupt young minds like Harley's even when I have to venture back into the cold, cruel world to rectify the situation. For a moment I considered feeding myself first. But long-lost lovers don't come along every day, so with a martyred sigh, I clipped the leash onto woman's best friend's super-sized collar and tripped back out to my car.

It took only a few minutes to reach Tomcat Pet Warehouse, a mom-and-pop store larger than most third-world countries. Harlequin trotted alongside me, thwapping his tail at lesser canines and eyeing cats with enough interest to make the hair rise on their arched backs. A macaw riding on his owner's shoulder gave him pause. He tilted his blocky head at it, then gazed at me as if questioning the wisdom of allowing such an animal to remain uneaten, but before I could explain the intricacies of civilization, Harlequin was attacked by a lanky tornado.

I stumbled back a step, but the whirlwind had already morphed into some kind of hairy mongrel that had wrapped its forelegs around Harley's neck and seemed intent on gnawing off his right ear.

"Quit it," someone chided, and tugged at the mongrel's leash. The reprimand did nothing whatsoever to rectify the situation, but I followed the nylon cord to the hand that held it, zipped up the well-toned arm and across a broad shoulder to the face. "Hey, Chrissy."

"Eddie?" Eddie Friar and I go back to my early days in L.A. In fact, we dated for a time, but that was before we realized that he and I had more commonalities than differences... namely, an attraction to men. "What are you doing here?"

"Spending my life savings."

"What?"

"Khan," he said, nodding toward the animal that had wrestled Harlequin to the floor. They tussled joyfully, endless limbs paddling. "He eats enough to fuel a pack animal."

"Uh huh," I agreed.

"And he doesn't sleep. Ever. He's like a windup toy in hyperdrive." His voice sounded haunted, and I noticed for the first time that his handsome face was haggard. "Sophie's threatened to leave home."

I laughed. Sophie, believe it or not, is Eddie's greyhound. She's elegant and docile and, I'm quite certain, smarter than the vast majority of her two-legged counterparts. "You should have known the dangers of bringing a young male into your house by now."

"I'm a slow learner. Hey, tell you what," he said, gaze still on the wrestling hounds. "I'll feed him for a week if I can have him for a night."

"What?"

"Harley." He sounded desperate and a little crazy. "I'll take good care of him. You know I will. His own bowl. His own bone. His own...You know what? He can have my bed. I'll sack out on the couch."

"What are you talking about?"

"Khan's driving me out of my mind. I just need something to wear him down. And look at how happy they are."

Harley did look pretty thrilled, if his drunken expression and wriggly body language was any indication.

"I'll just give them a couple hours together, then separate them for the night. Tomorrow morning, they can play again...if Harley wants to. I'll return him when you're done with work."

"I don't know. He's pretty attached to me." Or, more accurately, I was attached to him. "Maybe I'd better—"

"T-bone steak. Organic and pasture fed."

I tilted my head at him. "For me or for him?"

"Both. Both of you. And remember my potatoes au gratin."

I did. Favorably. "What about them?"

"I'll make a double batch."

"With ham?"

He nodded. "Creamy in the middle and crunchy on the top. It'll be ready at seven o'clock tomorrow night if you want to come by."

I felt myself weakening. "Harley does like a nice potato dish."

In the end, he muscled dog food into both of our vehicles, then let the dogs hop into his backseat. I felt embarrassingly maudlin as he slammed the door and drove into the sunset.

In less than forty minutes, I was back home. Hoisting the dog-food bag out of the trunk was no small feat, but I am woman, watch me roar, and grunt, and—

"Hello."

I jerked my attention toward the sidewalk. A man in a dark windbreaker stood not twenty feet away. He looked disturbing like the guy from the gym parking lot.

"What are you doing here?" My tone was something between a snarl and a gasp.

Windbreaker smiled and took a step toward me. Something gleamed in his hand. I backed away, bumping into the Saturn's left taillight.

"I know this probably seems strange," he began, but that was the last I heard. Terror, powered by a dozen near-death experiences and my own possibly overactive imagination, fueled me. Dropping the dog food, I torpedoed toward the driver's side. For a moment, my fingers scrambled futilely against the handle, but finally I tore the door open and shot inside. Engaging the locks, I jerked my gaze to the rearview mirror.

He was coming! Stalking toward me.

I squawked and shoved my key in the ignition.

He had reached my bumper, but I was already yanking the Saturn into drive, leaving him behind.

I drove like a maniac, screeching around the turns, hands shaking on the wheel. But as far as I could tell, no one followed me. By the time I could think, I was squealing onto Rosehaven.

Jerking the Saturn into park, I raced toward Rivera's front door. It was locked. I rang the bell, then glanced breathlessly behind me.

No murdering thugs seemed to be lumbering up the walkway, but I wasn't about to take any chances on that fortuitous trend. I raised my fist to pound on the door just as it opened.

"McMullen!" I had a momentary impression of Rivera's shocked face before half falling, half stumbling inside.

He caught me. I pressed my face against the lieutenant's chest, shamelessly hiding from the world.

"What's wrong? Chrissy..." He closed the door and wrapped his arms around me.

I felt my eyes well up and my body shake like a battered piñata.

"Chrissy." He pushed me to arms' length. "What the hell happened?"

From the kitchen, his phone rang. I squawked and jerked away, knees buckling. He caught me before I hit the floor.

I'm not proud of the fact that he had to carry me into the living room. My legs had turned to flan, my mind to Jell-O, both sugary snacks not high on my to-be-eaten list. But still viable when there was no pecan pie in sight.

He set me carefully against the armrest of the couch, as if I were a ticking time bomb, then drew back. I clung to his hand, but he tugged away with a promise to return in a minute.

I watched him lock the front door and check the windows. His scowl was dark, his glances toward me worried, before he disappeared into his kitchen.

I drew my knees up to my chest and huddled against the cushions until he returned with a tumbler a quarter full of amber liquid.

"Drink this," he ordered, pressing it into my hand.

I took a sip and wrinkled my nose.

"All of it," he said.

"Are *you* trying to kill me, too?"

Stormy emotion shone in his dusky eyes but he set his jaw and tipped the glass to my lips. "Drink it."

I did so in one long gulp, then shuddered and set the tumbler aside.

"Tell me what happened."

I swallowed again. It was bile this time but still tasted marginally better than the whiskey. "I think... I think..." Now that it came down to it, I wasn't at all sure what I thought. Everything seemed sketchy.

"Start at the beginning," he ordered.

I nodded disjointedly. "The rhythm method isn't very reliable."

His scowl deepened. Had I not known the dark lieutenant on an intimate basis, I would have sworn that wasn't possible.

"They should have used an IUD or the pill or a diaphragm or maybe all of the above if they didn't want another—"

"Not that far back," he said, and sat down beside me. Practical. He had always been a practical man.

"You don't want to hear about my parents' failed contraception plans?" I fiddled with a pillow, glanced nervously toward the front door.

"Chrissy..."

"No. You're right." I shivered. "No one in his right mind would want to think about them copulating."

"You're okay now," he said. "Just tell me what happened."

I was willing to oblige but found it rather difficult to marshal a single coherent thought. I cleared my throat. "There was a man in a windbreaker by my garage."

Now that I said it, this didn't sound like the groundbreaking news it had seemed a few minutes earlier. It wasn't as if it was against city ordinances to have strangers pass by your house. Or to wear windbreakers, for that matter... although the fashion police frowned on such things.

I watched Rivera's face, waiting for a dismissive sneer, but his expression remained dour. Lieutenant Jack Rivera,

I've long known, has the kind of paranoia generally attributed to prey animals ... and cops. Inside his personal vehicle, he kept an anti-theft club for his anti-theft club.

"I think ..." I exhaled shakily. "I think he had a knife." Not that I wanted to add to that paranoia.

"Did he hurt you?"

"No. I jumped in the car, locked the door. Came straight here."

He nodded his approval. "Was it someone you knew?"

"No. Yes. I ..." I nodded, belatedly remembering why I had been so freaked out. "I saw him. Outside the gym."

"When?"

"An hour ago. There was another man." I described him briefly. "But I don't think they were together. He seemed happy to get out of there, but Windbreaker Guy offered to help me change my tire."

"You had a flat?"

I nodded.

"Was it slashed?"

I caught my breath. Despite my own paranoia exhibited in the parking lot I had somehow never considered that possibility. "How would I know?"

"You wouldn't," he said.

I blinked at him. "Then I don't know."

"What happened after that?"

"I said I didn't need help. So he left, or at least I think he did. I changed it myself."

"Why didn't you call me?"

"Because we broke up."

He scowled but didn't argue. "Did you go straight home?"

"Yes."

"And he was there?"

"Yes. No," I corrected. "Harley was out of food, so we went to Tomcat."

His brows quirked. "The strip club or the—"

"The pet-food store."

He watched, maybe not quite believing. Which was, perhaps, fair enough. I've been known to spend some time at the Strip Please, where male dancers like to strut their stuff, but only in a professional capacity, of course.

"On Lowell," I added, remembering to drag out my snooty voice just in time.

He gave me a look but let it slide. "Did anything out of the ordinary happen while you were there?"

"The cashier wasn't rude to me."

He raised a brow.

"And Eddie was there."

"Eddie?" A carnivorous growl of jealousy sweetened his tone, but I tried not to enjoy it too much.

"Eddie Friar."

"Your gay ex?"

"He wasn't gay when we dated."

The left corner of his mouth twitched a little, but he refrained from laughing. It was a good choice on his part. Stress tends to make me a little unpredictable... and somewhat vicious.

"He took Harley home for a play date with his puppy."

I could practically see his mind processing that information. "Anything else happen?"

"Not really."

"You didn't see the guy in the windbreaker?"

"Not until I got home." I shivered again, even though my story seemed a little less terrifying in the safety of Rivera's cozy living room.

"Where was he when you first saw him?"

"In the parking lot. Not—"

"When you got home. Where was he then?"

"On the sidewalk."

"Did he have a vehicle?"

Another question I had failed to consider. "I don't know."

"Was he there when you arrived or did he follow you?"

"I'm not sure."

"Did he speak?"

"He said hello."

"Hello or hi?"

I paused a beat. "Are you serious?"

His brows quirked with impatience. "What else did he say?"

"Something about..." I matched him scowl for scowl, thinking hard, remembering things, little facts that hadn't quite surfaced before. "Something about how I might think this was strange."

"What was strange?"

"I don't know." I was starting to feel kind of silly, realizing, rather belatedly perhaps, that it might have been possible that the guy in the parking lot and the guy on the sidewalk were two entirely different individuals. Truth be told, my skittering mind hadn't absorbed much more than the fact that they both wore dark windbreakers. But I wasn't quite ready to explain that to the glowering lieutenant. "That he was there, maybe. After seeing him at the gym."

His gaze felt hot.

"How'd he look?"

"Windbreaker Guy?" Maybe I was stalling. "See, that's the thing..." I tried an ingratiating smile. It might have looked more like a frenzied snarl.

"What's the thing?"

"I may have been mistaken."

"What?"

"I may have ..." I shook my head a little, as if disavowing the possibility I was about to share. "When one is sufficiently inundated with adrenaline, one can sometimes misinterpret the situation." And if one is *really* fucked up, sometimes she'll manufacture a crisis so as to have a reason to seek out the one person she desires above all others. But of course that wasn't the case here; I'm a licensed psychologist. "Even go so far as to manifest a miscreant when—"

"What the hell are you talking about?"

"I panicked! Okay? I panicked."

His expression suggested this might not be the startling news I thought it to be. "And?"

I took a deep breath. "Maybe they weren't the same guy."

He didn't even bother to look peeved. His patience was beginning to worry me almost as much as the probable ... possible ... actually not very likely ... attempt on my life. "You think there were two different men wearing windbreakers?"

"Could be."

"What color were they?"

"The windbreakers or the men?"

"Let's start with the men."

I fidgeted. "He ... they ... wore baseball caps. I couldn't tell much about their features."

"Describe the gym guy. Start at his cap and work your way down."

"Red. I think it was red. Or—"

"Or?"

"I'm not sure."

Exhaustion was setting in.

"What about his hair? Was it—"

"Blond," I said, excited now that I had an actual memory. "And long enough to see past his cap."

"Light blond?"

"About the same as Tony's."

"Your boy-toy at The Blvd?"

I ignored the jibe. "Yes."

"Was it him?"

"Of course not."

"It was dark. His face was obscured. How can you be sure?"

I gave him a look. "Because I'm not completely psychotic."

He neither denied nor confirmed.

"Tony's taller," I explained. "Windbreaker Guy was only medium height."

"Windbreaker could have been slouching."

"Tony's younger."

"How old was Windbreaker?"

"At least thirty."

He didn't grit his teeth, but it kind of looked like he wanted to.

"And Tony wouldn't wear a windbreaker if his—"

"Chrissy—"

I didn't give him time to tell me that was the most asinine reasoning he had ever heard. "It wasn't him," I said.

He scowled but continued on as if he believed me. "What about the other guy at the gym?"

"He wasn't Tony either."

He returned the look I had given him earlier. "Describe him."

"Short, handsome." I don't know why I added that. Not just to watch him bristle, I'm sure. Although no one has ever accused me of being *overly* mature. "Hispanic, I think."

"You think or you know?"

I considered that for a moment. "I know."

He nodded, moving on. "You never saw him again after he left?"

"No."

"And he and Windbreaker didn't seem to know each other?"

"I have no reason to think they did."

"Tell me exactly what happened."

I explained the entire incident from the time I exited the gym, seeing no reason to recap my embarrassing fantasy about the guy with the glutes and the imagined invitation to fun.

No, I assured him. Neither of the men in the parking lot had accosted me or made any indication that he meant to. One was short and dark. The other was medium height and blond. The short one wore a green T-shirt and black sweatpants. The other wore the windbreaker. I was beginning to believe that the LAPD probably wasn't going to run out to apprehend men on the basis of poor fashion sense alone.

I moved through the story like a robot on sedatives. It was beginning to sound more boring than scary.

"All right, let's talk about your arrival at your house. Did you notice anything suspicious when you first got there?"

"No."

"You're sure."

"Yes."

"So you entered by the front door."

"Correct."

"Where was Harley?"

"He, um ... he met me at the door."

"Does he usually?"

"Yes."

"Did he seem agitated?"

"No."

"He wasn't pacing or fidgeting or biting his nails?"

"No, no, and what the hell?" I was beginning to wish Windbreaker Guy had pulled out a gun and shot me in the head.

Rivera's frustration matched mine. "I can't help you if you don't answer my questions."

"I've answered them all forty-seven times."

"You have not answered—" He stopped himself, held up a palm. "So you didn't see Windbreaker Guy again until you returned from the store?"

"Correct," I said, calming my tone in concert with his.

"Did he have the knife when you first saw him or did he draw it later?"

I pursed my lips, trying to figure out how to phrase my thoughts. "About that..."

He flattened his lips into a thin line.

"I've been thinking..." I paused, wobbled my head at the unlikeliness of that scenario.

"What about him?"

"I realize I may have given you the impression that after my arrival at home, the gentleman—"

"Just spit it the hell out, McMullen."

"He wasn't threatening me!"

His brows shot up. He tilted his head as if an askew position might help him make sense of me.

I cleared my throat. "My bedroom window's been sticking."

"And you think the gentleman with the knife intended to scare it into opening?"

I forced a laugh. "I'm glad you see the humor in the situation."

He dropped his head a fraction of an inch, like a wolf preparing for the kill.

I refrained from fiddling with the piping on the couch ... and hiding under it. "It could have been ... Now that I've had sufficient time to consider the situation ... I begin to believe that the weapon in question might actually have been a ... screwdriver."

Rivera stared at me in silence for five full seconds, then jerked to his feet and paced away. At the end of his self-imposed tether, he turned to stare at me again.

I gave him my most winning smile, followed by a barely controlled wince. "I might have mentioned the sticky-window problem to Shirley a few days ago."

He narrowed his already narrowed eyes.

"She might have mentioned that fact to her nephew."

"Shirley's nephew is white?"

"And medium height," I added.

His dark brows dipped.

"And blond." I tensed, waiting for him to blast me. I had learned some time ago that cops don't particularly like it when folks cry wolf. Go figure. "And, you know, mid-thirties."

He inhaled deeply, exhaled slowly. As an exercise to maintain self-control, it was fairly effective. Still, I reminded myself to suggest a few other tools to defuse his temper in the future. He would probably find Dr. Dirkx's chapter thirteen quite enlightening. In fact, he might find the entire book helpful if he were to—

"I need a favor."

I blinked, thoughts tumbling to a halt. Since when did Lieutenant Jack Rivera ask for favors instead of delivering edicts, accusations, or threats?

"I want you to leave town," he said.

Chapter 8

People *will* surprise you, Pork Chop. But mostly, they'll just piss you off.

—Glen McMullen, delivering yet another life lesson to an impressionable Chrissy

I caught my breath. Leave town? Why would he want me to—

But the truth dawned on me: Rivera was mocking me, making light of my foolish phobias.

"Very funny," I said, and rose to my feet. My knees hardly shook at all. Such is the resilience of Christina McMullen, PhD. "Well... I'm glad I've amused you, Lieutenant. But I want you to consider this..." I raised a haughty brow. "Perhaps I have reason for my paranoia. Perhaps if the LAPD had protected me in the past—"

"Michael's moved out of your parents' house, hasn't he?"

I managed a confused expression.

"And Peter hasn't moved back in?"

I narrowed my eyes, suspicions firing up like Dad's bottle rockets.

"What do my moronic brothers' whereabouts have to do with anything?"

"Your old bedroom is empty."

"And that is significant because..."

"I'm sure you'd be welcome there."

My jaw dropped. My eyes opened wide, and for a second I almost believed he was serious. But even Rivera couldn't be deluded enough to think I would rather live with my family than be murdered by strangers. He had, after all, met them.

"If you wanted me out of your life all you had to do was ask," I said, and headed for the door, but he caught my arm in a grip that was neither amusing nor gentle.

"And you call yourself a therapist."

I stared at him.

"You think I'm trying to get rid of you, McMullen? Is that actually what you believe?" His voice was low and deadly earnest.

I waited, breath held, trying to figure out where this was heading. But the fire in his eyes made it difficult to think.

"Good God, look at you, you're..." He breathed the words, then gritted his teeth, almost stepping toward me but not quite. He pulled air into his lungs, chest expanding. "Have you heard of the Black Flames?"

His tone was ultra-serious. Too serious. He was putting me on... having a little laugh at my expense. "I'm afraid I don't have time to familiarize myself with all the boy bands that—"

"It's an Asian gang. Daiki's gang."

We stared at each other. My heart had slowed to the speed of an Irish dirge. "Why are you telling me this?" I asked, but truth to tell, I didn't really want to hear the answer.

"They're relatively new to L.A." He released my arm, scrubbed his face with his right hand. I hadn't realized until then how exhausted he looked. "Not warm and fuzzy, like the Crips or the Bloods. No scruples at all. No—"

"Rivera!" I felt panic bubbling up again. "Why—"

"They'll take out babies, children. Hell, they'll take out a whole city block if they're pissed enough." He clenched his jaw. "Their L.A. cartel is gaining power."

I blinked. "If you're trying to mess with my head, I think it might be working."

He only stared at me.

I licked my lips. "So that's what you've been working on? That's why I haven't seen you?"

"We arrested one of their key players last night. There will be repercussions." He let the statement fade. I searched his face, certain he was toying with me, but his expression suggested otherwise.

"So you were...you were involved in the arrest?" I was trying to be brave, or at least to refrain from peeing in my pants.

A muscle jumped in his jaw. "They like to have leverage."

The house was absolutely silent. I felt a little sick to my stomach. "Leverage?"

"Hostages."

"Holy shit," I breathed, and felt my bladder quiver.

"They keep them sedated...most of the time."

"Sedated?"

"Opiates, mainly. They're old-fashioned that way."

"You're making this up," I said, but the accusation was weak.

"Sometimes parts of the victims are found. A tongue. A—"

"I get the picture," I snapped, then desperately searched his face. It told me nothing I wanted to believe. I nodded once, backed away a step, then peeled off toward the bathroom. I reached the toilet an instant before my stomach rejected its contents.

By the time my legs were steady enough to carry me into the kitchen, Rivera was scrambling eggs. His fingers looked long and strangely elegant against the whisk's stainless steel handle. Our gazes met. Neither of us spoke. He lowered his gaze and dumped the eggs into a frying pan filled with cooked rice.

"You should have told me," I said.

"Why?" He didn't look up as he mixed the concoction with a wooden spoon. "So that you could pry into my business? So that you could do some dumb-ass thing that puts your life at risk? Again?"

"*Your* life's at—"

"I'm a cop!" The words were rife with frustration, hot with anger. "It's my job! I'm trained to keep you safe. Paid to keep you—" He waved a hand at the world, then clenched his fist and lowered it slowly. It shook.

I went to him like an apparition in a bad movie, steps stilted, body all but unmoving.

"Hey." My voice was soft.

His gaze met mine. Haunted. Tortured.

"I'm safe," I said. "I'm okay."

He closed his eyes. The spoon rattled to the stove. He shut off the burner like one in a trance.

"I'm all right," I said again.

He bumped a nod. I took his hand and led him back to the couch.

"How long has it been since you've eaten?" I asked.

"You have to leave," he said.

"Just..." I took a deep breath. "Just slow down a little."

"There's no time for slow."

I returned to his kitchen. Some time ago, he'd installed a granite-topped center island. Gleaming copper kettles hung from a metal grid attached to the ceiling. The room looked like *Better Homes and Gardens* porn. If I had a clean cup in my entire house it was a red-letter day.

After emptying the fried rice onto a plate I'd taken from his cupboard, I fished a fork out of a nearby drawer and took it to him.

"Eat," I said, setting the meal on the armrest.

He gazed at me, then pulled me down beside him and captured my hands.

"Promise you'll go."

I forced a laugh. "I can't go running back to my parents."

For a second, I thought he'd argue, but he jerked to his feet and paced away. "You're right. Somewhere else. Somewhere even I can't find you. Can't give you away no matter what happens."

"What do you mean, no matter what happens? What might happen? What—"

He pivoted toward me. "Do you know anyone in Switzerland?"

"Switzer—" I laughed. Sure, absolutely *positive*, that he was joking. "Very funny. Ho ho ho. But you've had your fun now. I'm sorry I panicked, okay? I'm sorry I—"

"Tell me you'll go." His eyes were mesmerizing, haunting. "Tell me you'll go, keep your head down, stay off the radar."

"I have clients."

A muscle jumped in his lean jaw. "Last I heard, psychologists weren't very effective without their tongues."

The air left my lungs in a hard rush. Blood evacuated my extremities.

"Harlequin," I said softly.

Rivera's face was hard now, his eyes flat. "He'll be happy with Eddie. And when things calm down, I'll pick him up."

"What about—"

"Shirley can take care of herself."

"If she can, so can I," I said, but he didn't even bother to argue.

"You've got to go. Pack light. Just the necessities," he said, tugging me toward the door. I dragged him to a halt.

"Quit it! Will you..." He turned toward me. I huffed a laugh. "This is insane. I can't just drop everything."

"If there was a better option I'd suggest that." His gaze burned into mine.

I swallowed. "When would I have to leave?"

"Tonight. Tomorrow at the latest. And you have to stay gone. A month. Maybe more. I'll let you know when you can come back."

"A month! Let me know... How?" The question was little more than a hiss of air. "You said you don't want to know where I am."

"When it's safe, I'll find you."

It sounded so *Last of the Mohicans* that I almost laughed.

"That's crazy. Don't you—"

"Please." The single word was soft but intense. "Please do this for me. So I can think. So I can keep my head, knowing you're safe." Then he kissed me.

"This is ridiculous." I was breathless now, from the fear, from the soul-searing kiss. "What about the other cops? They have girlfriends. They have families."

"I don't love them," he said.

I stared wordlessly for a second, and then I jumped him, kissing him with a *Fifty Shades* kind of frenzy.

He kissed me back.

I ripped at his shirt. He grabbed my ass. The world receded in a clash of smoldering passion, but suddenly he jerked his lips from mine.

"No!" I'm not proud of the fact that I whimpered the word.

Rivera didn't even glance toward me. Instead, his attention was riveted on the kitchen door. On the opposite side of that room was a small porch that led outside.

I froze, breath held. He unwound my legs from around his waist. I dropped my feet to the floor. His eyes were as hard as agates as he pushed me behind him. A gun appeared in his hand, possibly retrieved from an orifice only possessed by cops and Hollywood cowboys.

"Call nine-one-one." His voice was low and deadly.

I searched frantically for my purse, but I hadn't brought it in. The sound of breaking glass shattered me.

I gasped. Rivera pushed me down beside the couch.

Something scraped against a wall.

I stifled a scream. Rivera dropped down beside me, slipped his fingers behind my neck, and kissed me. His hand was steady now, his voice dead level, his eyes the same. "Leave," he ordered.

"I—"

"Now." His voice never wavered. "The garage is secure. When I stand up, I want you to get there as fast as you can. My keys are—"

"No!" I shook my head, but he caught my jaw, forced me to meet his gaze.

"My keys are on the hook next to the steps."

"I can't—"

He tightened his grip on my chin. "Get in my car."

Something banged against the wall of the porch. I flinched, heart pounding, but he didn't move. "Get in my car," he repeated, "lock the doors, and start the engine."

I was breathing hard and fast now.

"Do you hear me?" he asked. "Start the engine and hit the gas."

"What if they get in before—"

"Don't wait for the door to open. Don't look back. Just go."

I heard a whisper outside the kitchen window and gasped an expletive.

"Chrissy. Listen to me. You can do this."

My heart was beating a hole in my chest. "Where?" I whispered. "Where do I go?"

"Where no one can find you. Where *I* can't find you."

"But... My phone. My—"

"Leave it! Leave everything."

Footsteps! I could hear them creeping around the outside of the house, surrounding us.

"Do you understand me, McMullen?" He drew me back to him. "You have to disappear."

"I can't—"

"You can. For me." He smiled grimly, the slightest curve of irresistible lips. "You can do anything."

"I—" I began, but a noise boomed from the porch.

I shrieked. Rivera yanked me to my feet and shoved me toward the garage. I tripped, almost fell, and lunged forward. I grabbed the door handle. It was locked, but I managed to tear it open and then I was through. My fingers, numb as cucumbers, dropped the keys.

I fell to my knees, searching wildly. There! Under the folding chair. A gunshot echoed in the house behind me. I snatched up the keys and stumbled toward Rivera's car. The engine roared to life. I jabbed at the garage-door opener on the visor, slammed the Jeep into drive, and screamed away, taking half the door with me. Someone jumped out of the way and somersaulted to one side. Shots were fired. I careened onto the street and tore away, but I could see someone already lurching into a white sedan behind me.

I took the next turn on two wheels and sped into the night.

Chapter 9

I'm not lost. I just don't know where the hell I am.

—*James McMullen, in an atypically honest but typically stupid moment*

I sat up, groggy and disoriented. Outside, stunted trees and scrubby cactus surrounded me. It took me several seconds to realize the nightmare of just a few hours before had been real. I remained absolutely still, enveloped by rancid terror, but the morning was silent.

A car cruised past me on the right, half hidden by the scruffy underbrush, thick as L.A. narcissists, between me and the road. I held my breath, but the car didn't stop. And a good thing. The Jeep had virtually no fuel. I had lost the white sedan in less than a mile but hadn't slowed down for hours.

I'd been running on hope and fumes for what seemed like an eternity. Still dressed in spandex shorts, tank top, and tattered hoodie, I was cold and exhausted and stiff. I'd had no way to refill the Jeep's tank. No cash, no credit cards, nothing to barter. My only real skill was as a therapist, and I rather doubted someone in Where-the-Hell-Am-I was going to fill up my tank in exchange for being asked about his relationship with his mother.

I wanted nothing more than to remain in hiding ... unless it was to learn that the whole ordeal had been some horrible mistake I would later laugh at over cinnamon-swirl French toast and thick-ass bacon. But my bladder reminded me in no uncertain terms that other needs were even more essential than breakfast.

Peering around me, I unlocked the driver's door and stepped cautiously outside, but all remained quiet. I took a step forward.

Something sprang for me from the trees. I yanked back with a shriek of terror. But my attacker morphed into a blue jay and flew away with a startled caw slightly more dulcet than my own.

Steadying my hands, I thanked the organ gods for a strong bladder and hurried into the woods. In a moment, I was relieving myself behind a bad-tempered succulent.

"Don't move."

I gasped. My much-lauded bladder trembled. The voice was guttural and came from close behind me. My hands remained where they were, clasping my shorts. How had the Black Flames found me? I'd driven all night, checked my mirrors a million times. Had they put some kind of tracking device on Rivera's Jeep? My mind spun with questions, but the answers hardly mattered. They had me dead to rights. But I wouldn't go down without a fight. I skimmed the woods, desperate for some kind of weapon ... Nothing but prickly plants and the occasional nerve-racking blue jay.

"Think you're pretty smart, don't ya?"

I straightened, but I was too scared to turn around. "Who are you? How'd you find me? Why ... why are you doing this?" My voice shook. I'd like to believe I was just acting, planning to keep him talking until I could devise some ingenious plan of escape. Hollywood has made a cool gazillion by banking on that very idea. But I'm afraid the truth is a little more embarrassing; I was scared out of my mind and blabbering like a lunatic. My hands shook, but I managed to pull up my shorts. I would not die with my bum hanging out. It seemed little enough to ask of my last moments of life, but my knuckles brushed the inside of my sweatshirt's pocket. It hung low, bulging.

"Why?" he asked, and snorted. The sound was low and evil. "I think ya know the answer to that."

I could hear his footsteps in the brush behind me and swallowed. Time was running out and there was no weapon in sight. Nothing within reach, unless...What did I have in my pocket? Memory burst in my brain. Yogurt. I had purchased it at the gym. My workout twelve hours before seemed like a lifetime ago, the relative safety of the parking lot, a sanctuary.

"Turn around," he said. "So I can see your face."

I gritted my teeth, calling on any latent modicum of courage I might have overlooked. It was now or never. Snatching the yogurt from my pocket, I twisted and threw with all my might.

My aim was shockingly accurate. The carton, warm from my body, exploded in my assailant's face like an overripe egg. I spun away, leaping through the brush. Twigs scraped my legs. Branches tore at my hair. But I reached the Jeep. My fingers clutched spastically at the door handle. I clawed it open, leapt inside, and fired up the engine.

It wasn't until then that I saw the old man sitting on the ground, legs bent at awkward angles like a broken doll's. I scanned the area. No hulking criminals seemed to be ferreted away in the trees. No ninjas were leaping toward me like...well, like ninjas.

I remained immobile, heart thumping in my chest as the scrawny figure creaked to his feet. His hands were empty, entirely bereft of the cannon I was certain he carried. I scanned the area again. Nothing disturbed the stillness.

When he spoke, I couldn't hear his words. Peach goop was splattered across his face and chest. His camouflage cargo pants hung low on practically imaginary hips and he wore two plaid shirts, both buttoned incorrectly. I was still breathing hard, still feeling shaky, but I was nothing if not stupidly curious.

Making certain my locks were engaged, I powered down the driver's window, engine still running.

"Why'd you go and do that?" His voice was scratchy, his brows beetled over a pemmican face.

I darted my eyes this way and that. He seemed to be entirely alone. "Who are you?"

"Me! Who in blazes are *you*?"

I scanned the woods again. Still no WMDs. "I asked first." It seemed that I had, at a moment's notice, returned to my usual level of immaturity.

"I'm the owner of this here property."

"Are you Asian?"

He swiped a hand across his face, then propped his fists on the baggy waistband of his camo pants. "What the devil are you talking about, girl?"

"You're not..." A noise crackled off to the right. I jumped, but it was just another bird, trying to scare the liver out of me. "You're not a Black Flame?"

He shook his head. "Could be you're even crazier than the others," he said.

"So you're not trying to kill me?"

"Didn't plan on it," he said, and bent to retrieve the plastic bucket he'd dropped during the yogurt attack. "Gotta get back for the breakfast rush. But maybe tomorrow if I ain't too busy." He snorted at his own wit, then shambled away, muttering about kids and respect and people who should be horsewhipped.

But I was uninsulted. The word *breakfast* had stuck like a burr in my underfed brain. I was suddenly ravenous, and the only sustenance I had possessed was spattered across the old man's face.

Surveying the area one more time, I stepped out of the Jeep. "Hey!" I raised my voice, feeling exposed and pee-in-my-pants scared. I kept my hand on the door handle in case the old man morphed into a gun-wielding gangbanger with a vengeance. "Did you say something about breakfast?"

He twisted toward me, grumpy as hell and looking ridiculous with peach slop plastered across his nose and cheeks. "You plannin' to steal that too?"

"What?"

"There ain't no reason to play dumb," he said, and turned away with a disgruntled snort.

"I'm not playing. Listen ..." I stumbled after him. "I need help."

He swung back toward me. "Why would I help you when you was planning to steal my morels?"

"What would I do with your morels?" I shambled to a halt. "I hardly even use my own."

He chuffed a heavy breath. "You as dumb as you act?"

"How dumb do I act?"

"Pretty damn. Come on," he said, and changing course, headed for the still-running Jeep. "You can give me a ride. Serve ya right if they see ya."

"Who?" I asked, but he just clambered into the passenger seat and stashed his bucket between him and the door

"Let's get a wiggle on. I ain't got all day," he said.

"It'll serve me right if who sees me?"

"The dense duo."

"The dense..."

"My grandsons. We gonna get going or what?"

I climbed into the driver's seat. "So you're not...you're not Asian, right?"

"Asian...Holy nuts, girl! Is your blood sugar low or somethin'?"

"My everything's low. Just..." I stared across the seat at him. "Please. Answer my question."

"Name's Eli," he said finally. "Eli Hughes."

I scowled, trying to think, but I was running on ashy terror and two hours of sleep. "Is that Irish?"

He glared at me. "Like it ain't bad enough you steal my mushrooms."

"I wasn't stealing anything," I said, and shifted into drive. "How can there be mushrooms in the desert anyway?"

"Who says there was?" he asked, and hugged the bucket to his side.

"You sure you're not Irish?" I asked, remembering my idiot brothers' idiotic behavior.

He snorted and pointed a crooked finger toward the north. "Take a right up here."

Nothing more was said until we turned onto a long, bumpy lane that wound up a short hill to a low wooden shed. It was surrounded by a barren, dusty lot as big as a football field.

Hughes was already scrambling out of the Jeep before I shifted into Park. The building toward which he shambled might have been called a shack, if one was feeling particularly generous...and somewhat intoxicated. I was just about to slam the door when Paul Bunyan appeared on the porch. He was tall and blond with a small head, a wide chest, and hips that seemed to have been whittled down to toothpick proportions. His legs were long, his smile lascivious. "Gamps, you shouldn't have."

"I didn't," the old man huffed, and ambled up the ramshackle stairs.

But the grin never left Bunyan's face. "I got eyes," he said, gaze roving over me like dirty hands. "And I can see ya brung me a gift."

My eyebrows shot into my hairline as he trotted down the tilted wooden steps, but a thwack of sound from the right caught my attention. Not fifty feet away, a chicken danced across the hard-packed sand, jerked spasmodically, then fell, dead as a turkey baster, on the ground. A woman, or what might have passed for one, if they made them big as SUVs and scary as hell out here in the sticks, retrieved the headless corpse by its legs and hauled it unceremoniously into the shack. I felt the bile rise in my throat like a geyser.

"Wanna have some fun?"

"What?" I jerked my attention to Bunyan, but I was pretty sure that, unlike the Adonis at my athletic club, he really had spoken those exact words. "No." My answer was unequivocal.

He grinned as he prowled toward me.

"Thank you anyway." I crowded back against Jeep's still-open door. "But I hate fun."

"Come on, sweet thing," he drawled. "There's a party in my pants. And you're invited."

Chapter 10

> If God only gives you as much as you can handle, I wish to hell he didn't think I was such a badass.
>
> —*Peter McMullen, following a confrontation with a couple of angry husbands*

I would like to say, in my defense, that I seriously considered springing back into the Jeep and roaring off down the road at that point, but I'm a practical woman. A practical woman with an all-but-empty fuel tank, no money, and not a clue where the hell I was.

Although I suspected hell was a pretty good bet.

But if I was hoping the old man would help me out, I was about to be sorely disappointed. He had already disappeared inside. What hadn't disappeared was the seductive smell of frying bacon. Perhaps the fact that it kept me rooted to the ground despite Bunyan's dumb-ass come-on was proof that the trauma of the last few hours had rendered me brain dead.

"What's your name, sweet cakes?"

He was close now. Less than ten feet away and big as a yeti.

"I'm..." I paused, realizing with belated clarity that I couldn't very well use my real name. Breath held, I noticed a cardinal just flitting to a nearby branch. "Scarlet."

He raised his brows and broadened his grin.

"Scarlet," he said, and upped the wattage of his smile. "Sounds like a stripper name. You a stripper, darlin'?"

The first sip of indignation flowed through me. "As a matter of fact, I'm not," I said, and raised my brows.

"A hooker?"

"No," I said. "How about you? Might you be an ass?"

I don't know why those particular words fell out of my mouth. I was, after all, at the mercy of strangers, but this guy immediately put my back up. Maybe that was because he reminded me of my brothers in some fundamentally disturbing way. Yes, he was taller, beefier, and blonder, but I instinctively knew they would share a boneheaded sense of humor.

His grin never faltered. "You got a last name, firecracker, or are you one of them one-name chickadees, like Cher or Madonna?"

My mind buzzed, trying to scare up a believable surname, but just then a second man stepped out of the shack. He was short one shirt. His chest was broad enough to dine on. "Maybe it's Lolita," he said, and snapping a dish towel over one brawny shoulder, descended the steps.

"That it?" Number One asked. "Have you only got the one name?"

"Of course not," I said.

"Then what is it?"

Don't say O'Hara. Not O'Hara, I thought, but my mind was spinning. I pried my eyes from Number Two's chest. "O'Tara," I rasped.

"No shit?"

"None. Are you ... twins?"

"Uh uh," said One. "That there's my clone. I was so dang pretty, folks decided the world needed more of me. Only he's kinda a disappointment."

I narrowed my eyes as he drew closer. My fight-or-flight instincts were ticking like a time bomb.

"Where you come from, Miss Scarlet? The wind blow you in?" he asked, stepping even closer.

According to Dr. Dirkx, the average person's comfort zone for strangers ends at about twelve feet. Closer than that and the amygdala in the exterior extremity of the frontal lobe begins to fret. Thing One was closer than that, with Thing Two closing in; my amygdala was going bat-shit.

I retreated a pace, skirting the Jeep's open door.

"She does look kinda windblown," said Two.

"Fiddle dee dee," said One, and reached for me.

My hand shot sideways without ever interfacing with my brain. One minute, I was being relatively civil, and the next, I had Rivera's anti-theft club jacked up against Thing One's nether parts.

He hiked up on his toes, mouth open in a wordless O, brows raised in surprise as he awaited my next move.

"Here's the deal," I said, and shifted my gaze from one cretin to the next, trying to figure out just what the deal might be as I tightened my grip on the impromptu weapon. "I had a bad day, followed by a worse night, and topped off by a hell of a morning. Do you know what I'm saying?"

Thing One nodded. Carefully.

"But I'm not looking for trouble."

One shook his head. Cautiously.

"I just want to be left alone. Do you understand me?"

He nodded again. Slowly.

I shifted my gaze to the dunderhead that remained behind him. The world seemed to stand still, except for the smell of bacon. That wafted toward me like a siren's irresistible song. "And breakfast," I added.

"You like bacon?" One asked. His voice had risen by a few octaves.

I narrowed my eyes at him, wondering if he was joking... Everybody with half a brain cell and functioning taste buds likes bacon. But I had learned early on, even before my stint as a cocktail waitress, that if you hike a man up by his balls, things generally stay pretty serious.

"Yeah," I said. "Bacon's all right."

One nodded, arms held stiffly away from his sides, as if he would spontaneously combust should they touch his hips. "We cut it extra thick," he said. "And Gamps makes pretty decent flapjacks." His brow looked a little moist, his lips dry. He licked them.

I skimmed my gaze to his brother and back. "I can't pay you."

He shook his head again. "Don't matter," he said. "Don't matter at all. We wouldn't take your money no how."

"Pretty little thing like you," said Two, slithering toward me. "I'm sure we can think of some way for you to work it off."

I lifted the club a little, hitching One up on his toes another notch as I realized his sibling was unable to fully comprehend the situation, hidden as we were behind the driver's door.

"Tell him not to be a numbnuts," I warned.

"Re!" he snarled. "Back the hell off."

"What?" He ambled closer. Finally realizing the state of affairs, he stopped short, widened his eyes, and laughed like a hyena.

One growled and twisted toward him but I tightened my grip on the club, effectively jacking him a little higher.

"You," I said, jerking my head toward Two. "Get me some breakfast before your brother's a eunuch."

Confusion mixed with happy humor on his broad face. "We don't have no sheep no more. So I—"

"Not a ewe's neck, you fuckup. A—Just do it!" One croaked. Sweat had found its way onto his neck.

Two shrugged, grinned, and sauntered away.

Seconds ticked by as I watched the door of the shack, but no one reappeared to devour me.

"Scuse me," said One, polite as a Girl Scout. "But my legs are cramping up some."

I eased the club away from his balls and stepped back a quick pace.

"Geez," he said, and rubbed the offended area. "PMS much?"

I raised the bar marginally and tried to feel guilty when he flinched. Nothing. "Do you get the *L.A. Times*?"

"What?"

"It's a newspaper." He still looked baffled. Either he was dumber than I thought, or his thinking apparatus was directly linked to his testicular area. "Large sheet of paper with words written on it?"

"I know what a newspaper is."

I thought of a half-dozen nasty rejoinders. There was, apparently, something about idiot brothers that brought out my fairly substantial mean streak, but I fought it back. "Do you get it or not?"

"If you put that thing away I'll take a look," he said.

The smell of maple syrup juxtaposed against fried pork and nitrates was wafting out of the building and interfering with my concentration. I lowered the club distractedly and wandered, nose first, toward the porch. But at the last second I remembered that men whose nether parts have been threatened by a hard object sometimes hold a grudge; I motioned Thing One past me with my impromptu weapon.

He hurried ahead, shooting me nervous glances and muttering about poor manners and the unfortunate lack of a sense of humor.

Once inside, I scanned the area. The building was divided into three rooms, but there seemed to be no interior doors. Two of the chambers appeared to be filled with mismatched tables, some of which had been built out of makeshift objects: a sheet of plywood atop two low barrels, a car hood balanced on hay bales, two ... ah, the missing doors ... there they were, propped on tilting saw horses. Three men sat around the nearest door. They glanced up as I came in, faces smeared with grease. I couldn't help but wonder if this was where novelist James Dickey had found his questionable inspiration for *Deliverance.*

"Sit down," One said, motioning irritably toward what appeared to be a window propped on what might have been a discarded vanity.

I eased onto the piano bench that ran the length of it. The cushion felt a little sticky, but before I could react, Thing Two came through the doorway to my right. He was carrying a pair of plates. One was covered in ragged-looking pancakes the size of my head. The other was filled with bacon and what looked to be a variety of cheeses hacked into irregular chunks.

"A loaf of bread, a jug of wine, and thou," he said.

I swung my gaze up from the dubious-looking meal and scowled.

"My apologies for Rom." He grinned, slithering closer. "He's been off his nut some for the past ..." He wiggled his head. "Twenty-two years or so."

I curled my fist around the nearest fork as he invaded my aforementioned body bubble.

"I'm the oldest," he informed me. "By forty-three minutes and thirteen—"

"Set down the plates and no one'll get hurt," I said.

He grinned and slid the dishes onto the window/table, then sat down across from me on a seat that may or may not have once occupied a tractor. "I like a girl can play hard to get," he said.

"Where am I?" I asked, and drowning the cakes with syrup from a nearby bottle, shoveled breakfast into my mouth with my erstwhile weapon.

"Well, you ain't in heaven no more."

I narrowed my eyes at him. "How about hell? Am I there?" I asked, but the pancakes were surprisingly tasty, so I was pretty sure I had not yet descended past purgatory.

"Get it?" he asked as I sampled the bacon. "I says you're not in heaven anymore cuz you must be an—"

"Who made this?" The bacon was flavored with apple ... and a hint of ambrosia.

"Gamps. Not bad, huh? Ya oughta try his kitchen-sink scrambler."

"Is there bacon in that too?"

"There's everything in that."

"Where'd you get it?"

"My devilish good looks?"

"The bacon."

He shrugged. "Rom cured it, but I—"

"Wait a minute," I said, continuing to chew. Being raised with the Troglodyte Trio had long ago made me a multitasker. "He's Rom and you're ..." I took another bite of bacon and wondered how quickly one could become addicted to smoked pork. "Re?"

"At your service." He grinned. "You can interpret that any way you want, love bucket."

"As in Romulus and Remus?"

"Roman gods," he said.

Demigods, if I remembered my mythology correctly, but I was a little too consumed consuming the fruits of their mutual labor to make mention. "And you two made this?"

"I wouldn't lie to no angel."

"Uh huh. Why the cheese?" I asked, and stabbed my fork toward the irregular chunks.

"Taste it."

I did so without taking my gaze off him. It was tangy and sharp, complimenting the bacon, setting the pancakes on their proverbial ear.

"Where'd it come from?"

"My rugged—"

"The cheese," I said.

"Frita and Whinnie."

"Where's that?"

"In the barn. It's got a dandy hayloft. Wanna see?"

I quit chewing for a moment. "You keep your cheese in the barn?"

He chuckled. "Frita and Whinnie are goats."

So they had made it themselves. A couple dozen questions sprang into my head, but the cheese was singing its siren song, fuzzing my concentration. I took another bite. "Where am I?"

"Well ya ain't—"

"Don't make me stab you," I said.

He grinned. "I like 'em feisty," he said.

I raised my fork.

He chuckled. "You're home, dream dumplin'."

I didn't bother to glance around, but I did slow my mastication for an instant. "There aren't any bedrooms."

"Not our home. *The* Home. The Home Place. You gonna eat that last piece of bacon?" he asked, and reached out.

I gave him the glare I had tested on my idiot brothers and sharpened on a hundred inebriated Warthog patrons. "If you're fond of those fingers you'll keep them to yourself."

Romulus, hitherto known as Thing One, chuckled as he entered the room. "Looks like sweet cakes has her some taste, brother. So ya best back off. She's mine."

"The hell she is," said Re and rose to his impressive height.

"The hell she ain't," Rom said. "I saw her—"

"Get outta here! Both of ya!" someone growled.

I turned to the right. The biggest woman I had ever seen had just entered the room. Her hair was the color of pomegranates... except the two-inch roots, which more closely resembled ashes. She wasn't necessarily fat, but tall and broad and... okay, under her posy-sprigged housedress, she was fat, too. But I'd rather have had my spleen removed with a salad fork than share that little factoid with her. Especially once I recognized her as the bulging-biceps chicken killer I had seen outside.

"Yes, ma'am."

"Sorry, Momma," the twins muttered, and slunk away like scolded collies.

She was six feet three inches of shoe leather cooked in cactus sap, and when she turned her glare on me, I felt myself shrink to wart-sized proportions.

I swallowed. She glared.

"So you're a thief *and* a freeloader."

The men at the door/table beside me stared, unblinking, seeming braced for a speedy exodus. I abandoned my breakfast with only a small whimper.

"I..." The squeaky sound that escaped my lips was embarrassing. After all, I had just managed to face off a mammoth-sized portion of Tweedle Dee and Tweedle Dope. But perhaps that was only because men are so desperately fond of their balls. This creature didn't have any balls to worry about...maybe. "I, um..." My mind was spinning as I remembered Rivera's desperate plea for me to remain hidden. "I'm afraid I left my wallet at the..." I thought wildly for a likely story: laundromat, coffee bar, soccer match—all seemed a little tame for this alternate universe. "Cock fight?"

Quizzical didn't quite describe the look she gave me. *What the fuck* might have better summed up her expression. But she moved on, stabbing her gaze through the window/table at my bare legs.

"You sickly?"

I raised my brows, waiting for her to continue, but I wasn't rude enough...or anywhere near *brave* enough...to demand an explanation from this backwater Amazon.

"Why else would ya be so skinny?" she asked, making me realize with sudden clarity that for a backwater Amazon, she was pretty perceptive.

"No. No." I cleared my throat. "I'm perfectly healthy."

"Then ya got yourself a job. Minimum wage."

I opened my mouth. Maybe to object. Maybe to inform her that I had a PhD. Maybe to inhale my unfinished breakfast, but she thumped a tire-sized palm against the table, causing me, the other customers, and perhaps the rest of the planet to jump.

"But you keep your hands off my boys." She leaned in, breathing hard. I leaned back; her forearms weren't the only things strong enough to take down a rhino. "I don't want none of your loosey-goosey ways seepin' into 'em. Ya understand?"

I nodded, though I can honestly say I understood nothing.

"Good, then finish eatin', cuz I don't care how scrawny you are, there won't be no faintin' once you start takin' orders."

"Orders?"

"Waitressing," she said. "You got enough brain cells twittering around in that pretty head of yours to do that, don't ya?"

Chapter 11

> If her feelings for bacon were any stronger, the relationship'd be condemned by the Pope.
>
> —*Peter McMullen, who, for a troglodyte, knew his sister pretty well*

The next thirty-six hours passed in a blur of king-sized orders and an oil tanker of beer.

I had slept in Rivera's Jeep, consumed another breakfast that would make a vegan weep, and jumped back to work.

"A cheddar bacon omelet with a side of steak and extra rolls," I said, slapping the order onto the pass-through window that looked like it had been hacked out of the wall with a fireman's ax. "A taco salad with a side of steak. And one burger. Rare, with a side of steak and—"

"I do not make burgers."

I glanced up, stunned. An unknown man returned my stare, steel-blue eyes impassive, cappuccino hair pulled back in a man bun. He would have looked hipster perfect except for the scar that nicked across his forehead and into his hairline. And those kill-me-now eyes. "Where's Eli?"

"I do not make burgers," he repeated. His face, a honey-gold hue that suggested a mad-dash fusion of exotic races, was absolutely expressionless.

I glowered. I'd been on my feet for approximately two eons. Breakfast was but a distant dream. Lunch had been a feeding orgy at Hades' favorite trough. I had no idea how so many people could have learned about this place. As far as I knew, the establishment didn't boast so much as a Post-it Note to draw in passersby. But maybe there was some kind of bacon-flavored homing beacon I knew nothing about.

"Who are you?" I scowled through the serving window at him.

"Hiro."

"Is that your name or your occupation?"

What passed for his expression suggested he didn't find me particularly amusing. He looked as cool as a cucumber. I felt as hot as banana flambé. Hot, exhausted, and just about ready to tear someone's head off. His was the only one currently within my line of vision.

"No burgers," he repeated. He was only slightly taller than I was and not particularly muscular. I was pretty sure I could take him if he used that better-than-thou tone again.

"The guy at the car hood wants a burger."

"That is not my concern." Despite my instant dislike for him—I mean, a man bun and a knuckle-sized rough-cut earring... really? In numbfuck nowhere?—I admit, although reluctantly, that his features were somewhat intriguing. Native American, maybe, with a dollop of Polynesian. But what the hell was he doing in that weird-ass poet's shirt? And his accent. It was... Okay, truth to tell, I wasn't entirely sure he had an accent. Neither did I care. He could have been President Obama's conjoined twin and I still would have wanted to whack him upside the head with a dining room chair. See how well I was reconnecting with my redneck roots? I was even adopting an accent of my own. I called it southern discomfort. What better disguise for the elite Christina McMullen, PhD?

"He said he had two yesterday," I parried. "For breakfast."

He held my gaze with unblinking steadiness. "One must cease living in the past to fully embrace the present," he said, and turned away.

"Listen!" I leaned over the pass-through. "If ya don't wanna embrace my—"

"He said he don't make burgers!"

I jumped like a spanked spaniel. Big Bess, aka Momma Hughes, stood glaring at me from three feet away. How she moved around like a powder puff on her size-forty-seven feet, I had no idea, but it was as creepy as hell.

"And if Hiro Jonovich Danshov says he don't make burgers..." She tilted her impressive bulk toward me a little. "He don't make burgers."

"But the guy at the car hood—" I began. She cut me off at the pass.

"Had better not be unhappy with the service in *my* establishment."

I needed this job and/or a ride out of perdition, but my temper was beginning to make some serious inroads into my fear. "Then Confucius there better start fryin' up some beef patties before—"

She took a step closer, crowding me toward the serving window. "What'd you call him?"

"Ahhhh..." I'm no wilting daisy, but all things are relative. She was relatively the size of a Humvee on steroids, and I was beginning to suspect she might have the hot and heavies for her short-order cook. "Confucius?"

Her brows lowered like angry hedgehogs.

"Cuz he's so..." I would have liked to shift my gaze to the object of her affection, but I didn't dare take my eyes off her, lest she mistake me for a chicken and find something other than my neck to hold up my head. "Insightful?"

"Convince 'em to order the lasagna," she said.

"Yes, ma'am," I agreed.

I didn't have much choice but to return to the car hood.

"I'm sorry, sir," I said. "Sir" was a balding gentleman wearing a pair of overalls that looked as if they might have, at one point, been used to clean radiators. Ditto for what remained of his hair, however, so I was trying not to preemptively pass judgment. He was bookended by a pair of fellows who were half his size and a quarter his weight. "I'm afraid burgers ain't on the menu today."

He nodded laconically, glanced at his flatware, then shyly raised his gaze to mine. It wasn't until then that I noticed his eyes. Dark brown and Johnny Depp soulful, they drew me in like linguine in burgundy sauce.

It was also at that moment that I wondered how I had sunk into the ninth circle of hell so quickly. It hadn't been forty-eight hours since I'd left L.A., and here I was comparing this behemoth to one of Hollywood's sexiest sons. This behemoth who, by the by, may have actually *eaten* Johnny Depp.

"How 'bout you?" he asked.

I canted my head. "Beg yer pardon?"

"You on the menu?"

Soulful eyes or not, I prepared to blast him out of his steel-toed work boots. But just then, Bess cleared her throat. It sounded like a foghorn through Appalachian mist. And somewhere from my past, during the time I had spent schlepping drinks at the Warthog and defending my honor... or not, I remembered a couple of lines that I had used on more than one inauspicious occasion. "I ain't very heart healthy,"

I said, and glanced at him through my lashes, stubby and unenhanced though they were.

I felt my employer's glower darken. My spleen quivered in response as I remembered the hapless...and headless... chicken, but I continued on.

"If ya order the lasagna, though, I promise to get yer system racing when I deliver it."

The fellow on his left snorted, threatening to spew beer from his nose. The other one just gaped.

"I guess I kinda do have a hankerin' for Italian," he said.

By the end of the day, my feet throbbed, my back ached, and my brain felt dirty, but I had survived a million-hour shift. Plus, after disrobing down to my tank top, the gratuities had improved considerably; I had scored a pocket of change and a Texaco coupon. Clutching the crumpled voucher to my chest like a dying friend, I limped out to the Jeep. Slumping into the driver's seat felt heavenly. I sighed, immediately slipping into a haze. But I roused myself with effort. I didn't know where to go or what to do, but I was certain of one thing: I had to leave Hillbilly Haven.

The Jeep rumbled when I turned the key. Muttering my thanks to every deity ever conceived by guilt-riddled minds, I shifted into drive and turned the wheel. But before I had even reached the bumpy lane, the engine coughed, sputtered, and droned to a gasping death.

Alternatingly cursing and praying, I turned the key again. But there was no hope. It wouldn't start. Apparently, deities are jealous little bastards who don't like to share prayers. I dropped my head against the steering wheel, but I was too angry to cry. Too tired to sleep.

That was the last thought I had before sliding into oblivion.

"Holy fuck, you're beautiful," Rivera said, and he was right. I was lean, clean, and well-dressed. Even my hair looked good. That's how I knew I was dreaming.

"And you're an ass," I said.

He grinned, bite-me lips kicking up a little at the corners. "But you still want to do me."

"Do not."

"Oh come on..." He sauntered toward me, shoulders, hips, attitude, all moving in synchronized seduction. "You can do better than that."

I raised my chin, fighting down the inferno of desire. "I don't know what you're talking about."

"Lying." He was close now. Close enough to see the Butter Brickle flecks in his dark chocolate eyes, to feel the smoldering pheromones fly off him like wind-blown sparks. "I know you can do better. Hell..." He lifted one long-fingered hand, touched my cheek. "Harley *can do better."*

"Harlequin." My voice sounded funny, but his touch had always turned my brain to mush, my inhibitions to ash. "How is he?"

"Safe."

Tears burned my eyes. "Make sure he gets his soup bone. And that... and that Eddie brushes his teeth."

He slid his palm across my cheek, caressing my ear, massaging my scalp. "Who would have thought that's what would do it for me?"

"What?"

"I've dated heiresses, geniuses, starlets. There might have even been a few who were prettier than you."

"Screw—" I hissed, but he tightened his fingers in my hair and pulled me in for a kiss, searing my lips, setting fire to my libido.

"But none of them loved a Great Dane with a flatulence problem and suicidal tendencies. None of them loved like you." His eyes

burned into mine, seeing through my carefully erected walls to my trembling soul.

"He's not suicidal." It was difficult to speak, almost impossible to remain upright.

"No?" He kissed my jaw with such sweet slowness that I felt myself melting from the inside out.

I tilted my head back a fraction of an inch. "He's just..."

He'd found the pulse in my throat. It thrummed like a kick drum against his lips. "Dense?"

"No."

"Yeah." He breathed the word against my sensitized skin. "He is. But you love him anyway. Makes me think there might be hope for me." Drawing back, he found my eyes with his. "For us."

"Rivera..." My throat felt tight. I gripped his shirt in frantic fingers. "Yeah?"

"Don't die. Promise me."

His lips twisted up in succulent, irreverent humor. "On one condition."

I nodded, too hopped up on emotional angst to speak.

"Stay gone," he said.

"But I—"

"Until I come for you."

"But how—"

"Stay gone," he repeated, sliding his hand down my back to cup my derriere, "and I swear to God I'll make it worth your while."

I awoke in the backseat, curled up on Rivera's leather jacket like a lovesick kitten. I breathed in the scent of him, wanting to remain there forever, to believe his whispered words. But my urinary system would not be ignored. I sat up. The Jeep's windshield was dripping with condensation, but in the wakening dawn I thought I could see the sketchy outline of a building hidden by scraggly trees and an asymmetrical hill.

Thinking anywhere would be better than Home, I scanned the area in all directions. There wasn't a soul in sight. Popping the locks, I stepped to the ground and headed into the woods.

The barn was tall, devoid of paint, and slightly lopsided. In short, it was in only marginally better shape than the restaurant.

Desperately hoping there were facilities inside, I hurried to the door and set my hand on the latch.

Something honked in my ear. I jerked around, heart stammering, but the donkey that eyed me from a few feet away looked unaggressive and ridiculous.

I pressed my hand to my boobs and managed to keep the contents of my chest where they belonged. But my bladder was not going to be so easily contained.

The scare had almost made a restroom superfluous.

Turning rapidly, I yanked the door open and stumbled into the barn. Inside, it was as dark as an Irishman's soul, but I could make out a few rundown stalls and the tools necessary to clean them.

Hurrying past pegs holding everything from pitchforks to curry combs, I rushed into the nearest enclosure, squatted behind fifty-pound bags of who knows what, and answered nature's primitive call. From between the planks of the adjacent stall, a pig the size of Denmark watched me with squinty-eyed curiosity, but I didn't care.

My shoulders slumped with relief. Heaving a sigh, I scanned my surroundings: straw bales to my left, hay to my right, and just past those, wooden rungs rising to an overhead loft. A glimmer of light shone from above. I straightened, curious.

"My kingdom for a dollar bill."

I squawked like a plucked duck and spun around, dragging my shorts up as I did so.

One of the Things grinned from ten feet away. "Cuz that's the best show I seen in years."

I lowered my head, face hot. "What are you doing here?"

"I just come by for a little ass," he said, and took a step toward me.

"Don't come any closer," I warned, and grappling for my keys, held them in the defensive position touted by those who were, apparently, against arming women with rocket launchers.

He grinned at my feeble courage and took another step. "But I gotta," he said, "cuz she's hungry."

I narrowed my eyes and he laughed.

"Josephine," he said, and chuckled as the donkey brayed again. "My ass... I come to feed her. Guess it's just good fortune that I saw one, too."

"Not quite so lucky that you are one," I said, feeling my defenses wilt, but when I moved to sidle past him, he stepped into my path. Fear was cranking up inside of me again, but I did my best to contain it and tilted my chin up at a jaunty angle.

"Remus, isn't it?" I asked.

He smiled. "Most folks can't tell us apart. But you musta noticed that I'm the handsomest, huh?"

I looked up through my lashes at him. "Well, Rom and I already went clubbing together, so I figured he wouldn't be stupid enough to try somethin' again." I tried to move around him, but he took one step to the right, effectively blocking my exit.

"Where you goin' in such a hurry?"

"Somewhere with smarter company." I smiled. "I thought I'd try the pasture."

He grinned. "Them stallions is pretty bright. But I'm better hung. Wanna see?"

"I'd rather eat dirt." Which, thanks to my idiot brothers, I had done on more than one occasion.

His grin was carnivorous. "Come on, sugar melon, all the gals round here want a piece of Remus."

"I'd like a teeny piece, too," I said, and fluttered my stubby lashes. "But ya might miss the part I'd hack off."

"Now that's not very nice," he scolded, and stepped toward me.

I shuttled backward, bumping into the corner of a stall. It was then that I saw Hiro Danshov through the broad doorway. He stared at me, glanced at the behemoth blocking my exit, then strode on past like it was a fine Sunday in Mayberry.

Remus grinned. "Looks like it's just you and me, firecracker."

"Looks like it," I rasped. Dropping my keys, I grabbed a nearby pitchfork and stabbed.

He screamed, high-pitched and energetic, then stumbled into the open, cradling his thigh with both hands. Dropping the fork, I snatched up my keys and darted past him. But I needn't have hurried. He had fallen on the ground, still shrieking like Janet Leigh at the sight of a shower.

From the comparable safety of the Jeep, I saw that Danshov hadn't even stopped to glance behind him.

By the time I had screwed up enough courage to return to the Home Place, the breakfast rush was in full swing. Bess growled an order and I hopped to, hoping she wouldn't be offended by the fact that I had, possibly, killed her eldest-by-forty-three-minutes son.

When the last oddly hirsute patron departed, I dropped into the nearest chair with three slices of cinnamon-swirl French toast. Say what you will about Hiro the profoundly unheroic, he could really *parlez vous* toast.

"That comes out of your pay," Bess said.

I was too tired to be pissy, so I nodded my listless agreement. She was gone in a moment, but I could still feel eyes on me and glanced up.

Danshov was watching me through the serving window.

Anger and sarcasm spurted up in equally caustic measures. "Thanks for your help this morning."

One arched eyebrow rose a fraction of a millimeter. He was dressed in a loose-weave V-necked shirt and simple drawstring pants, and he was spooning up the contents of a ceramic bowl. It might have been oatmeal, but from my vantage point, it looked as appetizing as sawdust. Moron.

"He did not appear to need my assistance," he said.

I snorted. As luck would have it, Remus took that precise opportunity to limp past the window. He spared me one accusatory glance before hiking laboriously across the porch to who knows where.

"I guess you were wrong," I said, and found that, despite my usual maturity, I wasn't entirely able to quell the spurt of happy pride that rushed through me at the evidence of my antagonist's agony.

"Perhaps you might consider modesty."

I shifted my attention to the cook. "What?"

"Modesty," he said, and dragged his disparaging gaze over my scantily clad body. "You have heard of it?"

Catholic guilt rushed through me, but I had learned to squash that bug before my christening. Besides, it wasn't as if I was wearing workout shorts and a lung-squeezing tank top because of my love affair with spandex. "Blaming the victim…some call it the coward's means of justifying their own turpitude," I said.

He narrowed his eyes, showing his first spark of interest in me. "Tell me, Miss… O'Tara." The slightest curve of a smile lifted the corner of his lips. They resembled Cupid's bow to a ridiculous degree. "Might you be a psychotherapist?"

I felt myself blanch as memories of gunshots and terror stormed through my head. I had vowed to remain incognita for a reason; I made a *psffft*ing noise. "Like a shrink or somethin'? You leggin' me?"

He set aside his bowl of sawdust. I yammered on.

"You think I'd be slummin' out here in Nowheresville if I had a PhD or…" I waved a vacant hand. "Whatever? That'd make me dumber than a bag of balls. Stupid as a…" I tried to catch my breath, to find the perfect insult, but it was too late. He had already left the building.

Chapter 12

You have the right to remain stupid. Don't abuse it.

—*Lieutenant Jack Rivera*

I found a discarded copy of the previous day's *L.A. Times* that night. With shaking hands, I skimmed every story by the Jeep's dome lights. But there was nothing about the death or injury of an LAPD officer. Relief sluiced through me, until I realized there was no story regarding *any* type of disturbance at Rivera's house. Surely an attack on a police lieutenant's home would be newsworthy even on the day following the incident. Unless I was losing my mind, the shootout had happened. So why hadn't anything been written about it? Had dirty cops orchestrated some kind of police cover-up? Police could go bad; I had experienced that on a very personal level. Or were the Black Flames powerful enough to keep their nefarious deeds out of the news? Were they so powerful that even now they knew where to find a quivering psychologist who—

A bullet whizzed past my ear.

I shrieked and twisted to my left, only to see the missile materialize into Big Bess's knuckles. She gave me a what-the-fuck look and made a cranking motion with her turkey-sized hand.

I fumbled the key twice before I was able to get it into the ignition, then powered down the window a miserly two inches.

She watched me like I was a couple cherries short of a cobbler. "Ya can't sleep out here."

"What? Why not?"

"My sons are good boys, but they ain't no saints."

I stared at her, nasty ripostes racing through my head like nasty little weasels. But Big Bess Hughes wasn't exactly the type of woman I wanted to antagonize. Hell, she wasn't even the type I wanted to *meet.*

"I'd check into a hotel," I said. "But my employer hasn't paid me yet."

"Tell ya what. I'll let you a room here ... for a price."

I narrowed my eyes. *"Here?"*

"In the big house."

"Big house?" I was beginning to sound kind of brain damaged.

"Back behind them trees," she said, and gave a Big Bird–type nod west.

"You've got a house?"

"You think we slept in a cave or somethin'?"

I didn't answer, on account of it might have been a trick question. "How much you askin'?"

"Fifty dollars."

"A *night*?"

"Maybe you're used to payin' by the hour?"

I was ungodly tempted to inform her that her sons were philandering perverts and she would make a mountain gorilla look like a prima ballerina, but I wasn't that brave.

"Twenty," I said, "if it's got a good lock on the door."

"Deadbolt and regular. But I won't take less than forty," she countered.

"If it's got a decent mattress I'll give you twenty-five."

"Double-sized Beautyrest. And you'll pay thirty-five."

"Twenty-seven with my own bathroom."

"Pedestal sink and Waterpik showerhead. Thirty-two."

"Twenty-nine," I said. "With use of a washer and dryer."

"Thirty, and you buy your own soap."

"Twenty-nine fifty and access to the Internet."

"Internet!" She spat the word. "I don't allow none of that stuff 'round here. What do ya think I am, some sort of L.A. floozy?"

I raised my brows at her. "Floozy?"

"Immoral peddler of sexual ... Hey!" She squinted at me, eyes as small as marbles. "Did you bang up my Remus?"

"Bang up ..." Memories of our tussle in the barn assailed me. All semblance of the sassy me disappeared like banana peels down a garbage disposal. I don't respect a lot of things, but I'm not one to fool with the maternal instinct. My own mother might have been mean enough to devour her young whole, but even *she* took offense when others offended us. "No! I don't even ... Whatever are you talking about?"

"He's been walkin' kinda funny." She raised her chin, glaring at me from another angle. "You do the dirty with 'im, girl?"

"The dirty ..." I managed to shake my head.

"Bandicootin', swankie-swirlin', grummettin', wrasslin' the—"

"No!" I said, afraid to hear any more.

"You sure?"

"Absolutely."

"You know what I'm talkin' 'bout?"

"Yeah, I think I ... I think I get the picture."

"And you promise you ain't rode the monkey with my boy?"

Oh dear Lord! "Scout's honor."

"Huh." She was still scowling, but she shrugged. "He musta had hisself another eating accident, then."

"Eating..." Curiosity almost overwhelmed my sense of self-preservation, but she motioned me out of the Jeep before I could voice any potentially deadly questions.

"Come on."

I did as ordered, following her down a rocky path through inhospitable vegetation until we came to a turn-of-the-century two-story surrounded by twisted sycamores. The porch was wide, the stairs steep, but I was steeped in fatigue and barely noticed my surroundings.

The room she put me in was pink on pink. Like the love child of Pepto Bismol and Barbie. The frothy décor wasn't quite my style, but the Schlage on the door was right up my alley.

I slept like a cadaver that night. And in the morning, it all began again. I shed my old self like a snake slipping its skin. Flirting became second nature, teasing, an art form; the tips increased exponentially.

"I could use another glass of wine when you get a chance, Scarlet, love."

The fact that the Home Place served wine was not the most surprising part of this dialogue. The real shocker was the speaker himself: A lean forty-something, William Holsten was dressed with neat conservatism, possessed all his incisors, and, judging from the tattered paperback beside his neatly refolded napkin, was literate. A veritable gem in these parts.

"Coming right up," I said, and gave him a smile before heading for the kitchen.

"Whatcha doing?" Remus asked, stepping into the doorway behind me. My heart jumped like a skittish bunny, though he was still limping a little.

It was late. The restaurant was all but empty. Even Danshov had left for the night, probably to sit cross-legged by the lake and hum like an underfed Buddha. Poser. The fact that he did so alone in the dark and never spoke of it to anyone had no bearing whatsoever on my certainty that he was an outrageous showoff.

"My job," I said, and poured a glass of red.

"It's closing time."

I didn't bother glancing at the clock above the stove. "What about the Home's mantra?"

"What ya talkin' 'bout?"

"If people have money... take it," I said, and sauntered back into the dining area to hand off the wine.

"Oh." Holsten set *To Kill a Mockingbird* aside. "Thank you, my dear."

The British in his voice called mournfully to the Christina I longed to be.

"Are you a teacher or is that just one of your favorites?" I nodded toward his paperback.

He shifted back in surprise. "Aren't you the intuitive one? I *am* a professor, actually, but I'm frightfully unfamiliar with the American classics."

Thing One was scowling at me from the kitchen. I took my time with Mr. Holsten, nevertheless. Or maybe because of.

"How do you like it?"

"It's interesting, isn't it?" he said, eyes alight, one palm lifting as if to grasp the dynamics of the novel. "The juxtaposition of good and evil captured against the backdrop of your country's old South. Racism, hope, stereotyping, kindness, all enmeshed in such a simple..." He laughed and lowered his hand. "Listen to me rambling on like a right duffer just because you're too much the peach to tell me to sod off.

My apologies." He lifted the glass and took a sip. "Please do go about your business, I'll be gone in a jiff."

"No hurry," I assured him, and gathering up a few remaining dishes, returned to the kitchen.

"I don't trust that guy," Remus said.

I raised a brow at him. "Not puerile enough for you?"

"What?"

I shrugged and slunk back into my hillbilly act, a little happier for the use of my ten-dollar word. There's nothing like a catty remark to put some bounce in a girl's step. Well, that and a full rack of barbeque pork ribs, which I just happened to have set aside for my own consumption. After taking the plate from the fridge, I tugged a stool up to the counter and fell to. But I'd barely taste tested it before the Thing pulled a chair up beside mine.

"You got that good an appetite for other things, too?"

I ignored the insult, though I had seen *him* eat, and honest to God, it was not something to witness on an empty stomach.

"You can thank me later," he said, and settling into the chair, propped it back on two legs.

I glanced up, barely taking time to swallow. "For what?"

"I'm gonna walk ya home."

"No, yer not."

"Gotta," he said. "Don't want nothin' to happen to ya."

I gave him a jaundiced stare over top of my bus-sized meal. "How do ya feel about somethin' happening to *you*?"

His brows dipped into a scowl. "I was just bein' friendly. I don't know why ya have ta be so mean," he said, and rubbed his thigh a little.

"And I don't know why you can't take a hint."

He grinned. "You got some spark, I'll give ya that, but I still can't let you walk home unescorted."

I masticated as I studied him.

"You musta heard about the Carver," he said.

I stopped chewing. "The what?"

"The Carver. Guy's been terrorizin' the area for a month a Sundays now. Grabbin' gals at oil stations, in parkin' lots ... on their way home from work ..." He let the statement dangle and grinned at me.

I swallowed the pork. It seemed a little dry suddenly. "Why's he called that?"

"The Carver? Well, it ain't cuz of his prime rib recipe."

I felt my gorge rising.

"Fact is, it could be more than one fella, cuz the descriptions have been kinda iffy. But you don't need to worry, sweet cheeks. I'll take care of you."

I took another bite of pork and tried for nonchalant. "The Carver's starting to sound more charming by the minute."

He grinned. "If I wasn't so discernin' I might think you wasn't interested in me."

"No!" I tried to put a little disbelief into my tone.

"All I want's a little air."

I stared at him, then licked stray sauce off my fingers. "Air?"

"Some folks know it by other things."

Ahh, a blow job. "Listen, Remus, if the planet was about to explode and I could save the entire world ..." I paused as if considering. "Still wouldn't do it."

He tilted his head at me. "I been doing some thinkin'."

"Soon as I'm done here, I'll call the paramedics."

He chuckled. "What's a pretty little dewdrop like you doin' out here in the boons, that's what I'm wonderin'."

"Just polishin' up my social skills."

He narrowed his eyes in sly consideration. "You got yourself a secret, honey buns."

Fear had replaced my appetite, but I belched softly and refrained from wetting myself. "You're right, I do have a secret."

He grinned and rolled his hips, letting his knees fall apart a little. "Is it the fact that you got it bad for a good-lookin' stud muffin that's hung like an elephant?"

I leaned toward him and blinked like a dewy-eyed Bambi. It was a little something I had practiced in high school and perfected while trolling for tips. "I'm gay," I said, and leaving the remains of my meal, turned sharply away. But he caught me by the wrist. I twisted back toward him.

"You're lyin'," he rasped.

I forced a smile. "If Hoover Dam busts open I can probably save the valley."

He lowered his brows.

"Cuz I'm a dyke." I ground my teeth and tugged at my arm. It was like trying to escape from a crocodile.

"You shittin' me?"

"Not the tiniest turd." I tugged again. Still nothing.

"Well, listen ..." He snagged me a little closer. "I betcha I can help you with that, too."

I had been trying to act cool, calm, and collected, but he was big, broad, and boorish. Plus, we were very close now, with me crammed between his sequoia-sized thighs.

"Thanks anyway," I said.

"A little Remus will make you good as new."

"I *am* as good as new." I sounded breathless now. My mind was screaming for me to fight like a cornered wolverine. But he was far stronger than I. So I lurched forward instead. His chair teetered backward. I tried to pull free, but suddenly we were both falling. My boobs slapped his face. I hissed a curse and scrambled backward, but there was no need.

He remained exactly where he was, half sprawled on the chair, half slumped on the floor. I shuffled back another uncertain step. He didn't move. Sangria-dark blood trickled onto the floor. But it was his eyes, wide and unblinking, that scared the bejesus out of me.

Chapter 13

If you think breaking a mirror causes a shitstorm, try wreckin' a condom.

—Peter McMullen, whose daughter (as that bitch, kurma, would have it) is just like him

"Shit!" I breathed the mild curse, but Remus remained exactly as he was, sprawled like a broken doll on the floor. A giant broken doll, limbs flung out in all directions.

Every wild instinct insisted that I run. But to where?

Before I could arrive at a satisfactory answer, footsteps fluttered up from behind.

I jerked toward the sound just as Big Bess appeared like a glowering troll in the doorway. Our gazes caught and fused. For one crazy-ass second I thought she might not notice her oversized son stretched out on the barn-wood floor, but finally her eyes lowered.

I held my breath as a hundred disclaimers whizzed through my mind. A thousand lies scrambled along on their heels, but none of them seemed satisfactory. "I'm sorry," I rasped. She was already hurrying toward the possible corpse.

I held my breath and backed away, but she speared me with porcine eyes, pinning me in place. "What happened?"

"I..." Couldn't seem to push out a plausible lie, but I had long ago learned the underwhelming usefulness of absolute honesty and knew beyond a shadow of a doubt that taking the blame caused herpes. "He ... I think he hit his head."

She snorted like a palsied hyena. "You mean he ain't just sleepin'?"

For one irrational second, I actually hoped she was being earnest, but she stopped me before I could travel too far down Stupid Street.

"I know he hit his noggin, Einstein. What I wanna know is, how'd it happen?"

I was shaking my head, denying everything. "Maybe we should call an ambulance."

She propped her meaty fists on good-sized hips. "A what?"

I blinked and motioned vaguely toward his leaking scalp. "Head injuries can be..." I felt sick to my stomach. I'm not overly fond of seeing blood, even my brothers'—and those fucktards deserved to lose it by the gallon. "Bad."

"Well, don't seem likely that they'd be good, does it?" She huffed another snort and bent. "Re! Remus." She nudged him a little with the toe of her work boot. "Wake up."

No reaction.

She glanced at me again, scowled, then dropped her gaze to my boobs. "You. Jezebel." She motioned toward me like I was a cattle dog gone astray. "Bend down here."

"Wh ... what? Why?"

"Cuz I ain't got no linguine in clam sauce handy. Come 'ere and bend over."

I'm not sure why I did as told. Maybe because a girl can get a little discombobulated when she thinks she may have caused the death of another human being ... or one suspected of being human. In any event, I bent, boobs dangling.

It was then that Hiro Danshov appeared beside me, face devoid of curiosity. It was also then that Remus sniffed, twitched like a dreaming terrier, and turned his head, nose pointing toward my cleavage. His extremities stirred. I stared in fascination.

"What do ya think yer doin'? Ya want to give him a heart attack? Get outta here," she ordered, and I did, scuttling out of the restaurant and through the woods toward my Pepto Bismol refuge.

The next morning, I opened my bedroom door slowly and glanced in both directions. The hallway was blessedly empty, but when I stepped out of my room, I stumbled over something. A pile of clothes lay on the carpet. I bent down to discover men's garments. Tighty whiteys, a flannel shirt, and a pair of camo pants. Eli's clothes. Obviously, someone believed I should wear them. The thought was ludicrous. I'd look ridiculous. On the other hand, perhaps it was better than having men accost me every waking moment.

With that lovely thought burning a hole in my brain, I did a quick change. In a few minutes, I was examining myself in the full-length mirror tacked to the inside of the closet door. Sexy, I was not. In fact, if I slapped on a bird's-nest beard and a headband I could probably be inducted into the Dynasty of the Ducks. Nevertheless, the lovely no-accosting fantasy convinced me to spend the day so attired.

I got more than a few double takes from the breakfast crowd. Romulus was testy. Remus didn't show at all. Apparently, he was nursing a headache and trying to remember where things had gone awry; kitchen chairs weren't usually so persnickety.

By noon, I was hot and grouchy and had seen a decided decrease in gratuities. But at least the men were leaving me alone. Even Gizzard Manks, the lazy-eyed mechanic who cleaned his teeth with a pocketknife, ignored me.

I popped the top button on my borrowed flannel shirt and carried on. The tips improved considerably.

When nine o'clock rolled around, my dogs were yipping like a sled team. Limping through the moonlight, I slipped behind the Jeep's steering wheel and debated what to do next. I could walk to the nearest gas station, purchase fuel, then return here for Rivera's vehicle. But I didn't have a solid idea where that gas station was, how I would find it in the dark, or if my whining puppies would carry me that far.

So perhaps I should wait it out.

On the other hand, I wasn't particularly fond of the idea of giving the Terrible Twins time to regroup. Although, I had to admit, Rom seemed to have given up. Or maybe he was just waiting for me to let down my guard.

I should probably go.

On the *other* other hand, I had promised Rivera I would remain in hiding until he contacted me. But how would he do that? I didn't have a phone and *he* didn't know my whereabouts. And maybe he was injured, or worse, despite the promises he had whispered in my erotic dream.

I should *definitely* go.

Then again, who was going to take care of Harley if I returned to L.A. and was dismembered by the Black Flames before ever reaching my front door?

With that thought in mind, Hillbilly Hell didn't seem so bad.

Except, what about Laney? She had almost certainly tried to contact me by now. She was probably worried sick.

What if she traveled to L.A. in an attempt to figure things out and was compromised because of me?

I *had* to go.

Mind made up, I reached up to flip on the overhead lights so as to count my money, but nothing happened: The Jeep's battery was dead, probably due to the fact that I had left those very same lights on some nights before.

Anger and despair boiled inside me. I prepared to drop my head dramatically against the steering wheel, but a movement caught my eye.

Danshov was passing by in the darkness. A good-sized shadow traveled along beside him. A bear? A wolverine? Or just a dog. Probably a dog. I liked dogs, I reminded myself, and stepped out of the car.

"Wait!" My voice sounded more panicked than I had intended. He kept walking.

"Hey, if I get some gas, do you have jumper cables I could use?"

He didn't even pause. My ire ratcheted up a notch. I hate being interrupted, getting shot isn't on my entertainment short list, and if you tease me, the repercussions are likely to be swift and juvenile. But being ignored has always brought out the monkey in me. Still, in retrospect, it might have been a mistake to rush up behind him and grab his arm. Because there wasn't a stuttering second between reaching out and finding my back yanked up against his chest. I couldn't breathe, couldn't move. His right arm, I realized with minimal clarity, was wrapped around my throat, while the thumb of his left hand seemed to be pressed against an extremely sensitive point in my neck that I had not formerly known existed.

"Holy hell!" The words were emitted in a rusty croak. I was certain I was going to die, which made me think that perhaps a more enlightened person would apologize at that juncture. But I had to assume that those progressive individuals had not been raised with siblings from the Pleistocene era. Siblings whose never-ending practical jokes forced a thinking person to use her apologies judiciously, like when it was conclusively determined that I was, in fact, the one who'd stapled my brother's detention notice to his forehead.

Danshov held me immobilized for three endless seconds before loosening his grip and pushing me roughly away. I stumbled, caught my balance, then turned shakily and rubbed my throat.

"Who are you?" The words sounded as if they had been scraped off the bottom of somebody's boot. I just hoped my tone suggested more accusation than awe. Because I wasn't awed. Awed would be stupid. I was angry.

Judging from Danshov's expression, he wasn't exactly euphoric himself. He stared at me from beneath beetled brows for another couple seconds, then turned with an economy of motion and strode away. The wolf-dog remained a second longer, growled a rumbled warning, and trotted up beside him.

The enlightened individual mentioned earlier would probably have thanked her lucky stars for her continued survival and went her merry way, preferably in the opposite direction. I, on the other hand, followed him. I can't say why exactly. Maybe it was because despite the fact that he barely exceeded my own perfectly acceptable weight, he had disabled me without breaking a sweat or mussing his man bun.

"Teach me how you did that," I said.

He didn't even bother to refuse.

"Help me," I demanded. "Or I'll tell them the truth."

He stopped, then pivoted slowly toward me. His expression wasn't exactly terrified. In fact, he barely managed to appear conscious.

"And what... Miss O'Tara... is that truth?"

Okay, maybe it wasn't the best alias I could have invented, but I met him eye to eye. "You're a wanted man," I said.

Seconds ticked away. His lips curled a little. The expression made him look as cuddly as a cobra. I swallowed but pressed on. Persistence—it's one of the things that made me a pretty decent therapist... and an extremely irritating individual. "You're wanted for... something."

He lowered his head. For a moment, I was pretty sure he was going to kill me, but then he turned away. What a pleasant surprise. I felt it as a nice little tingle near my solar plexus. What was neither so surprising nor so pleasant was that I felt the burning, and perhaps somewhat suicidal, need to follow him.

"Listen, I don't have to learn how to... you know..." Even I didn't know what I was trying to say, but that had never stopped me before and failed to do so now. "You don't have to teach me to *kill* anybody. Not that I think *you* have killed someone..." I tried a chuckle. Dear Baby Jesus, what was wrong with me? "I just want to know how to defend myself."

He didn't stop. Neither did I.

"Help me," I said. I meant it to sound demanding and put upon, but in retrospect it might have come out whiny and a little ape-shit crazy.

"Why?"

Maybe the surprise caused by his response made me trip. Maybe it was that the trail was as dark as Satan's sidewalk. Either way, I hit my knees, scrambled to my feet, and lurched after him. "Human kindness?" I guessed.

"Not my strength." We had reached a steep hill. I stumbled up it, wheezing like an asthmatic chimpanzee.

"You don't want me as an enemy." I meant it as a warning. It probably sounded more like a dumb-ass joke; we'd only been climbing for about five seconds, but my heart was already in overdrive.

The trail dipped mercifully. Glancing down, I spotted what could have been the outline of a building set in a small clearing. It was small and dark, crouching like an evil gargoyle, seeming to suck in any glimmer of light from its surroundings.

It was spooky as hell, but I kept trudging, grunting when the trail ascended, stumbling when it roughened.

"Teach me that trick and I'll leave you alone," I promised, and winced as we entered the building's shadow.

He breathed a truncated snort, stepped into the cabin, and slammed the door in my face.

For reasons not entirely clear to me, I couldn't sleep that night. Maybe it was the heat. It was unseasonably warm, but I'd opened the window beside the twisted sycamore, and the northern breeze kept the temperature bearable. So maybe it was those pesky attacks on my person that were bothering me. But truth to tell, certain individuals have been trying to off me for most of my adult life and I generally sleep like an inebriated infant. Now, however, I lay in my popsicle-pink room and stared at the ceiling, missing my old life and wondering why the hell weird shit kept happening to me.

I had been minding my own business. Doing my job, working out, buying dog food. Doing all the mundane things that should ensure a long, if monumentally boring, existence. So why did people keep trying to kill me? I was a good person. Well, I was an okay person, if one's standards weren't too lofty...which, luckily, mine weren't.

So why had I been chased out of my city of choice and forced to live on the lam with a gaggle of inbred Neanderthals? Neanderthals who eschewed technology.

Neanderthals who didn't have so much as an antiquated typewriter, for God's sake.

But wait. Just because Bess disapproved of technology didn't necessarily mean her sons shunned it. Apparently, she wasn't a big fan of sex outside of marriage either, but I had a sneaking suspicion her offspring didn't share that sentiment.

So if they had a computer, where would they hide—

The barn! The answer hit me like a blow from Thor's mighty hammer. Ah, Thor... It wasn't his massive muscles that appealed to me, of course. It was his determination, his devotion, the way he gazed at Natalie Portman with knee-weakening adoration. Although a couple straining biceps and an Aussie accent didn't exactly shove him into the chopped-liver category. Okay, maybe fatigue was making me a little loopy. I struggled to wrangle my mind back on track: technology and the lack thereof.

Just a few days before, I thought I had seen a light shining from the barn's loft. Had I imagined it? I sat up in bed, remembered the encounter that had involved pitchforks and a shrieking Thing, and lay back down. But the thoughts wouldn't leave me alone. I knew a little something about animal husbandry from my childhood, when Laney and I had frequented (some said terrorized) nearby stables, stables where the hay had habitually been stored in lofts.

The twins' fodder had been stacked in the aisle. Why? What was up above? Might it be an office of sorts? An office with a PC that could give me some insight into L.A.'s events?

I sat up again, then paused, perhaps waiting for sanity to find me. When that failed to occur, I swung my legs over the side of the bed. The floor felt cool against my bare feet. I slipped into the flannel shirt and camos I had discarded earlier, then pattered silently to my door. It opened almost soundlessly.

In a matter of moments, I was slithering down the hall, heart hammering like a gong in my chest. I stubbed my toe twice before reaching the stairs. The first one moaned like a tortured ghost when I stepped on it. The second one sounded a little less tormented. I speeded up. If Bess were going to hear me, it would probably be best if I didn't act as if I planned to steal the family jewels.

I reached the main floor without incident. Once there, I stopped, held my breath, and waited to be dead. When my heart was still beating overtime fifteen seconds later, I considered myself lucky and thought about my next move. I had read somewhere (maybe in a cheap mystery novel written by someone who almost no one ever tried to kill) that when searching, one must do so methodically. Perhaps, then, I should begin in the house. It was, after all, closer than the barn, and I was, by nature, as lazy as a slug. But further consideration, and the terrifying idea of Big Bess sneaking through the dark on her giant powder-puff feet, disabused me of that idea.

The front door was unlocked. The path to the barn, as black as the devil's codpiece.

I felt my way carefully through the darkness. In the pasture, Josephine cranked her gigantic ears toward me but remained silent. No light shone from the barn. I eased inside, bumped into the stack of hay bales, then shuffled around them and forward. My knees felt a little unsteady, but I was nothing if not determined to an asinine degree. Eventually, my fingers touched a wooden rung. Heart pumping, I glanced up, but I could see next to nothing. Still, I slipped my foot onto the first step and thrust myself upward. By the time I reached the top of the ladder, I was breathless but strangely euphoric. Grappling my way onto the loft, I rose cautiously to my feet. The moon shone through a hole in the wall, illuminating my surroundings: more bales, a washing machine, a couple dozen items I couldn't identify, and a door that led to a small room. I stumbled forward, surprised as hell that I had been right. Perhaps I was dreaming, as is often the case when I find myself to be correct—but just then I struck my elbow on what appeared to be a bass fiddle atop a motorcycle. Even in my dreams, I couldn't make this crap up. I reached for the doorknob.

Inside, moonlight glowed through an open window, casting a gray glow. I slithered in, shut the door silently behind me, and glanced about. I had been right. Incredibly, entirely right. It was an office. An office where—

"Shhh!" The whisper was loud enough to wake the catatonic.

I froze.

Someone giggled.

"Wait a minute. Hold on, girl."

Oh fuck, oh fuck, oh fuck. I could hear them, noisy as mating pachyderms, on the dirt floor below. But maybe they wouldn't come up here. Maybe they were just planning to go for a midnight ride ... together ... on a donkey the size of a retriever.

"Not here! Not here," rasped a labored voice. "I got me a little room up top."

His words snapped me into action. I spurted across the floor, frantically searching the grayness for somewhere to hide. But it was impossible to see. Still, I thought I could make out a boxy piece of furniture not twelve feet away. I spurted forward and ricocheted off its corner. Pain radiated through my hip, temporarily stunning me, but a clambering noise from below catapulted me back into action. I managed to jam myself between the wall and a desk just as the pair stumbled past the open door.

I held my breath.

"Whoa, there, whoa, sweetheart," he crooned, and suddenly they were inside the room with me. I closed my eyes and apologized to all the deities I had offended earlier. None of them struck the couple dead on the spot. Then again, nobody fried me to crispy-critter consistency either. I considered it a win.

Until I heard the unmistakable zip of an opening fly.

Chapter 14

If you think God ain't got no sense of humor, get naked and take a good long look in the mirror.

—Momma Hughes, aka Big Bess

He groaned. She giggled. Mother-of-pearl snaps sprung open like the lid on a jack-in-the-box. The pair stumbled across the room, well into my line of sight. She was bent backward. He was bowed forward. Her hair was long and blond, her boobs thrust upward.

It took him only a second to set them free. I was about to be tremendously intimidated by the sheer magnetism of her bosom, but just at that moment something hit me in the face. I was sure it was a bullet, but in retrospect, I think it might have been one of her buttons. Regardless, I gasped.

"What was that?" she huffed.

"What?" He jerked upright, entirely abandoning his mission.

Weird. In my experience, nothing short of a nuclear blast can jostle men from their boob quest once they're on course, but he had frozen like roadkill, attention riveted on the door.

"I thought I heard a noise." Her voice was sex wrapped in velvet, but he pushed her unceremoniously out of the way, opened the door a crack, and peeked out.

"Not there." His sigh made his shoulders sag.

"Who? Who's not there?" Vengeful jealousy was already firing up in Blondie's voice.

"Momma." He moved closer to her. They were hidden from me now, but I heard the rustle of clothes, the sigh of their bodies as they met. "You didn't think there was someone else, did you, sweet cakes?"

She moaned. "Tell me there ain't, Rom."

"There ain't."

"You promise?"

"Course I do."

"Cross your heart and hope your thingie'll fall off?"

Her phraseology was sophomoric and disgusting. Classy Christina reminded herself of that while Crazy Chrissy simultaneously stored away the memory for any solemn vows that might be called for in the future... if she had a future.

"Shit, you're a dirty little—Ah," he said. Apparently, she had found the organ most susceptible to fall-offage.

"So you ain't worried about your brother?" Her contralto had softened a little.

"That scrawny little runt? Why would I be?"

"I meant, won't it hurt his feelin's if he finds out we been... ya know... doin' it in the hay loft... and the corn crib... and the trunk of his car?"

The trunk of his...

"After all, I'm sorta supposed to be *his* girl."

"Ya, but he ain't got..." There was an expectant pause. "This!"

"Ohh!" she gasped. "Rom, that's the cutest little thing ever was."

"Little!"

"I meant the barbell. Did ya get it pierced just for me?"

"Well... ya said ya wouldn't do it no more if I didn't find a way to prove my true feelin's."

"Well..." She purred the word like a stretching feline. "I'll do it now for—"

"Careful!" he croaked, then got ahold of himself. "It's still a mite sore."

"But you can still—"

"Ya bet your world class tits I can!" he growled.

Half a second later, a shirt landed three inches from my feet. Jeans followed. Apparently, the underclothes were better for distance shots. I picked his boxers off my left shoulder with gritted teeth and balled them in one hand.

Then they were going at it like spinner dolphins. At least, that was my assumption. I couldn't see them, but from their mating-walrus noises, I was pretty confident of my deductions.

Not that I *wanted* to see. I'm far too classy to wish to witness something so disgusting. On the other hand, I hadn't seen anything really disgusting for a long time. And *couldn't*, no matter how I craned my neck, see more than a right foot and a left elbow. The pairing seemed odd, but I haven't *been* disgusting for a long time either, so maybe I had forgotten how to do it properly.

What I lacked in visuals, however, I more than gained in audio.

Their performance seemed to go on forever. The panting, the groaning, a slapping sound similar to an oar in rough water.

"Harder! Harder!" she insisted, and despite all probability, he managed to do just that.

After that, there was some wildcat screeching, a lot of growling, and the inevitable collapse. I dropped my head against the wall behind me and tried to be as silent as the furniture, but there was no point; if a 747 had careened through one window and out the other, I'm pretty sure its flight would have gone unnoticed by the sexletes.

But in a matter of moments, she spoke. "Wanna do it again?"

My eyes nearly popped out of my head. I've never been more surprised ... until *he* spoke.

"Why not?"

"So, you can get it up?"

"Course I ... What was that?" he rasped.

"What?"

"I thought I heard somethin'."

I strained to hear. Perhaps a distant rumble reached my ears.

"Was it a truck?" Her voice had risen to Minnie Mouse range. "A diesel? With twin cylinders and a hemi?" She sat up, scooting into my line of view, eyes as wide as chicken eggs. "Where was it? On the road? In the yard? Coming through the trees?"

"Through the trees?" He chuckled. "Don't be silly, love bucket. The woods is too thick. There couldn't be no—"

"If he can drive through a window, he can drive through the trees." She was on her feet now, scrambling around like a monkey. A naked monkey. Damn! Some of those monkeys have really impressive boobs.

A rumble came from below.

She squeaked a noise only heard by Chihuahuas and women hiding behind desks. "Oh Christ! It's my husband!"

"You're *married*?"

She was *married*? And dating Thing One?

"Sorta." She grappled for her clothes while I held my breath, hoping she'd find the bra I'd tossed out before she found me.

"Huh," he grunted. "I suppose he'd get kinda riled if he knew?" He plucked her shirt off the floor and handed it to her.

She pulled it over her head, apparently forgoing her bra for more important, or at least more visible, garments.

"Kinda riled? Kinda riled! Where's my shoe? Where's... There!" She grabbed it from somewhere above her head. "Underwear. Under—"

He handed them to her. She shoved them into a pocket of the shorts she was still yanking up, then hopped into the one shoe that had been removed. "That was..." She was panting.

"Spectaculent?"

"Yeah," she said, but she was already searching the room, head spinning like Linda Blair sans exorcist.

"I'm pretty good, huh?"

"Yeah, yeah. Hung like a donkey. How do I get out of here?"

He glanced around, calm as Sunday. "Window?"

"How high—Never mind." She yanked it open. In a second, she was gone. There was a little *umf* of pain as she hit the ground, then a clambering sound, a few pitiful whimpers, and silence.

I remained where I was, wishing rather fervently that I had taken the same route some time before.

As for the Spectaculent Thing One, he sighed in satisfaction, then plopped down on the couch. I held my breath, sure I couldn't be so unlucky as to have him think now would be a good time to unwind in the barn/office/sex shack. But I was wrong. He groped around for a moment, then raised his arm.

A noise blurted beside me. I almost erupted from my hiding place like Vesuvius on a bender. But the noise belonged to nothing deadlier than a television. I calmed myself with Herculean effort, and a second later, the Thing was totally reclined.

I closed my eyes in misery, determined to wait it out. In my disappointingly limited experience, men are generally catatonic seconds after coitus, and though those seconds seemed to stretch into millennia, in reality less than two minutes had probably passed before he was snoring like a hippo in need of a tonsillectomy. I held my breath, listening, and waited for another eternal five minutes.

He didn't stir. Exhaling quietly, I jacked up my nerve, dropped to my hands and knees, and crept forward half an inch. That's when my camos betrayed me. They brushed noisily against the couch.

The giant snuffled to wakefulness. I jerked back into my corner. He sat up groggily, then, rising to his feet, he stretched, scratched, and scanned the room. It was then that I realized I had failed to eject his underwear a satisfactory distance from my hiding spot. They were lying at the corner of the couch, and if retrieved, would put his face just about level with mine.

He turned one circle, saw his boxers, and reached for them. I held my breath, hoping against hope ... but our eyes met. The world stood still. My heart slammed against my ribs. My brain, still stunned by the up-close sex-a-thon, was whirling like a pinwheel, trying to come up with an explanation or an excuse or a ...

He straightened, tugged his pants on commando style, retrieved his shirt from a nearby lamp, and sauntered from the room.

I will never know how he missed me. My only explanation was that, in my terror, my senses were heightened, while his, in post-coital stupor, were dulled. Whatever the reason, gratitude washed over me. The deities had forgiven me. Still, I waited several minutes, remaining in the corner until the world went completely silent. Then, quiet as a carrot seed, I crept from hiding. It was a relief to straighten my back, better yet to—

Light flooded the room. I spun around just as the giant stepped inside. His brows winged upward, his eyes widened, and then he grinned, slow and Machiavellian, as he shut the door behind him.

Chapter 15

Some people have an unfair advantage in the game of playing dumb.

—*Father Pat, perpetually impressed by Chrissy's innate abilities*

Thing One stood absolutely still, table-sized chest naked, feet bare, and expression going from WTF to IWSN.

"Well, fiddle dee dee, if it ain't Miss O'Tara." His voice was smooth as custard.

I stood my ground, though my knees felt kind of wiggly.

"So you finally come for a little taste o' heaven?" he said, stepping toward me.

I raised my chin, searching for courage. "I don't believe heaven is something one can taste."

He chuckled, still advancing.

"Wait!" I held up a hand, then motioned spastically toward nowhere. "I think I heard something. An ... an angry husband, maybe."

He remained silent for a second, then grinned. "So ya saw the whole thing, huh?"

"What?" I blinked, looking innocent, or possibly myopic.

He snorted softly. "Was you hiding in here the whole time?"

"What whole time?" I asked, but my voice squeaked like a rubber ducky in distress.

"Where was you? Beside the desk?"

I neither confirmed nor denied. Possibly because my heart had crowded up against my larynx.

"Bet you got yourself an eyeful, huh?"

"I thought I heard someone," I repeated hopefully, but didn't quit backing away.

"Sometimes, when Pork Chop dreams, it sounds like a three-quarter-ton diesel."

"I do not," I said.

"What?"

"What?" I repeated, realizing, belatedly, that he probably wasn't privy to my high school nickname.

"I was talkin' about our boar. Pork Chop," he said. "What was you talkin' 'bout?"

I shook my head, but my nimble little brain was already patching together seemingly unrelated facts. "Why did you want to get rid of her?"

"You got any idea what Momma does if she finds folks creepin' round her property without permission?"

I ignored that. "Why?" Maybe it was the therapist in me that made me need to understand his reasoning, or maybe I'm just nosy. Or maybe they're the same thing.

"I guess she's kinda private and don't like—"

"Why didn't you want her to stay?" I asked. "You seemed to be ... enjoying—"

"I tell you what, honey cakes, I won't tell Momma what ya been up to if—"

"What about Remus?" Meeting his eyes wasn't easy, but I had learned long ago to either take the bull by the horns or be skewered by the same.

"What about 'im?"

"I don't suppose he's going to be too thrilled to learn about your nocturnal exploits."

"Huh?"

"He's gonna be mad when I tell him you were doing the hump and bump with his girl."

"Well, sweet tits..." His voice was steady, but a light flashed in his eyes. "I guess you gotta do what you gotta do."

What? Since when? And why was he so sanguine about the situation? If I wasn't mistaken, men could get kind of peeved about this sort of...

My mind spun to a halt.

He wanted Remus to learn the truth. What was the fun of screwing your brother if said brother didn't even know about the screwage?

"Guess I'll just tell your momma instead," I said, and turned away, but he grabbed my arm.

"What do ya want?" he rasped, voice desperate, brow already damp.

I stored away my evil grin, sure I'd want it later. "A computer."

"What?" He sounded honestly surprised.

"A computer," I repeated. "You must have heard of them."

"Of course I heard of 'em," he hissed. "They're implements of the devil."

I raised a brow.

"They cause folks to wander from the path of righteousness."

"Are you kidding me?"

"There's all sorts of stuff on them things. Even..." He glanced right and left, then leaned close to whisper, "Pornography."

"Porn..." I stared at him from a WTF angle. "You're worried about a little porn when you were just..." I motioned wildly toward the spot where they had gone at it like rutting Labradors. "With your brother's..." I was bumbling badly. "Who happens to be a married woman?"

"Well, she got me all revved up. You can't stop no man then."

"What?"

"Ya stop 'im and his dingle'll fall off."

"Are you out of your mind?"

"It's a proven fact."

"That you're certifiable?"

"That a fella's gotta follow through once he's riled. And just looking at you in them camo pants..." He shook his head, eyes alight.

"Swear to God, if you touch me—"

"Get out!"

"What?"

"Out the window!" he rasped

"I'm not—"

"Momma's comin'."

Fear swooshed through me like a shot of tequila. "How do you know?"

"Cuz I can't hear nothin'."

"That doesn't even—" I began, but he grabbed me and shoved me out the window like so much fermenting garbage.

I hit the ground a second before I heard the door creak open in the little office.

"What ya doin' in here, boy?"

"I was just about to watch some TV, Momma."

"TV ain't no good for you. It'll make you go blind," she said, then paused as if skimming his half-naked body. "Just like other things'll do."

"I thought I'd see if Jimmy Bakker is back on CBN yet."

"You're a good boy, Rom."

"I try to be, Momma."

I heard the door squeak as she turned away, but after a moment she spoke again. "You happen ta know where your brother's run off to?"

"I ain't seen him since supper."

"He wasn't in his bedroom." Another pause. "He better not be with that skanky blonde."

"What skanky blonde is that, Momma?" If his voice were any more innocent, he'd be putting his hair in pigtails to the tune of "I'm a Little Teapot."

There was a whisper of noise, as if she'd turned away, but she spoke again.

"You don't suppose he's with that city gal I hired, do you?"

"Miss O'Tara?"

"You think he's lyin' with her?"

"Golly, I hope not. Fornicatin's wrong."

Silence ticked away. "*You* ain't interested in her, are ya, boy?"

"Me? Course not, Momma."

"Good, cuz if she ain't in her room, I'm gonna kill her."

Chapter 16

> Today's mood: annoyed, with a fair chance of I'm-gonna-bitch-slap-you-into-Sunday.
>
> —*Chrissy, on multiple occasions*

I scrambled through the bushes like a wild ape. But there was no way I was going to make it through the front door and up the stairs without being seen. My teenage years had taught me my limitations. True, I had been fifty pounds heavier, but even then I had been something of an expert at gauging how best to escape authoritarian figures, and it was clear from the get-go that the only way I could perform this particular feat involved the sycamore beside my bedroom window.

The lowest branch was seven feet off the ground, and I'm no tree squirrel, but necessity is the mother of dumb-ass attempts. I jumped at it, missed, tried again, and wrestled myself aboard. From there it was just a matter of shimmying up the slanted trunk, leaping sideways, and dragging myself through the window. I flopped to the floor like a hooked mackerel, stumbled drunkenly to my feet, then hauled the window closed before leaping for the bed. I had snagged the covers up to my chin a second before the lights sprang on.

Shielding my eyes with my right hand, I blinked as if stunned. This wasn't my first rodeo.

"Mrs. Hughes?" My tone was wonderfully breathy. "What're ya doing here?"

She glared at me, then shifted her gaze toward the window. "I was just worryin' 'bout ya." Striding into the room, she bent double and glanced under the bed. "Ya doin' all right?"

My mind was spinning. What to do? Play innocent? Play dumb? Play dead? I skimmed the possibilities. My innocent act had never been my most convincing role, but I tried it anyway. "That's sure nice of ya, but I'm dandier than—"

"What's that in your hair?" she asked, straightening abruptly.

Breath held, hand not quite steady, I came away with a sycamore leaf between my forefinger and thumb. Damn it! My mind was spinning up a dozen explanations, a hundred weak-kneed apologies, but then I remembered my roots: I lied like an Irishman. Sticking the foliage back into my hair at what surely was a jaunty angle, I said, "Rao leaf."

Her brows lowered, nearly obliterating her eyes completely. "What the devil you talkin' about, girl? You been creepin' around outside?"

"I beg yer pardon?"

"You playin' hide the zucchini with my boys?"

"Hide the..." I huffed a sound that might have been taken as outrage. Or indigestion. "What I've been doin' is workin' my tail off."

"Yeah?" She peered at me from uncomfortably close quarters. "What else you been doing with your tail when—"

"Workin' like a slave for hours on end. I've been patted and leered at and pinched. The last thing I want is to be playin' anything with anyone."

"So what ya been doin' for the past hour or so?"

"I came straight up here and gave myself a nice Rao-leaf hair treatment."

She leaned in, eyes narrowed, as if she could divine the truth through her pores. "Are you lying to me, girl?"

I tried to dredge up some honest-to-God outrage, but her breath, clearly set on "stun," was making it hard to think. I pulled the covers a little closer to my chin. "It's organic…'specially good for chemically treated hair."

Her glare deepened.

I raised my chin and tried to convince my heart to saunter back into my chest. It was getting pretty cramped in my throat. "I can let you try it. If you've ever colored your hair, it'll help—"

"Colored my hair!" She snapped upright like a church steeple. "What do you think I am? One of them loosey-goosey New York gals? I ain't never dyed my hair a day in my life. This here's all natural," she said, and lifted a pomegranate-colored tress from her chins.

"No," I said.

She stared at me, probably wondering if she should slap me just for kicks and giggles. "Go to sleep," she ordered finally, and tromping across the room, left me with a pounding heart and a decade off my life expectancy.

The following day was hell on my…everything. News of Danshov's culinary expertise was spreading like cheap mayonnaise.

Every man from the tri-county area seemed to pass through the Home's battered front door. I was getting to know more than a few of them on a first-name basis. The rest I christened myself: Oily, Gimpy, Blinky, Restless, Pine Sol, Knuckles…If I could score a Sneezy or a Doc I'd have myself a mining crew. But the truth was, overall, they didn't seem a bad lot. On the other hand, any one of them could be the Carver. Or maybe Remus had simply invented a serial mutilator just to torment me.

Regardless, I was afforded little time to dwell on my fears, past or present, during my shift. But later, when I had finally retired to my frothy room, half-remembered stories of people in the witness protection program nagged me. It's a well-documented fact (at least according to Hollywood) that a disconcerting number of people in those programs have been found by their enemies despite the FBI's best efforts. All sorts of things could trip a witness up—a hobby they couldn't give up, an old acquaintance they wanted to see just one more time. But more often than not, it was their habits that got them in trouble.

It made sense when I thought about it. You could alter the color of your hair, change your wardrobe, tweak your voice, but deep down in the darkest recesses of yourself, you are what you are. I was learning that more profoundly the longer I spent in Hillbilly Holler, and I wasn't sure I was all that thrilled about my dark recesses. Perhaps I had quelled my baser instincts for a time, fighting them off with ten-dollar words and secondhand designer ensembles. But the truth was... maybe I wasn't quite as classy as I had hoped. Lying, for instance, came with awe-inspiring ease. And jacking an anti-theft club up against Rom's tender bits had, perhaps, felt a little more exhilarating than it should have.

But what bothered me most were the continuing dreams involving Rivera. It would have made sense if I had nightmares regarding his well-being. Instead, my midnight meanderings were generally more carnal and often confusing. The latest featured him as a chef and me as a flounder. But it probably didn't mean I was the lustful catch of the day longing to be stuffed. In fact, if I knew anything about dream analysis—which, of course, I do, since I have a

PhD and years of clinical experience—I surmised that such dreams were nothing more than a symbol of my willing separation from Rivera. We had become so far removed from each other that we no longer shared so much as a species, despite how he had looked in nothing but his apron and semi-erect chef's hat.

Nevertheless, he had given me his treasured Jeep and sent me from his house in an attempt to protect me.

But if that was true, why hadn't the *L.A. Times* featured so much as a sidebar about the incident?

I paced the short distance of my bedroom, roaming past the frilly curtains like a caged hound in a lollipop factory. I needed information before I went mad. I needed—

I stopped dead in my tracks. In the darkness below, I could just make out a form trekking through the sparse trees...Danshov, heading off to meditate by the lake, as I had seen him do in the past.

Who was he? And why was he here? Rivera had said he would find me. But if he was capable of locating me, could the Black Flames do the same? Had they, in fact, done just that? Was Hiro Jonovich Danshov a member of that despotic gang, come to murder me? But if that were the case, why would he wait?

The agony of not knowing was making me crazy. Maybe it was that craziness that prompted my next action. In retrospect, I see that it might have been wiser to strategize, to think things through. But the irritating little Zen was leaving his cabin empty, allowing any passing lunatic to invade his privacy.

Turns out, I knew just such a lunatic. Stiffening my spine, I waited to the count of fifty (thirty, actually, patience not being my best quality), then crept back through the window. In a matter of moments, I was in the woods. Beneath the tortured trees, it was as dark and spooky as my senior prom. A hundred small noises suggested hidden eyes at every turn. But I hurried through the underbrush, heart thumping, mind running wild. Still, I reached his domicile without being torn to shreds by any of the sundry monsters scared up by an overactive imagination.

A small, dilapidated Volkswagen was parked beneath a twisted pine. I assumed it was Danshov's, though I'd never seen him drive it. Peering through the passenger window netted me no information except for the fact that he fostered a deplorable lack of clutter. Where were the fast-food wrappers? The mystery novels? The undergarments he'd shimmied out of and shoved between the seats?

Peeved and twitchy, I moved on to the cabin. Unlike the main house, it was locked. Glancing nervously behind me, I slunk around the corner and gazed into the window on the far side of the building, but I could see nothing.

A scrape of noise sounded to my right. I spun around, ready to spout apologies or explanations or pleas for mercy, whichever would save my sorry hide, but the opossum that squinted at me from the shadows seemed to be doing no more than spying on me. I stared at him. He stared at me, and then, in silent accord, we hurried off in opposite directions, him into the woods, me around the corner of the house.

It took several minutes for my heart rate to bump down to normal, for me to continue my quest. But every window was covered. I could see nothing inside. Maybe if I bent double and peeked—

"Hello."

I squawked, twisted, and bounced off the window frame.

Danshov stood not six feet away. His dog was marginally closer, lips curled silently away from exposed fangs. I couldn't figure out which one to fear more. Even the marsupial spy seemed benevolent by comparison.

"Holy shit, ya scared the crap outta me."

Only the left side of his face was visible, making his head appear disconnected from his body. "Yes," he said, tone a velvety threat in the darkness. "I should not be creeping around my own house."

"I suppose..." I shook my head, though I have no idea why. "This probably seems odd to ya."

He said nothing.

I cleared my throat, searching for an explanation for my uninvited presence there. Nothing, absolutely nothing, came to mind.

"Perhaps I could help you search," he said.

"Wh...what?"

"I assume you have lost something?"

"Lost..." It was ridiculous, of course. But I had nothing better. "Oh, yeah. I've lost...something."

He raised one brow a hair's width, waiting.

"You're probably wondering what it is." And possibly planning to decapitate me and use my head for a torch.

The hound stood beside him, silver eyes steady, white teeth gleaming.

"Shikoku is."

I blinked, shook my head.

"The dog," he explained. "She is wondering what it is you have lost."

"Oh." I laughed again. He didn't join me. Neither did the dog. "The truth is..." That I was certifiably insane. "I'm lookin' for a computer."

"When did you last have it?"

I didn't try the laugh again. The sound of my last attempt had scared me almost more than the dog did. "I guess I shoulda said I *need* a computer."

"So you thought you would take mine?"

"Do you have one?" Maybe the fact that he owned a computer wasn't the salient point here. His tone, after all, was about as welcoming as an open grave. "I mean..." I found some semblance of good sense. "No! I'm not going to *take* yours. That'd be wrong. I just thought... I thought maybe I could *use* it."

The hell wolf growled. The sound reverberated in her throat like a rumble from the underworld, making my hair stand on end.

"But I can see this isn't a good time. So I'll just—" I backed away. The hound followed me with liquid-silver eyes.

"Now is fine."

It took all my effort to pull my gaze from hound to Hiro. "Wh... what?"

"Now is a good time. Come." He motioned toward the door.

I glanced in that direction. The house looked as black as death. "You know, it's late and I—"

"Come in," he repeated. The beast growled in concert. "So that Shikoku can learn to know you."

I glanced at the dog, clearly a wolf in wolf's clothing. "To know how I *taste* or..." I let the words trail off.

He smiled, the slightest lift of plum-honey lips. His corner incisors were sharp and slightly tilted, like a budding vampire's. "She will not harm you... if I do not tell her to do so."

"Oh, well, that's... comforting."

"Come in," he said again.

"I'd love to. Really. But..." I stretched my arms over my head and faked a gargantuan yawn. "It's late. I should be gettin' on." True. So true, and yet I couldn't seem to force myself to turn my back on him. "I'll let ya return to ..." Don't say "making a head torch." "Whatever ya were doing."

"I am afraid I must insist."

"No." I managed to force my arms back down to my sides, to shake my head. "Ya don't. Really. Ya don't."

The dog lowered her head and took one calculated step toward me.

"Shikoku is quite territorial. We must convince her that you are not a threat." Reaching out, he took my arm and steered me toward the door.

Perhaps I should have screamed. I'm aces at screaming under normal circumstances. But this was hell and gone from normal, and my breath seemed to be stuck like a cork in a bottle.

Inside, he switched on the lights. The floor plan was simple: bedroom, kitchen, and living area all shared space. The interior was as clean and uncluttered as the inside of a conch. The furniture was utilitarian. There wasn't a dish on the counter or a sock on the floor. Even the logs near the fireplace were orderly.

I took in the tidiness with suspicion. Where were the TBR piles of novels, the mounds of clothes that would be put away "any day now"? The normal, all-American detritus. "How long have you been here?" I asked.

He held my gaze. "Three days."

"No. I meant, how long have you lived in ... wherever we are?"

He didn't even blink. Why the hell did the man never blink? "Three days," he repeated.

I was sure he was wrong. The horrifying working conditions of the Home Place had caused some sort of intentional dementia. Obviously, he'd arrived before me. And yet I felt the blood leave my face in a rush. "What?"

"Thursday was my first day of employment."

I shook my head. He couldn't have arrived thirty-six hours after a tongue-severing Chinese gang had tried to annihilate me. That would be too coincidental. Wouldn't it? "Why are you here?" My voice creaked like an opening crypt.

"To cook."

I shook my head, numb with premonition.

"I believe you have seen evidence to support the theory."

"Why here?"

"Why not?"

So many reasons, but I began with the safest of the lot.

"A chef with your abilities should be in New Orleans or New York or New—" I began, but a glint of light caught my attention. I jerked my gaze to the right. Five steel blades lay perfectly aligned on a rough-hewn kitchen table. I swallowed my bile.

"Are you ... making soup?" I guessed.

He tilted his head the slightest degree.

"Chopping vegetables for ..." I swallowed. I'm sorry to say that more than one person has thought it a dandy idea to try to kill me with a sharp instrument. "Soup or stir-fry or maybe ..." I shrugged. "I'm a big fan of teriyaki."

"Why are *you* here, Miss O'Tara?" His voice was very soft, but I heard him loud and clear. Even my tongue was listening.

"I ..." I cleared my throat. "Like I said, I was just out for a stroll."

"In shark-infested waters?"

"In ..." Had he made a joke? Was he quoting one of my favorite movies of all time? "You're a *Princess Bride* fan?"

Any fan of my sweet Westley couldn't be all bad. Could he? Unless... The breath clogged in my chest. Did he know about my obsession? And if so, how? I didn't glance toward the knives again, for fear that the sight of them in all their surgical grimness might change my mind about the goodness of anyone *Bride* related.

"Why," he asked again and stepped forward, crowding me a little, "have *you* come here?"

"I... I was just... tired of the same old, same old. Had to... had to get away... for a while. Ya know how it is. The noise and the stress."

"Most bring a change of clothing, do they not?"

I didn't dare break eye contact, but I had yet to see a single pair of shoes in *his* domicile. "I just had to get outta the city. I'm a... I'm a country gal at heart." I wished quite fervently that I hadn't drawn attention to any internal organs he might plan to remove with those horrifically mesmerizing knives.

"What city is that?"

My mind raced like a hamster on a rusty wheel. "Uh... Vegas?" I shouldn't have said it like a question. It wasn't a question. "Vegas," I corrected.

Both brows lifted a fraction of a millimeter. "Are you a showgirl, Miss O'Tara?"

"A—" My well-educated mind screeched to a blistering halt at the idea, but perhaps, suggested the lightly used practical side of my mind, I should be a little more concerned about keeping my head above my clavicle than about maligning myself. "There ain't nothin' wrong with entertaining folks," I said.

He tilted his head at me, then reached back without turning and locked the door. I zipped my gaze from the door to the knives to him. Door, knives, him. "What act?" he said.

"What?" My throat felt dry, my underwear wet.

"In Las Vegas," he said. "What was your act?"

"Oh." Dear God Almighty, the knives glistened like a dentist's torture tools. "You probably haven't heard of it."

"Perhaps I am more cosmopolitan than you think," he said, and waited.

I didn't know anything about Vegas acts. I mean, come on, if I wanted to see a pair of boobs I'd look in the mirror. Ditto if I wanted to catch a glimpse of a singular boob. But some time ago, while trying to extradite Laney's super-dweeby soon-to-be husband from a similarly hideous situation, I had met a performer who had been dubbed, possibly by himself, as mystical. And as long as I was stealing other people's identities...

"I was a magician's assistant," I said, remembering Athena, Mr. Mystical's go-to gal.

He glanced at me from the corner of his eye as he headed toward the table. I held my breath, waiting for him to call me a liar... or kill me dead in my tracks.

"Ever work with knives?" he asked, and lifted one of the blades from amongst its fellows.

Oh dear God, he was the Carver! Of course he was the Carver! Why hadn't I thought of him immediately? Nerves. Probably just nerves.

"Listen, I'd love to stay and chat with ya. But I gotta go." I turned jerkily toward the door.

"Don't leave," he said.

I closed my eyes and hoped for a miracle, but the elves failed to whisk me into the magic kingdom. Damn lazy-ass elves.

"For whom did you work?" he asked.

I swallowed and tried like hell to think. When I spoke to the magician's real-life assistant, better known offstage as Gertrude Nelson, she'd been studying for her premed exams. "The Mystical Menkaura."

"Was he?" he asked, and fingered the nearest blade. The entire unit was steel. Light whisked from tip to handle.

I would have passed out if I weren't so scared of what he might do to me while I was unconscious. "What?"

"Was he mystical?"

"Oh." I couldn't quit staring at the knife. The one in his hand seemed particularly mesmerizing. "The horse was better."

"He had a horse?"

"Yeah."

"On stage?"

"Weird, right?"

The left corner of his lips twitched just a little. Was it anger or humor? Anger or humor? "What did he call *you*?"

"Menke or the horse?"

"Was it a talking horse?"

"Talking horses are pretty rare ... even in Vegas."

"The magician, then," he said, and rotated the knife slowly in his hand.

"Scarlet."

"I thought you performers had stage names."

"Oh. You meant my ..." The mesmerizing sheen of the knife was making it difficult to remember my real name, much less try to think of another alias. "Athena."

"And the name of the hotel?"

I would never hold up under torture. He hadn't even brought out the bamboo slivers yet and I was ready to turn over blood kin. Of course, if he was willing to torture my brothers I would have been happy to hand him the instruments, so maybe that wasn't a true test. "The um, the Pyramide."

"So you'll be listed on their website?"

My bladder quivered. Menkaura Qufti's real assistant had been hotter than hell, with bushels of blond hair and boobs like cannonballs. "They, ah ..." My voice was squeaky. Almost as if I was lying through my teeth. "They've probably replaced me already."

"In four days?"

I tried a smile. It was gritty at best. "That's Vegas for ya."

"Did you steal from him?"

"What?" I stepped back a pace.

"Take his ..." He shrugged. The motion was almost negligible. "Rabbit or something?"

"No, I—"

"Were you trespassing?"

"Why would I ... Oh," I said, remembering I had kind of been doing just that when he caught me. "No." I shook my head. "I had my own computer."

He stared at me, maybe thinking I was nuts. Maybe he was right. But if so, it was justifiable insanity. "Where is it now?"

"My computer?"

"Was that not what we were discussing?"

God only knew. "It's at home."

"In Reno?"

I almost agreed, but recognized the trap and caught myself before it snapped. "Vegas. A little condo on ... Mulberry Street." Enough! No more bogus information, my mind screamed, but my mouth seemed to be functioning without the dubious benefit of my brain. "Just up the road from ah ..."

"Sesame Street?"

"What?"

"Why'd he fire you?"

I raised my chin a little and tried desperately to catalog the area around me without turning my head. Surely there was something I could use to defend myself.

"What makes you think he did?" I asked. "What makes you think I didn't..." He ran his thumb along the edge of a blade. Fainting was looking like a more viable option all the time. "What makes you think I didn't just quit?"

He examined me in silence for a hopeless eternity. "You do not strike me as a quitter."

"I would never strike you," I said, but it was a lie. If I thought I could get away with it, I'd hit him with everything but the dog.

For a second, I actually thought he might laugh. But he spoke instead, using that scary-as-hell quiet tone that set my hair on edge. "So you quit?"

"He..." My mind spun for some kind of story. Some kind of lie. Some kind of anything that would keep him talking. "He made a pass."

"And?"

"He wasn't as attractive as the horse."

An elongated moment of silence passed before he drew an electronic tablet from a drawer. Setting it on the table beside the knives, he bent, fingers flying on the keyboard.

In an instant, the image of the Mystical Menke was smiling at me from the screen. I swallowed my bile and glanced at the door.

"I can do a six-minute mile," he said. I jerked my attention toward him; he didn't bother to raise his gaze from the screen. "Faster if the footing is favorable."

I believed him, but even though it generally takes me about an hour to cover the same distance, I thought I might be able to beat him; fear changes everything.

"Shikoku is considerably faster."

I glanced at the dog. She smiled evilly, silver eyes shining.

I fisted my hands and steadied my bladder. "What do you want from me?"

He glanced up, casual as a cactus. "You might try the truth."

"I told you the truth."

He raised his brows, first at the screen, then at me. "Gertrude Nelson is a blonde."

I fisted my hands beside my thighs and tried like hell to be strong. "Madam Clairol."

"Tall."

"High heels."

"And extremely well-endowed." He gazed at the screen for several seconds. "Hard to fake that when you are bereft of a shirt."

I pursed my lips. "I don't gotta explain myself to you." Maybe I was going for hillbilly haughty. Maybe I had entirely lost my mind.

He straightened to his full height, which, quite suddenly, seemed pretty full. "How long have you known Cal?"

"Cal?" I had no idea what he was talking about. It was nice not to have to play stupid. So much easier to employ the real deal.

"Big man," he explained. "Crooked nose. Likes to break arms."

"I don't know Cal. And I don't believe I'd like him very well if I did." I tipped my nose toward the ceiling and took a step to the rear. He followed.

"What's your specialty?"

"Specialty?" I didn't know what the hell he meant, but an answer of some sort seemed to be a great idea. "I was really good at being cut in half."

His face didn't do a lot of expressions. Moderately quizzical was a nice change of pace.

"For the great—"

"Menkaura," he finished for me.

"And pretty good at prideful awe," I added.

Quizzical was leaning toward dumbfounded.

"Ta da," I said, and lifted both hands toward the right, as if extolling the magical powers of some unseen performer.

There was a moment of silence, then, "Who sent you?"

"What do you—" I began, but there was no time to finish the sentence. He had already thrown the knife.

Chapter 17

Build man fire, he be warm for a day. Set man on fire, he be warm for rest of life.

—*Confucius... maybe*

I jerked to the right. The blade sliced past my nose. I lunged for the door, grappling for the lock, but Hiro was right behind me. There was no hope of escape. I pivoted toward him, trapped. The knife reverberated in the timbers beside my head, but I barely spared it a glance; his eyes, so close, so silvery blue, held me spellbound.

Without glancing away, he tugged the blade from the wall. Light flashed along the razor-sharp edge.

"Don't!" I pressed my back against the wall, groveling and sniveling. "Please."

"Thirty-two seconds," he said, and touched the tip of the blade to my throat.

I would like to say he looked insane. But bored would be a more accurate description. Did that mean he was especially crazy? I swallowed, closed my eyes for an instant, and attempted to calm my clattering nerves. It was like trying to civilize L.A. "What?" I said.

"Do not play stupid."

"I'm not..." I managed to shake my head the smallest degree without slicing my own throat. "I'm not playing."

"Thirty-two seconds. That is how long it takes to bleed out when the saphenous artery is severed."

"Then I'd like to request... respectfully... that ya refrain from doing that." My voice was barely a whisper.

He stared at me, an impossible mix of intensity and boredom, then pulled the knife away abruptly and stepped back a pace. "Who are you?"

I swallowed, hoping I wouldn't throw up. "I'm Scar—"

"Don't say Scarlet."

I licked my lips. "Okay."

"If Cal didn't send you, who did?"

I searched rather hopelessly for an answer that wouldn't get me dead. It was impossible to guess what that might be.

"Were you simply sent to find me? Is that it?"

"I—"

"You are not equipped to kill me."

My fingernails curled against the wall behind me. "You *do* irritate me," I admitted. "But most people do, and I've never killed any of 'em. I mean, Bomstad's death was just bad luck. And Peachtree... he was really old. Altove, I'm sorry about that one, but it wasn't my fault. He had a gun... and a grudge and... and Albertson... you gotta admit, dirty cops..." I stopped myself, breathed, licked my lips. "I don't wanna kill you," I said, as if recapping my rambling message. "I don't want to kill anyone." Hardly.

His eyes took on a vague what-the-fuck-are-you-talking-about quality. I'm fairly familiar with the expression.

"I don't even know who you are," I added.

The world stood absolutely still for what seemed like an eternity, and then he drew back a couple more inches. "Go sit on the couch."

"If I do, do you promise not to kill me?"

He contemplated that for several seconds. I don't like to be fussy, but I would have been happier with an immediate response. "I will not kill you today."

I nodded, cautiously hopeful. "Do you mean ... like ... until midnight or for a full twenty-four hours?"

"Gott!" He said the word with quiet exasperation. I didn't know what it meant, but if he was cursing me he had lasted longer than most men in my acquaintance.

"I mean ..." I began, careful not to upset him further. "I'm just wondering how long I have before I should panic."

"You have not panicked yet?"

"This is actually me being stoic."

"Sit down," he said. "I will not kill you before dawn."

I actually felt myself relax, then chided myself for my low standards. A woman with a PhD and secondhand Manolos should probably aim higher. "You're not going to torture me until then, are you?"

"I will ask the questions."

I tried to nod and found with some satisfaction that my neck was just able to manage the necessary motion.

Shuffling toward the couch was more difficult. My knees seemed wooden, my muscles oddly flaccid. I turned, sat, gazed up at him.

"Cal did not send you," he said.

I shook my head.

"Manato would have taught you the location of the saphenous artery."

I scowled. "It's not in my neck?"

A strange blend of disdain and awe flickered across his face. "You are ignorant," he said. "So Arseny would not have hired you."

I almost argued, but I try not to be stupid even when I'm being called stupid.

"Which means you are hiding from someone," he said, and speared me with his ever-knowing eyes.

It took me a moment to realize I should object. "What? Hiding…" I tried a hissing sound, but my mouth was too dry. It ended up sounding a little like a lisping stutter. "What would I possibly have to be—"

He raised a hand. It still held the knife, but the motion was almost casual, as if he'd forgotten its existence.

"Did you…" He frowned. "Surely, you were not foolish enough to cross D."

I swallowed, mind tumbling over memories of one Dagwood Dean Daly, the gangster I had met years before and with whom I still shared a dysfunctional relationship. He's fascinating in a scare-the-pants-off-you sort of way. "What?"

"You are from Chicago," he said. It wasn't a question; still, I felt a need to object.

"No. I told ya. I been in Las—"

"Bartlett, perhaps." He ignored me completely, pacing a little. "Or Elgin."

I almost opened my mouth to ask how he could possibly guess so accurately, but again with the trying not to be stupid.

"You left some time ago. Why?" He stopped his pacing to stare at me. "Was it D's presence that precipitated your move?"

I shook my head.

"But you know him."

I prepared to shake my head again, but he beat me to the punch with a warning glance and an order. "Do not lie to me."

"I know him," I admitted.

"Biblically?"

I did shake my head now.

"So you work for him."

I shook again, pretty much all over.

He drew a deep breath, bending back slightly as if to fill his lungs to full capacity.

"I shall make an agreement with you," he said. "If you tell me how you know D, I will vow not to kill you for a full twenty-four hours."

"Forty-eight." The counteroffer slipped out as if we were bidding on a steamer trunk at Granny's Antiques.

He scowled. "Thirty-six."

"Okay." I'm ashamed to admit the amount of relief that sluiced through me. I mean, really, a girl should probably hold out for more than thirty-six hours of continued survival, but beggars and all that..."What about—"

"Torture is a great deal of work."

"I don't really..." I folded my hands in my lap and tried to be inoffensive. It's easier for some than others. "I guess I'm not really concerned with whether it's strenuous or not," I said. "I'd prefer you didn't do it anyway.

"In fact"—I said this like it was a brainstorm shooting lightning through my cranium—"how about if I tell you the truth, and you let me go?"

"That will depend on the truth," he said.

I licked my lips and opened my mouth, but my mind had been bled dry. "What was the question again?"

"How did you become acquainted with D?"

"Oh." I nodded and swallowed, thinking back to the first time I had met the gangster (or, as he liked to be called, collection engineer) on Chicago's famous Gold Coast. "I... uh... paid him some money."

He watched me narrowly. His dog did the same. "A cheating boyfriend?"

I blinked, confused.

"He is a good person to know if you want someone to discontinue breathing."

"I … no," I said, and shook my head vigorously. As long as it was still attached, I might as well use it. "No, I didn't hire him to …" I glanced at the knives and swallowed. "I was just paying him back."

"Perhaps you should start at the beginning."

I nodded. It was a dumb-ass story and kind of long-winded, but maybe that just meant I could postpone my own demise. Though stretching it out past thirty-six hours seemed difficult. "I have brothers. Three of 'em," I said.

He watched me in silence, as if that wasn't reason enough to pay a trained assassin. Others might agree with him … but only if they hadn't met the brothers in question.

"They're, um …" I probably shouldn't slander my family during the final day and a half of my life. I tried to think of something positive to say, but he'd been pretty specific about wanting the truth. "They're idiots. One of them … Pete …" I cleared my throat. "Peter John, he borrowed money from D." There was a shitload more to this little tale, of course. But I wanted to keep some of my dirty laundry for later. "And, um, failed to pay it back."

Hiro raised his brows a good quarter of an inch. It was like a shouted expletive from an Irishman. "Your brother does not know where the saphenous artery is either, does he?"

It took me a moment to realize his implication. "Lots of people don't know where that stupid artery is. It don't mean we're dumb." I drew a breath and continued on. "Could be it wasn't one of Pete's best decisions," I said. But, honest to God, it was light-years from his worst.

He watched me. "Are you aware that D has been known to take people's livers without their consent?"

"Well, to be fair, who would consent?" I asked, and wondered vaguely when I had begun justifying the actions of an organ thief.

"What of your brother? Was he aware?"

"I kinda think so."

"Yet he borrowed the money."

"Yeah."

"And left you to send the payment."

I shifted my gaze sideways. Silence echoed around us. His brows rose another quarter of a millimeter.

"Do not tell me you delivered it in person."

"Okay."

"Did you?"

I didn't respond. I've never been good at taking orders, but I was desperately trying to turn over a new leaf.

"Even knowing about his liver fetish," he added.

For a moment, I considered informing him that I was as brave as Natalie Portman and as fully deserving of Thor's adoration... or maybe I was just a really devoted sister, but in the end I settled for honesty. "Mom woulda blamed me."

That quizzical brow rose again.

"If Pete went missing, she woulda blamed me."

A quiet rumble issued from his caramel-colored throat. If I hadn't known better I would have sworn it was a chuckle. "How much did he owe?"

"Twenty thousand dollars."

"You must have been quite good at 'ta da.' "

I tried my utmost to make sense of his words, but my mind was shutting down.

"Your former occupation."

I blinked.

"With the Mystical Menkaura. I assume you paid your idiotic but fortunate brother's bill for him."

I didn't respond immediately because, while I consider defaming my family as entertaining as a Jagger concert, I don't like to share the fun with others. "What makes you think he didn't get the money together by himself?"

He didn't even bother to address that ridiculous notion. Which was fair; so long as there was beer to be purchased, brother Pete wouldn't have enough dollar bills to kindle a campfire.

I cleared my throat. "I borrowed the money from a friend."

"What friend?"

I froze. Yes, I would have been willing to serve up my brothers with apples in their mouths, but Laney had been the one to foot the bill, and she was in a league of her own. Mind whirring, I tried to invent a fictional friend, but he shook his head, already sensing the lie like a drug dog on a crack scent.

"I can't tell you that," I said.

"Because you have forgotten her name or because you are loyal?"

"Because she's perfect."

He watched me very closely, as if assessing everything I was. Everything I might be. "So you returned D's money."

I nodded, relieved he had moved on.

"But it wasn't enough."

My extremities jerked in surprise. "How did you know that?"

"So you agreed to find me for him."

"No." I lurched to my feet. He held the knife as if it was forgotten, but my memory's pretty sharp when it comes to cutlery. I sat abruptly, knees weak, voice the same. "That's when I… that's when I agreed to have dinner with him."

He scanned me: face, boobs, hips, thighs. Not with avarice or even with any real interest, but more as if he were questioning whether someone *else* might possibly be interested.

"When was that?"

I shrugged. Perhaps most folks would remember the exact date when they dined with a liver-stealing urban cowboy thug, but the rest of my life made such dates forgettable. "Eighteen months ago?"

"Was that the last time you saw him?"

"No, I… he, um, he showed up when I was in…" I paused, not too keen to share the tale about how he and Rivera had gone at it like mad dogs outside the Mandarin Hotel.

"The shower?" he guessed.

I shook my head.

"The circus? The attic? The sanitarium?"

"I'm not crazy," I reminded him, but the denial sounded a little uncertain.

I'm not sure if I saw doubt or humor in his eyes. "When you were what?" he asked.

"With my boyfriend." When I conjured up Rivera's memory—those high-octane eyes, that tight-muscled body, his sharp-edged intensity—it seemed a strange way to refer to him. Like claiming a shark for a pet. Or keeping a wolf on a—

"They fought over you," he said.

I jerked. "How do you know that?"

He raised his startling eyes to mine, but I held his gaze and remained where I was.

"How?" I whispered.

"Hand-to-hand combat over someone else's mate is D's favored activity," he said.

The idea made me feel funny. I don't know why. It's not as if I was jealous. D was certifiably insane. I would have to be the same to care that I wasn't the only girl over which he'd dueled.

"What happened to him?" he asked.

I snapped my mind back to the matter at hand. "D?"

"Your boyfriend."

"Oh." I fiddled with a loose thread on my camouflage pants. "He wasn't mine ... really."

"Out on loan?"

"We were just dating ... casually."

The cabin was silent.

"It was my idea to break up," I added.

He said nothing.

"He just ... we're not ..." I could feel my emotions winding up like tangled yarn. "What kind of man ..." I cleared my throat. What the hell was wrong with me? This guy was probably going to kill me in thirty-five and a half hours and I was telling him about my dates? "D didn't send me," I said finally. "That's a promise."

"Are you running from him?"

"From D? No."

True interest shone in his eyes now. "You know someone more likely to kill you than Dagwood Daly?"

"D's got his problems," I admitted. "But I believe the name given him at birth precipitated ..." I blinked, managing to stop myself. "No one's trying to kill me."

"You just grew tired of the city, I believe you said."

"That's right."

He shook his head. "You are a terrible liar."

"Am not."

He ignored me, stuck his knife, casual as sin, into the nearby end table, and paced, steps slow and panther smooth. "If neither Cal nor D sent you, who did?"

"No one."

"Trouble with the police, then," he said.

"What? No."

"So you won't mind if I call the LAPD and tell them I found a Lieutenant Rivera's Jeep?"

For a moment my mind went entirely numb, and then it sputtered to life like a Roman candle. A thousand thoughts whizzed through my brain: Dirty cops, vengeful octogenarians, disturbed clients ... who was trying to kill me this time?

But none of it made a lick of difference, because in the next second I snatched up his knife and faced him with a snarl.

Chapter 18

All you need is love? Really? Try going fourteen days without chocolate and get back to me to me on that.

—*Chrissy McMullen, who is not a particularly romantic individual*

Somehow my fingers had become curled like talons in his shirtfront, while my other hand thrust the knife up against his throat. "Who are you?" My voice was a breathy baritone.

Hiro stood very still, head cocked back as he watched me. His expression, God damn him to hell, was still bored. I tightened my grip. "You're the Carver, aren't you?"

"The what?"

"The Carver!"

He tilted his head as if only mildly curious. "This Carver, is he a friend of yours?"

"No! Why would I…Are you or aren't you?"

"Avery sent you. Did she not?"

"I don't know any…" I began, but just then I noticed the dog.

She was standing not three feet to my right, legs braced, attention riveted on my throat.

"Call off…" My voice squeaked. I tried again. "Call off your hound."

He watched me in silence for half a lifetime before he spoke. "*Wending*," he said finally.

The dog eased back a quarter of an inch. Her eyes matched her master's, attentive with a smattering of almost hidden amusement.

Nevertheless, I tightened my grip and focused. "How did you know where to find me?"

"So you did not want to be found?"

"How did you get here so fast?"

"You must relax, Ms. O'Tara. Find your inner quietude."

"Relax!" I laughed. It sounded five beans short of a full pot. "You want me to relax now that I've got the advantage?"

His right brow rose a millimeter, as if questioning my definition of the word. "I would suggest meditation."

"Shut up!" I snarled.

"That blade is quite sharp," he said, but his lips quirked up a little, as if the fact was nothing but amusing.

"I know it's sharp," I growled, and pushed the point into his skin. A droplet of blood swelled onto the tip and trickled down the blade. My stomach heaved in concert, but I held steady. "That's why you're gonna tell me everything."

If I was hoping he would start babbling like a cockatoo on crack, I was sadly disappointed. In fact, he said nothing. Nothing at all.

I licked my lips, uncertain where to begin with my planned interrogation; I wasn't sure how waterboarding worked, and I'd neglected to bring my favorite rack. "How much do you know?"

"I am rather ignorant on the subject of agribusiness."

"Don't get smart with me," I warned, and fidgeted a little, searching for my tough-guy stance. "I might seem like a harmless country bumpkin but I can get—"

I never saw him move. But suddenly the knife had been snatched away and I was thrust face-first against the wall. His body pressed into mine. Terror screamed through me. I didn't move a muscle. Not so much as a capillary. "You promised not to kill me." My voice had gone from baritone to whimper in an instant.

His was as steady as a metronome. "You believe me to be a murderer."

It wasn't a question, but I nodded anyway. Ever polite.

"Yet you think I would be averse to breaking a vow to someone who just threatened me with corporal retribution?"

It was a decent point. I licked my lips, mind spinning. "Honor among thieves?"

"You think me a thief, also?"

My left cheek was pressed up against the wall, while my right arm was twisted behind my back in a manner that suggested there might be a great deal of pain to come. "A thief?" I tried to make a *pfsst*ing sound, but my mouth had gone dry. "No. Of course not. Not that you *couldn't* be," I hurried to add. "I'm sure you could be anything you put your mind to. A pickpocket or a—"

"Who are you?"

I squeezed my eyes closed. "I can't tell you that."

"I do not like to break a vow," he said, and lifted my arm a smidgeon.

"Christina McMullen." I rasped the words and waited for him to kill me, but he spoke instead.

"Who?"

Does it seem strange that his ignorance infuriated me? "Christina McMullen," I gritted. "PhD."

"Yet you do not know the location of the saphenous artery?"

"Will you forget about that damned artery?" Sounding haughty is no simple task when your face is being pressed into the rough logs of a cabin wall.

"You truly *are* unfamiliar with Cal."

"I believe I've mentioned that."

"So who are you?"

"I told you I'm—"

"In a broader sense."

"I'm nobody." The truth hurt a little, but if it was going to save my life I was willing to give it a try.

He was still for several seconds. There was not a sound in the world. Finally, he released my arm and stepped back. "Nobody would not be as frightened as you."

I drew a deep breath and rubbed my neck. "I wish that were true."

"Who threatens you?"

In for a penny, in for a pound. "The Black Flames."

I thought I saw surprise sprint across his face, but all expression was gone before I was entirely sure. "What did you do?"

"Nothing!"

"Vicious gang members are not usually so bored as to target those who have done nothing."

"Rivera..." Saying his name made my throat close up. "Lieutenant Rivera was investigating them." I drew a deep breath, enjoying the feel of it. IMHO, people don't appreciate oxygen nearly enough. It's pretty close to chocolate on the must-have list. "He was afraid they intended to take me as a hostage."

I could almost see the thoughts running through his brain and headed off his next question. "I guess they didn't get the memo that we broke up."

"They came for you?"

I nodded.

"Where were you at the time?"

I cleared my throat, fighting back the terror the memories incited. "Rivera's house."

"Perhaps that was why they were confused about your separation."

"I was just there because..." I shook my head, remembering that I had run to Rivera at the first sign of trouble, but that maybe...just maybe...it had simply been an excuse to see him again, to be held in his arms. "It doesn't matter. He made me leave."

"To keep you safe?"

"Of course," I said, but a nagging little insect of doubt questioned the validity of that statement. Surely there must have been another way to ensure my well-being.

"So you plan to spend the remainder of your life in the employment of Bess Hughes?"

"No." I swallowed, exhaled, forced myself to say the truth I had just realized. "I'm going back to L.A. soon."

"To challenge the most bloodthirsty gang in modern history."

I raised my chin. "If I have to."

"I am certain your lieutenant will miss you."

Subtle. But I caught his meaning. "Maybe you underestimate me."

He watched me for an amused second, then turned and trekked quietly into the kitchen. "I have seen your skills."

I followed him. "Not everyone can be a deranged kil—" I stopped myself just in time. "Teach me to fight."

"No," he said, and opened the fridge.

I glanced at the malamute/demon. Harlequin likes to squeeze into my refrigerator at every possible opportunity, but Danshov's dog remained exactly where she was, not even mildly interested that he had opened the door to culinary delights. It was disturbing; even the hound had more self-control than I did.

"Teach me," I said, "and I won't tell anyone who you really are."

"And who am I, really?"

"I don't know. But I bet D does."

Our gazes met over his just-retrieved veggies.

"Tell me, Christina McMullen, are you trying to convince me to help you or to kill you?" he asked, and without dropping his gaze, chopped the stalks into small, perfectly identical segments.

If I hadn't been concerned that I was about to end up in whatever dish he was preparing, I would have been as impressed as hell. "I can pay you," I breathed.

"I do not need money," he said, and took a cutting board from a drawer.

"What? What do you mean, you don't need money? That's un-American."

"I am also not American."

"Then what do you need?" I asked, and grabbed his arm.

The world stood still between us. He gazed at my hand for an eternity, then lifted his indolent attention to my face. Blue fire sparked in his eyes.

"What do you offer?" he asked.

"I..." resisted squirming and looked up at him through stubby, unvarnished lashes. "I need help."

He nodded as if that was the only obvious truth in a world rife with uncertainty.

"*You* could help me," I said, and tightened my fingers on his biceps. They felt as taut and hard as the limbs of a sycamore. Beneath his simple garments, he was probably hotter than a pistol. But it wasn't as if I meant to seduce him or anything.

A little sexual allure, on the other hand, wouldn't hurt anything. "Please," I breathed.

He stared at my lips. I could feel the heat of his perusal and leaned in. I'm not proud of myself. But I was desperate. Desperate enough to kiss him.

And that's just what I did.

Chapter 19

Smarter than a fifth grader? I'd be thrilled to death if he could beat out dental floss.

—*Chrissy McMullen, regarding her amour du jour*

His lips were warm and firm. He tilted his head and slipped his fingers into my hair, pulling me closer. He smelled of power and dark chocolate, the greatest aphrodisiacs known to womankind. But I wasn't enjoying this. I was far too smart for that. I was playing him for all I was worth, leaning into the kiss, drawing him in.

That's when he stepped back.

I stumbled, unsteady in the wake of his reversal...and watched him shrug.

"I do not believe I can afford the price," he said, and nonchalantly turned away. In a moment, he was chopping veggies again. In that same span of time, I was tempted almost beyond control to hit him in the back of the head with a table, but I controlled myself with sterling aplomb.

Still, my mind was spinning. I don't like to brag, but back in my teenage days, I was said to have lips like a Hoover. I may have had acne. I may have had hips wide enough to sink a ship, proverbial or otherwise, but no one argued that I could kiss. And I wasn't ready to believe that eighty-odd men and a couple of decades had diminished that stellar ability. Which meant there was only one explanation.

"You could have told me you were gay. I wouldn't have judged you." My voice was admirably level, not even hinting at the insecurities and hormones that writhed like ugly snakes below the surface.

His lips quirked the slightest amount as he added bok choy and morel mushrooms to his growing pile of vegetables.

Laconic. Damn it. I hated laconic. Turns out, I'd rather deal with felonious. "So..." I leaned my ass against the table that might at any moment be called into service as a deadly weapon and tried to look cool. "If you're not interested in money or sex, what are you into?"

The cabin was silent to the beat of my ovaries pumping out estrogen like toxic gasses.

"Solitude," he said, making me realize my mistake. It would be so much easier to hit him with a chair than a table.

"Well," I said, and added a casual shrug to my chill repertoire, "the sooner you teach me self-defense, the sooner you'll be alone."

He glanced at me from beneath his brows. They were some low-ass brows, but not so much Cro-Magnon as say... early murderer.

"Unless you kill me," I said, attempting to make it sound like a joke. "But the police can be kind of intrusive when murder is involved." He still didn't speak. "Maybe you're already aware of that." I watched him add oil to a pan and tried for the life of me to read him. Who the hell was he? What was he doing here? How could I make him help me? "I suppose that's why you're here. To avoid certain... authorities?"

He inhaled deeply, causing his nostrils to flare in a manner that should not have been sexy. "Are you a fortune teller, Ms. McMullen?"

"Let's just stick to O'Tara. Scarlet," I said. "So as not to confuse the natives."

His eyes met mine. "Are you a fortune teller, Ms. O'Tara?"

I gave him a why-not shrug. "A psychologist."

He chuckled, low and quiet. I didn't know what it meant, but I gotta tell you, it didn't do a whole hell of a bunch to improve my mood.

I felt my brows lower a little. "I happen to be an excellent therapist."

Skepticism didn't quite sum up his expression. It was closer to a scoop of cynicism with a garnish of I-don't-give-a-rat's-ass. Retrieving a bowl of deveined shrimp, he dropped them into the pan. They sizzled merrily.

"I'm very intelligent," I said.

He glanced at me. If he was half as bored as he looked he would probably slip into a coma at any moment.

"And intuitive."

He gave no indication he had heard me, but I was on a roll. "You, for instance," I began, and narrowed my eyes as if thinking, though honest to God, I believe I may have given that up days before. "I would surmise that you have unresolved issues with your dad. A father complex, if you will." It was a safe bet. Even normal people, of which I've met several, tend to want to slap their old man now and again.

He didn't even bother to glance at me.

The shrimp were already turning pink, filling the air with the scent of ambrosia. He added a sprinkling of salt and a dab of what looked to be garlic butter. The man was clearly plagued with a buttload of disorders—dissocial, schizoaffective, derealization—but he was no idiot in the kitchen department.

"No father," he said, and tilting his cutting board, added freshly sliced veggies to the shellfish.

"Ever?"

He stirred, ignoring me.

"I don't think that's biologically possible," I said. "I mean, theoretically you must have had—"

"Go home," he said, and retrieving a bottle from the cupboard, swished sake into the mix. Steamy happiness swirled in the air. It's stupid how much I love food. But I focused on the dialogue at hand.

"Do you want to talk about them?" I asked.

He glanced up, as if vaguely surprised to find me still there.

"Your abandonment issues," I explained.

Reaching to the hook above his head, he retrieved a cast-iron kettle, filled it with water, and set it on the stove. In a minute, he was emptying the stir-fry onto a plate. There was only one. The shrimp were little curls of joy, the snow peas, inebriated happiness.

"Your family was poor," I said, and glanced at his left ear. Although I'm more familiar with Walmart than Tiffany and Co., I had a strong suspicion the rock there was worth a fair amount. Once, while supposedly studying for my mid-term exams, I'd read an article on precious stones. The chunk in his earlobe kind of looked like a ridiculously rare stone called painite to me. Why wear such a treasure in this setting except to remind himself how far he had come? "Your mother…" I canted my head, warming to the task. If I couldn't enjoy his stir-fry I might as well make sure he didn't either. "She was forced to work overtime to make ends meet. She loved you. I'm sure she did, Hiro." If he was moved by this proclamation, he was an excellent actor. "But she had so little time." I nodded at my own stupendous reasoning. I could see it all so clearly in my mind. Him, young and small and needy. Her, frazzled but heroic, trying to make a home but barely able to pay the bills. Thus, the care he took with his own surroundings. "It was a challenge for her to secure daycare. And her boyfriends—" I paused.

His face was set as if it had been cast in stone, but then his face was always set, so that didn't tell me much. But maybe his eyes had narrowed a little.

"It wasn't a boyfriend," I said, and something warmed in the pit of my stomach. "It was someone else. A woman, perhaps. Someone entrusted with the task of keeping you safe. She ..." I searched my mental files, reviewing a dozen similar cases ... cases where men had shut down, cases where they had turned to violence. "She compromised you. Allowed you to become—"

He slammed his palm against the tabletop.

I jerked back, heart pounding, but he only stared at me.

"It is time for you to leave," he said.

"I didn't mean to make you angry."

"I do not get angry."

I'll never figure out why he would say such a thing. It wasn't as if I needed the challenge. I would probably have tried to make him mad even without being goaded into it. It was the McMullen way. "It's okay to vent your emotions," I said. "You're only human."

An eyebrow rose a hair's breadth. "Do people truly pay you for this tripe?"

Again I resisted the urge to whack him across the head, but maybe my current self-restraint was caused more by the fact that he could kill me with a glance than by an excess of human kindness. Whatever the case, I continued on.

"Did that influence your sexual orientation, do you think?"

He said nothing.

"The fact that a woman failed you in your formative years...do you believe that determined your sexuality, or was it ordained from the start?" Pulling out a chair, I sat down and leaned forward, intent on his answer.

His gaze skimmed from my face to my boobs, marginally exposed between the buttons of my borrowed shirt. I almost straightened, but I was desperate and maybe...just maybe...a little bit insane.

He raised his eyes with slow regard to mine. "Men often find it difficult to embrace their emotions," he said. "You should not blame yourself."

"What?"

"Sometimes their own insecurities prohibit them from nurturing another's self-esteem...even if she is his daughter."

"I know what you're trying to do," I said, and laughed. "But believe me, I came to grips with familial disappointments long ago."

"I am sorry he failed you."

He was trying to turn the subject to me, to thrust a poker into my insecurities, but it wasn't going to work. I was far past caring about the fact that Dad had opted to refer to me as "the other white meat." "I somehow managed to survive."

"And move two thousand miles away so as not to be reminded of his disregard."

I smiled at his sloppy attempt to get inside my head. "Who are you supposed to be now? Montel Williams? My apologies, but I'm not going to break down and weep like an Oscar hopeful."

"He should have protected you."

I smirked and volleyed his raised brow back at him.

"From the barbarism of your brothers," he said. "He should have nurtured you instead of belittling you."

I smiled benevolently. "No one belittled—"

"He wished to help you. To shape you into the strong-minded woman he knew you could become. But he lacked the necessary tools. Hence his heartfelt but perhaps..." He shook his head with mournful understanding. "Misguided means of trying to point out your shortcomings while—"

"Pork Chop?" Perhaps I had snarled the word.

He paused. Silence dropped like a rock.

I felt a pulsing need to regale him with my father's casual disregard, but I reined myself in, cleared my throat, brushed an imaginary speck of dust from my shirt. "I believe we were discussing your need to—"

"He referred to you as Pork Chop?"

"What?" Embarrassment flooded me. "No! Pfffft. That would be asinine. What kind of barbaric—"

"Such callous insensitivity must have wounded your fledgling self-esteem."

"I'm afraid you're mistaken." My face felt warm. What the hell was wrong with me? "I was simply going to say that Daddy *enjoyed* a good pork chop now and again." *Daddy?* What the fuck was I doing now? I hadn't called him "Daddy" since I was four and trying to con him out of a second Twinkie. But I couldn't seem to stop my idiotic ramblings. "Mother tried to control his cholesterol, but some consider pork to be a white meat, and if trimmed properly it can be quite—"

"But perhaps that kind of hurtful jargon has, in the end, been advantageous," he said, and lifting his hand, brushed his knuckles, soft as breath, down my cheek.

I held myself steady, steady and strong. "You can't manipulate me, Danshov."

"And perhaps that, too, is because of your sire. Perhaps it was his hurtful but well-meaning taunts that made you what you are." He skimmed the flats of his nails down my throat. There was a dark magic to his touch, but I didn't believe in magic.

I laughed. "And what am I?"

"Resilient." His ever-clear eyes smiled. He pressed gentle fingertips against the pulse at the base of my throat. It seemed to slow its frantic pace. My head fell back the slightest degree.

"Strong, intuitive, and quite beautiful," he whispered, and leaned in.

Chapter 20

Follow your heart, but maybe invite your brain along, just to be on the safe side.

—Brainy Laney, once again living up to her sobriquet

Holy crap, this guy was hypnotic, like a cobra charmer or a really big portion of tiramisu. But he was right about one thing: I *am* strong.

"Only quite?" I asked, and remained exactly as I was, not leaning in, not leaning back, though his allure sucked me in.

A corner of his mouth lifted in unspoken regret. "But wounded."

"I'm not wounded."

"Here," he said, and ever so gently pushed two fingers beneath the neckline of my shirt to stroke my heart.

I stifled a shiver and tried to dredge up another disclaimer, but I felt myself weakening, drawn into the soulful promise of his eyes. His lips beckoned. His touch entranced.

"Perhaps that is why you feel the need to seduce gay men," he said.

I snapped away from him. "You're an ass."

A hint of amusement flickered in his eyes. "But I do not try to prove my allure by attempting to seduce—"

"I don't try to seduce gay guys!"

He watched me, gaze unflinching, as if he could read my thoughts, could draw them out of my head and dissect them like unfortunate frogs.

"Except..." I fidgeted a little. "Except for Eddie Friar, who ... to be fair ... didn't inform me of his sexual orientation until after we had ..." I winced.

He raised a brow. "After you had what?"

"None of your business," I said. It sounded as childish as a nursery rhyme, but at least I hadn't mentioned beeswax.

His lips, as full as a pair of damn plums, lifted the slightest degree. I watched their upward slant and reminded myself that he had a knife. So I couldn't kill him. Paradoxically, neither could I kiss him. "After you slept together?" he guessed.

"No," I said, and shifted my gaze away.

"What of the others?"

"Others!" I snapped my gaze back. "What others? There were no others."

His eyes crinkled at the corners.

"There were no others," I repeated. I was haughty now, but he said nothing. Seconds ticked away. Silence, as it turns out, eats haughty for lunch.

"You can't count Ben," I said.

Even the damn dog was silent. I gritted my teeth, searching for blessed reticence. But it wasn't in me.

"We're still friends," I said, and pushed a strand of frazzled hair behind my left ear. "Sometimes I watch Rover when he and Sal go out of town."

An eyebrow twitched. "Shall I assume that appellation is a shortened version of Salvador."

"Assume whatever you want," I said. Haughty had returned with a hard-assed vengeance.

"Ah ..." He nodded. "Sally, then."

"She's just a roommate!" I snapped. Although it had seemed kind of funny that she'd been wearing his shirt and little else when I'd returned their dog's leash. I waved a dismissive hand to assure him that her scanty ensemble mattered naught. "They have a very nice dog. A boxer. A little hyper sometimes. But you can't blame him. He's still a…I didn't try to seduce him," I snapped. "And I'm *certainly* not trying to seduce you."

He exhaled softly through his nose. It sounded a little like laughter, but maybe he was too smart for that. Bigger guys had been pantsed for lesser offenses.

"So the fact that your father failed to live up to your expectations has nothing to do with your deep-seated need to prove your worth?"

I gave him my best I-know-what-you're-trying-to-do smile. "Dad doesn't live up to anyone's expectations," I said, and amped up the wattage again. "He's Irish. But what about—"

"Are you hungry?"

"I…" Was starving.

"Help yourself to a plate," he said, and nodded toward the cupboard to his right.

Pride almost prevented me from accepting his offer. But pride can't hold a candle to shrimp in sake sauce. I found a fork neatly aligned in the appropriate drawer. He motioned toward a chair with an open hand. I sat and dished up, but I could feel him watching me.

"Am I wrong?" he asked. "Are fathers not meant to protect?"

I glanced up, having half forgotten our conversation. Food does that to me. Some addicts have their meth. Some their crack. I have stir-fry…and lasagna…and enchiladas ... and pastries so sweet they'll send you into a diabetic coma with one sidelong glance.

"That is how we've envisioned them from the dawn of time," he said. "Fair or not, we expect them to shield us from the hardships of the world."

I shrugged.

"He did not even protect you from your brothers."

I shook my head as I took my first crispy bite. It was insanely delicious. "Some theorize that we put too much pressure on fathers. That in a more natural setting, they would be all but superfluous. That women would form bands to care for their young in a more matriarchal society."

"Was there a band of nurturing women seeing to your care, Christina?"

"This is excellent," I said, perhaps to justify the fact that I was devouring the food like a hound on a hapless ... pork chop.

"If not, it was your father's duty to do so," he added.

I tightened my defenses against the memories. It wasn't as if I had been raised by rabid wolves. But living in the McMullen clan *had* been a little dog-eat-dog. "I can take care of myself."

He raised a dubious brow, reminding me of a half-dozen mishaps that had occurred in just the past few days.

"Under normal circumstances," I added.

"Then why date a police officer?"

I squirmed a little, which I resented because the meal was exquisite, making it almost impossible to multitask. "I'm not looking for a father figure, if that's what you're implying."

"So *he* doesn't protect you either?"

Harsh scenarios flashed through my mind. Rivera was saving my ass in each and every one of them. "That's his job," I said. "To protect and serve. Says so right in their credo ... or something."

He rose to pour tea, very precisely, into two fragile cups he'd taken from some hidden crevice.

"It's not just me," I said. "He's protecting and serving everyone." And wasn't that just the shits!

"And how does that make you feel?" he asked.

"I don't—" I stopped abruptly. Damn him. Damn him and his sneaky cobra ways. "Teach me to fight," I said.

"So you do not have to rely on another man who will fail to live up to your expectations?"

"So I don't end up dead," I said, but somewhere in the deepest part of me I wondered why men abandoned me.

"We all die sooner or later."

"I would prefer later."

He rested his hips against the counter behind him, leaving the remainder of his meal unattended. If I hadn't already known he was a psychopath that would have convinced me. "Why not return to Chicago?" he asked.

"Let me count the ways."

"Maybe you could abolish past demons while avoiding more current ones."

"No."

He watched me, and in the silence I could feel him cranking up a handful of inane questions with which to torment me.

"Fine!" I snapped. "You want to hear my sordid family history? I'll tell you. I have nothing to hide." And I had polished off my meal; I might as well talk. "My father was distant at best. He wanted a daughter about as much as he wanted a steak knife through the heart."

"Not many survive that," he said.

I opened my mouth, closed it, opened it again. "How do you know that?"

"Urban legend," he assured me.

I shook my head but couldn't quite ignore the questions that tumbled through my brain. Whose heart? Whose steak knife? I soldiered on. "I had acne, shock-victim hair, and an extra fifty pounds."

If he laughed, I fully intended to try that steak-knife scenario, but in all honesty, I wasn't even sure he knew how to laugh... or had a heart.

"I could barely fit inside my tuba."

No reaction.

"We played during halftime at the high school football games. It was Dad's job to drive me to the events."

"Your mother was otherwise occupied?"

I blinked in surprise. Thinking back, I wasn't sure what my mother was doing. Trying to pretend she'd never borne children, probably.

"Continue," he said.

I took a deep breath. "On one particular occasion, he took me but neglected to retrieve me. I finally called home to ask Mom if they were missing anything."

"Meaning you."

I nodded. "She said yeah, she couldn't find her cigarette lighter anywhere."

"She smoked?"

"But she was mad as a Scotsman when she discovered I had picked up the habit."

"One is considerably more likely to die from lung cancer than a punctured heart... statistically speaking."

"That's why I quit." I watched him. He had the kind of even-keeled temperament that would make a decent therapist, a good poker player, or a world-class killer. "Twenty or thirty times." I winced. Twitchy nerves made nicotine's siren song practically irresistible. "You wouldn't happen to have any Virginia Slims lying around, would you?"

His eyes shone as bright as mercury, but his expression never changed. Tough crowd.

"The last time I had a smoke was when Pete stayed with me."

"The brother who thought it wise to borrow money from one who covets livers?"

I nodded.

"He was living with you?"

I stared at him. The man might have been a murderer, but he didn't have to be mean; I wasn't stupid enough to allow my dumb-ass brother to cohabitate. "He was just visiting," I said.

"Is that why you risked your life to repay D?" he asked. "To remove him from your life?"

"No. I mean, Pete's a Neanderthal ... and a moron ... and a fucktard." I had almost forgotten how much I loved that word during my endless sojourn in Classyville and was thrilled to retrieve it. "*Really* a fucktard, but he's still my brother." I glanced up. "You know?"

He handed me a cup of tea.

I took a sip. It was weirdly tasty. "It's not as if Dad was much of a father to him either. And you know how mothers tend to favor their sons?"

He watched me in silence, making me wonder if he had any idea what I was talking about. Perhaps he hadn't had a mother either. Maybe he'd been chiseled out of granite.

"Not *our* mom," I said. "She didn't favor anyone. Maybe that's why Pete's been married about forty-seven times. Maybe that's why none of us have any idea how to build a decent relationship." I drank again and leaned back in my chair. "I guess if I were honest I'd have to say that I'd like to marry someday." I glanced at him. His fingers, artist pretty, were loose on the handle of his cup. "It might be nice to have a man who would..." I shrugged.

"Be there when you need him?" he asked.

I glanced up. Maybe there was pain on his face, but I was a little too immersed in my own angst to figure him out. "I thought Dr. Hawkins would be."

He remained silent, letting me find my verbal path.

I cleared my throat. "But in the end, he tried to kill me with a fillet knife. He might have gotten away with it, except for Rivera." I nodded at the realization, remembering how the lieutenant had looked in badass cop mode before I had passed out. Remembering how he had held me, gentle as a saint, when I'd awakened. "Then there was Peachtree. He tried to kill me with poison...and a poker...and a chair. Mean old bastard. Rivera..." I swallowed. "Saved me from him and Adams and..." I exhaled contemplatively. "I guess he's been there when I *need* him. But maybe it would be nice to have somewhere there when I *want* him."

"Lieutenant Rivera is not that man?"

Was it odd that I was discussing past relationships with a man whom I had recently convinced to allow me a few more hours of life? Quite possibly, but the sound of Rivera's name made it impossible for me to care. "He's got demons of his own."

"Cops..." he said, and shook his head.

"Right?" I put a lot of feeling into that single word. "They're a pain in the ass...all hardnosed and tougher than hell and impossible to talk to. Kind of like you."

He didn't mention that I seemed to be doing all right on the talking front.

"Still..." I said. My voice had gone soft.

"You love him."

"Y—No!" I snapped my gaze to his. "No. I don't love him. He's just so..." I curled my hand into a fist.

"Irritating?" he guessed.

"Yeah, irritating, but he's..." I searched wildly for the right word.

"Sexually alluring?"

"I didn't say that!"

He gave me an almost smile. "Is that the extent of his appeal?"

"Well... he's not exactly the kind you discuss Tolstoy with, but..." I shrugged. "He adores his mother... and dogs." I missed Harlequin with a fierce pang.

"Harlequin?"

"He brought me a Great Dane a while back... a Great Dane crossed with"—I shook my head—"a yeti, maybe." I swallowed, hoping to hell he was all right.

Not a sound disturbed the silence.

"He's, um..." I cleared my throat and turned my attention to the devil hound that was probably resting up so as to fully enjoy her meal of *therapist incognito.* Her silvery gaze had not left me for a moment. "It's not like he's a watch dog or anything." I hiccupped a laugh at the thought. "At first, I tried to get him to sleep by the front door. You know, like a last line of defense."

"Against..."

"I've had... I've had a few incidences, and I thought that his bark would probably be enough to scare off your average murderer-slash-rapist. But now..." I shrugged. "He ate a Brillo pad once."

He raised a questioning brow.

"The scraper thingie for cleaning dishes."

"Ahhh."

"Ate it whole. Got really sick. Sicker than a dog." I laughed at myself. "Dr. Kemah, his favorite vet, was afraid we were going to lose him after the surgery. She said he was slipping away, didn't have the will to..." I wiped my nose on my sleeve. "But when I rushed in to see him, he lifted his head and whapped his tail...just once. One single whap." I swallowed. "I took him home that night even though they worried about damage to his sutures. It took four of us to carry him out. It had to hurt. But he never even whined. And then once we got home...well, I could hardly make him sleep on the floor. Not after I almost lost..." I caught myself and tried to reel back the sappy. "Not after spending two grand to get him patched up. He's my most valuable asset...probably the real reason Rivera installed a security system."

"He got you a dog *and* a security system? And some say romance is dead."

I gave him a scowl. "He worries about me."

He said nothing.

"He *does*!"

"I did not suggest otherwise."

"You were thinking it. You were wondering why I'm here at the mercy of the numbfuck twins...and *you*...if he cares about my well-being."

"I am certain he cares," he said.

"Then why am I here?" I leaned across the table toward him.

"It was not to keep you safe?"

Insecurities were circling my head like sewage down a rusty toilet, but I quashed them. "Of course it was." I huffed a laugh. "What else?"

He didn't answer.

"I mean, it's not like he would have staged it."

"You are speaking of the attack on his house."

"Yeah, the attack!" I was up suddenly. Up and pacing. Shikoku rose slowly, watching me, but I was past caring. "*If* it was an attack." Let me just say at this juncture that when I let the crazy in, I don't just crack the window. I throw open the front door and invite its friends: paranoia, psychosis, and neurosis. "Maybe he just wanted to get rid of me."

"Does that not seem a bit dramatic?"

I swung toward him. "Not compared to staging his own death."

"Rivera staged—"

"Not Rivera! Geez. Try to keep up. K..." I stopped myself, felt the air leave my lungs in a hard whoosh. "No. No one did."

I shifted my gaze from him to the dog. Even *her* eyes were calling me a liar.

"Someone else probably paid for Kurt's obituary," I said. "And the coffin ... and the roses. And ... Anyway ..." I waved a dismissive hand. "You're right. Of course, you're right. I'm being ridiculous. Laney thinks Rivera cares about me. Says he's going to dig me a moat next to keep me safe. But maybe that's just the cop in him. You know? That whole serve-and-protect thing again."

"Laney?"

"Yeah. E—" I froze. Being nuts was all well and good, but when the crazy compromised Elaine, it had gone too far.

"The friend whose name you cannot divulge?" he asked.

"No. Laney, she's ... she's just an acquaintance."

"Short for Elaine?" he asked.

I shook my head, feeling manic. "Short for ... Lane. Lane Osterburg."

"That is long," he said.

"What?"

"Laney." He canted his head. "It is longer than Lane."

I tried to think of a plausible response, but panic had set in, full force and bat-shit crazy. "She doesn't have anything to do with this." My voice was a growl.

"Because she is nothing but an acquaintance."

"That's right."

He nodded, seemingly unconcerned, but something inside me had snapped.

"You won't touch her," I snarled, and rose jerkily to my feet. "You won't."

"And if I did?" His eyes were dead steady. Not a shred of human kindness shone in them.

"I'd kill you," I breathed, but he shook his head once, disavowing my ability.

"Then I'd die trying," I said.

"How would you do it, Christina? Knives? Guns?" And like some sort of black magic, he produced a short-nosed pistol from out of thin air.

I sucked in a breath, sure it was my last, but the gun had already disappeared.

"Pepper shaker?" he asked.

"Pepper ... ?"

"It can be done. Do you wish to see how?"

"Not..." I swallowed. "Not right now."

"You should not make threats you cannot keep."

"It was the stir-fry talking," I said, and backed away.

"And you should keep those threats you make."

I came to a stumbling halt as my back struck the wall behind me. "What?"

The silence was tense enough to kill. Almost.

He took a step toward me. "You should not say it if you do not mean it. It makes you appear weak."

I raised my chin. "I'm not weak."

His eyes suggested mild skepticism and a little bit of are-you-fucking-kidding-me incredulity.

"I've scared off Thing One and Thing Two," I said.

"Perhaps they are not as determined as the Carver."

The reminder of rumored atrocities made bile swirl in my stomach.

"Or perhaps the Things simply do not find you attractive enough to make the effort."

I drew myself up. "Rape is not about—"

"Like Eddie," he said.

"Eddie's gay."

"Or Ben."

"Ben's..." The memory of his "roomie's" spank-me attire made me pause a second. "Gay, too."

"Maybe your countless failed relationships explain your unusual affection for your dog. In truth—" he began, but just then I lost my mind and slapped him across the face.

We both halted. Then I scrambled like a wild monkey for the door.

Chapter 21

Generally, it's not until a mosquito lands on a man's nuts that he considers diplomacy.

—Lily Schultz, Chrissy's former employer and lifetime mentor

I didn't make it three feet before Danshov dragged me down. I tried to scream, but my back struck the floor, forcing the breath from my lungs.

I swiveled wildly, trying to knee him in the groin. He blocked it with a thigh. Then his hands were on my throat.

I bucked then I saw the firewood from the corner of my eye. Grappling to my right, I grabbed a log and swung. Blood spurted from his nose. He fell to his shoulder. I scrambled onto all fours, but before I could gain my feet, he was on me again. His weight pressed me to the floor. But it was the cold, sharp tip of a knife against my neck that made me freeze.

"I do not like to be touched." His voice was low, emotionless.

Mine was not quite so detached. "I'm sorry, I'm sorry, I'm so sorry."

"You will be," he said, and stabbed.

Pain shot through me. I jerked, gasping at the flaring intensity of it. My eyelids flickered shut. Unconsciousness tugged at me, pulling me down, rolling me under. I fought against it, then...

"You must be the aggressor," he said, and pulled his knife from the floor beside my ear.

It took me a moment to realize he was no longer on my back, a lifetime to understand that he was beside me, voice as casual as dawn. I blinked and twitched. My fingers worked. My legs moved. Still, I was certain there must be blood pooling beside my head. I lifted a hand to the tiny scratch beneath my right ear lobe.

"Get up," he said. "We shall try again."

I can't tell you how long it took for me to understand that I was basically uninjured. It took longer still to roll onto my back.

He stood over me, face impassive, body relaxed.

I drew a noisy breath. My lungs still worked. My muscles still flexed. I sat up and realized that even my bladder had done its job. Yay, bladder.

My legs felt wobbly as I pushed onto my feet.

"You are predictable," he said. "If you wish to survive you must learn to change that."

"That was..." I pressed my palms against my thighs. They shook like windsocks. "That was a test?"

"You said you wished to learn. Did you not?"

I nodded. Managing that much took Amazonian effort. "Yes. Yes, I did." I nodded again. Seemingly, my neck was also still functional. "You're a very good teacher," I began, but then the real me kicked in. "You fucking son of a bitch!" I snarled, and threw myself at him.

We went down in a tangle of limbs, me on top. My knee ended up somewhere in his midsection. I clubbed him on the side of the face with every ounce of enraged strength that was in me. His head struck the floor with a satisfying thump. But it was the look of surprise on his face that made life worth living. In the next second, however, he was gone, disappeared from beneath me. In the time it would have taken me to consider gloating, I was facedown on the floor again, staring at the hardwood from one rapidly swelling eye.

"That was somewhat better," he admitted. His voice was perfectly modulated. I was panting like a greyhound. My right arm was twisted up behind my back and my hipbones were being ground into the floorboards.

He stood up. It took me even longer to roll onto my back this time. My entire right side was numb and my left cheek was throbbing. Come to think of it, both left cheeks were throbbing.

I stared at his dispassionate face and wanted nothing so much as to kick him in the eye.

"You have a great deal of anger," he said.

"Yeah? Well..." I was still panting. "I get a little cranky when people stab me."

He opened his mouth to protest, but I snarled over him. "Or pretend to stab me."

"You must harness that rage," he said. "To compensate for your weakness."

I scrabbled to my feet, already missing the numbness with throbbing intensity. "I'm not—"

"And be rid of the fat," he said, gaze sweeping over me.

I huffed in outrage. "I'm not—"

Reaching out, he curled his fingers around my upper arm.

I swatted his hand away.

"If I am going to help you, you must become fit."

I narrowed my eyes at him. I hated getting fit. It was entirely possible that I'd rather get killed. "How?" I asked.

"Running to improve your cardiovascular system."

"I already run."

Dubious might describe his expression. *No fucking way* would have summed it up better. "How far?"

"Six miles." It was an out-and-out lie. I couldn't run six miles if a bear was biting at my ass.

"How often?"

I cleared my throat. "Two, maybe three times a week."

"You must learn to lie better."

"I'm not lying."

"That was even worse." He honestly sounded disappointed. "Deception must become your ally."

I opened my mouth to argue, then shrugged. Actually, lying was something I could get behind. "All right."

"And improve your speed. Your reflexes are all but nonexistent."

"They are not—" I began, but he slapped me across the face. Swear to God, I never even saw his hand move.

"You distracted me," I said.

His eyes were steady on mine. "I am going to slap you now," he said.

"What? Don't—" I began, but he had already tapped my opposite cheek.

"Quit—"

He slapped me again.

At which time I kicked him in the shin. Or at least I tried.

He stepped back with a scowl. I righted my balance and glared at him.

"Go to Chicago," he said.

"I'd rather be dead."

"Being dead is not the hard part," he said. "It is the dying that can be somewhat trying."

I felt the blood drain from my face. Still…"I can't." I whispered the words.

He stared at me, then shook his head and turned away. I'll never know exactly why I threw myself at him. But suddenly I was ripping forward, ready to tear his head from his body. He was, unfortunately, already gone. Simply out of my line of vision, and yet my body kept moving, circling wildly upward to land with shuddering impact on the hardwood.

My lungs exploded. My heart ceased to beat. I gasped for breath, body convulsing, until I was finally able to pull a scant molecule of oxygen into my bruised lungs.

It wasn't until then that I realized he was straddling me. And lo and behold, there was an expression on his face. I think it was contempt.

"Meet me at dawn," he said.

I was still struggling to get my wind back when he jerked me off the floor with a hand to my shirtfront. "What?"

"Near the black boulder by the lake," he said, and pushed me out the door. It closed silently behind me.

"Thanks," I told it, and turning, limped through the darkness toward the tree that led to my room.

Chapter 22

It's not the size of the dog in the fight, it's whether or not the mutt has an Uzi.

—Dagwood Dean Daly, ever practical but not particularly familiar with the canine species

I didn't have an alarm to wake me on the following morning. Nor did I have a phone, a roommate, or one of those often-sought-after husbands. But I had something far more reliable. Pain. It radiated from every joint, throbbed in every muscle, bitched on every inch of skin. I opened my eyes. Or rather, I opened my *eye.* The other one was a little slow on the uptake and not fully functional. I glanced toward the window. The first gray glimmer of light was just beginning to brighten the world. I closed my eye. Even that hurt. I took a couple careful inhalations, then held my breath and sat up slowly. New and interesting aches shot off in every direction, like fireworks on the Fourth of July. But it was too late to lie back down. That would hurt too. I was sure of it, so I levered myself out of bed and stood swaying on my feet. I was both pleased and disgusted to realize I had never changed clothes. One shoe, however, seemed to be AWOL.

I searched lethargically for a while, then finally struggled down the hall and limped along the trail toward the lake.

By the time I reached the water's edge, the sun had crested the eastern horizon and shone with foolish optimism on the glassy surface. It was a beautiful sight, even through one eye, but I was in no mood to appreciate the splendor of nature. I was more in the mood to kick some Asian ass ... if only I could see.

"You are late."

I squawked as I twisted to my right, then grabbed my ribs when Danshov rose like a mythical sea creature from the water. His wet hair, shiny sable in the morning light, was slicked back from his chiseled face. His shoulders were sculpted. A round scar marred the tight skin near his left clavicle, but beneath that his chest was perfect, his arms heavily veined and his belly as flat as Cold Stone's granite counter.

And below that ... I let my gaze slip lower. He was entirely naked. Not a stitch, not a thread, not a scandalous whisper of clothes. His hips were lean and taut his thighs muscular, and between them ... I jerked my gaze back to his face, my own warming fast.

"Remove your clothes," he said.

"Wh—what?" I asked, struggling to roll my tongue back into my mouth.

"Your clothes," he said, and tugging drawstring trousers from a nearby tree limb, slipped into them. "Take them off."

But why would I do that? Why, oh why, oh why? Especially now, when he was putting his on.

I shook my head. A growl issued from the right. I glanced frantically in that direction. Shikoku lowered her head and stalked me, but her master lifted a casual hand, stopping her advance.

He scowled. "Do you have a garment for swimming?"

I glanced down at my feet. "I don't even have two shoes."

For a moment, I thought he would question my reasons, but apparently he thought better of it.

"You may get wet," he said instead.

I blinked, mind already doubting what I had seen just moments before. Had he been naked? Had he been hung like a centerfold in some black-market equestrian magazine?

"I think I already..." I stopped myself, not entirely sure what he was talking about. I realize that some people might think that since one eye was swollen shut and I had abrasions over approximately five hundred percent of my body, I wouldn't particularly care about sex, but after my inadvertent sojourn in celibacy, that didn't seem to be entirely the case. However, I *was* lucid enough to forestall my current dialogue and find something more culturally acceptable. "That's all right," I said.

He scowled. "Come here," he ordered, and turned toward the water.

I swallowed. The mist was rising gently. I was quite sure that it would have been an inspiring vista if I had been in another frame of mind...or perhaps in an alternate universe. It would have been quite lovely on a postcard. But it was here right in front of me, and I couldn't see the far bank. Turns out, I like to see the far bank.

"I'm not a strong swimmer," I said.

He ignored me, which was probably just as well, since the truth was I could barely swim at all. A fact of which I'm not proud. But then I spotted the canoe. It was long and brown and tucked up between two boulders, reminding me uncomfortably of other things of considerable size.

"In," he said.

I brought my attention back to him with a start and shoved down the unacceptable images. "What's that?" I asked. Shikoku seemed to have chosen a spot at the front of the boat.

"Get in," he ordered. I didn't bother telling him I had never been in a canoe in my life. That much would probably be evident in a short while. And besides, how hard could it be? He stepped into the water, bare feet horrifically sexy against the sand. I pried my gaze away and toddled into the boat, managing, by sheer dint of embarrassment alone, not to upset it before we were free of the bank.

In a matter of seconds, we were slicing toward the open water. Hiro glanced back at me, brows low. I picked up a paddle. Muscles from every quadrant of my being screamed obscenities at me, but I mimicked his motions in a feeble attempt, while desperately trying to keep the movement from ripping off my limbs.

Still, my efforts yanked at every aching muscle, stretching hard across my back, but after a few minutes, I realized that I was required to do almost nothing. Hiro's strong, sure strokes took us smoothly toward the center of the lake, where he finally drew his paddle from the water and turned toward me. I took a firmer grip on the wood in an effort to pretend I was a functioning member of the team, but he didn't seem to particularly care. His eyes met mine, and in that second, I saw something in his gaze. Something almost hidden. Respect. True, I had failed last night, but I had fought valiantly, and because of that I seemed to have gained a smidgen of admiration. I waited for him to speak. To voice his true feelings.

"Last night was a mistake," he said.

I didn't say, "Hell, yeah"...just thought it.

"You were not ready."

No shit, Sherlock.

"I pushed you too fast."

Ya think? I remained demurely mute.

"I see now that we shall have to begin by improving your balance."

I breathed a sigh of relief. Truth to tell, I would have been happier if he had told me he was going to drive to L.A., gun down the people who had treated me poorly, then return to cook me a five-star dinner. But you know us beggars.

"Stand up," he said.

"What?" I was pretty sure I had heard him incorrectly. Brownie training 101 insists that you remain safely seated while aboard a vessel in open water. While 102 suggests you should try not to be a dumb ass. As you may have guessed, I didn't get very far as a Brownie. "Isn't that kind of dangerous?"

"You must learn to trust yourself if I am to help you." His eyes were earnest.

I sighed. My desire to learn to fight was long gone, driven away by moaning deltoids and not-so-laconic glutes, but if I remembered correctly, I had been somewhat adamant about learning to defend myself. I rose slowly to my feet. "Okay," I said, balancing carefully. "But don't rock too hard or I'll—"

I struck the surface of the lake face-first. It washed over my head in a shocking gush of cold. I screamed. Water streamed into my lungs. I closed my mouth and clawed, trying desperately to find the surface. It came at me sluggishly. But finally I burst into the air, gasping gratefully for every breath. A wave washed over me, driving me back under. Kicking frantically, I pushed myself back up. Danshov was already fifty feet away and paddling steadily toward the shore.

"Hey!" I yelled at him, but it was a poor effort, impeded by choppy water and sluggish muscles. I tried again, but waves slapped at me. I slipped under and came up sputtering. "Help!" Dirty water sloshed into my mouth. I coughed spasmodically.

By the time I recovered, the anti-Hiro and the damned phallic boat were almost out of sight.

Rage, as ferocious as a grizzly, was the only thing that got me to the distant shore.

By the time I dragged myself onto the sand, I was too exhausted to stand. I lay there for an eternity, trying to build up my strength. Finally, I rose to all fours and emptied my stomach onto the beach.

In the end, it was the seething need for revenge that made me limp toward the Home Place. I was going to live long enough to kill Hiro or die trying.

Chapter 23

Perhaps the fact that there is a highway to hell and only a stairway to heaven tells us something about the anticipated traffic flow.

—*Father Pat, upon being privy to a conversation regarding the comparative merits of classic-rock artists*

"What happened to you?" The man I referred to as Blinky voiced the question. He was twitchy and snaggletoothed, with a purple birthmark over his left eye and a comb-over that would make Donald Trump snazzy enough for a New York runway.

How bad did things have to be for Blinky to question my appearance? I wondered, and plopped his coq au vin on the table in front of him.

"I cut myself shaving," I said, ignoring the sympathetic glance Professor Holsten sent my way.

"You—" Blinky began, but I was already shuffling back toward the kitchen. It was 3:54 in the afternoon. I had been on the clock since eight a.m. In another six minutes, I fully intended to crawl into a hole and die. The sweet promise of revenge that had gotten me through the morning hours had been voided by the grinding ache that bitched in every living fiber. Revenge would have to wait, sweet, sour, or extra spicy.

"Eggs Florentine," Danshov said, and slid an order into the serving window.

I glared at him for all I was worth, but it wasn't my best effort. It takes a surprising amount of effort to glare properly, and I was one eye short.

"Drop dead," I said.

"Fifteen minutes," he countered.

"What?"

"You will get another chance to kill me in fifteen minutes. Meet me by the stables."

I delivered three more orders, all the while silently swearing that I had had enough. I was through. After this shift, I would demand payment, inform the Hughes clan that they were all a bunch of backwoods trolls, and march ... or limp ... off to ... somewhere. Anywhere would be better than this. Even the morgue held a certain amount of appeal.

But as I delivered my thousandth order of the day, my gaze fell on Gizzard Manks. He held his steak knife like a spear in one meaty hand and had, as always, ordered his tenderloin extra rare. Blood ran down his grizzly chin. I felt my stomach seize up. If there was no other reason to leave this God forsaken place he would be enough. But in the back of my mind, I knew the truth: The world was filled with Gizzard Mankses. I could maybe escape this one. But how long would it be before I ran into another? With my luck, it would be soon. Probably before sunset.

Stripping off my apron finally, I limped out the door and down the trail toward the barn I had discovered while relieving my bladder. That little nugget of embarrassment seemed like eons ago, but really only a few days had passed since ...

My musings snapped to a halt as a horse galloped into the clearing ahead. It was as black as onyx, arched and elegant and noble. Sliding to a stop, it reared slightly, tossing its ebon mane onto its rider's hands. Its rider, who sat as straight and tall as a...

Hiro Jonovich Danshov. I recognized him, snapped my mouth shut, and narrowed my eyes.

"Mount up," he ordered.

His voice was low and somber and stirred something deep in my primordial gut. Yes, I still hated him. He was a murderous son of a bitch with bad manners. But my sweet Westley, he looked good on that horse. Still, I wanted to ride with him about as much as I wanted to strip naked and sing the Redneck National Anthem at the Gator Bowl.

"Why?" I asked.

"Perhaps, following this morning's performance, you believe your balance to be impeccable?"

I eyed his mount, realizing for the first time that he was bareback. "I'll need help getting on," I said.

He scowled down at me as if I had lost my last dinner roll, then nodded to the left. "Your mount is there," he said.

I didn't even have to look to know he was talking about Josephine, the donkey with the ass-splitting spine.

I shook my head, first at Danshov, then at the donkey, silently denying he had suggested I ride such a beast, but I knew it was true. Sitting on a broken-down burro while he was mounted on an animal sent by the gods was just about the way my luck had been running for, oh... my entire life or so.

I stared at him for a second, wondering how hard it would be to pry him off the horse and beat him to death with the donkey.

In the end, I decided it would be more trouble than it was worth. So I gave the ass a jaundiced once-over. She was a mousy brown color, with a fish-tank head and a spine that rose from her motley back like the Sawtooth Mountains. To top it all off, she was staring at Hiro's mount with what I could only assume was hero worship.

"I can't ride that," I said.

"You cannot swim either," he said. His voice was deadpan, his body still as his horse danced a mincing minuet. "Yet you remain alive."

I gritted my teeth at him, venomous hatred rising to the surface like boiling lava, but he spoke before I could scald him with my justifiable vitriol.

"The decision is yours," he said. "You can become flexible in mind and body, skilled on multiple levels, or you can, once again, hope to find a man to save you from harm."

The world went silent. His fantasy stallion pranced in place.

"Which will it be?" he asked.

"I'm thinking," I growled, then on a wave of foolish independence, I turned and untied the donkey. Leading her to a nearby fence, I climbed carefully onto her back.

"Do not fall behind," Hiro ordered, and reined his mount toward the gnarly woods.

I was contemplating a half-dozen counter-comments about *his* behind when he nudged his mount into a trot. Josephine, longing to be with the fantasy horse, bumped into a hair-raising gait behind him.

I can't even begin to guess how long that went on. Sometimes it's difficult to judge time when you're performing a balancing act on the edge of a scapula while riding through perdition. But just when I was certain I would die if we trotted another step, Danshov and the dream horse broke into a gallop. Josephine, ugly little ass that she was, galumphed after. I grabbed for her scraggly mane, but my body, already tortured to the limit, could take no more. I slipped to the right. The ass went left. I hit the ground with a bone-jarring jolt and remained where I was, fully intending to rip Danshov's possibly nonexistent heart out when he returned to gloat.

Past performances, however, suggested killing him might be somewhat challenging. Instead, I thought, as I closed my eyes and settled more comfortably onto one tortured hip, I would pretend unconsciousness. Then, when he approached, I would roll over and kick him in the eyeball. But it only took me a few minutes to realize the truth.

He wasn't going to return for me.

Fine, I thought. Perfect. I'd just limp back to the Home Place, eat my weight in Eli's kitchen-sink scramble, and...

A growl rumbled through the woods. I opened my eyes, breath trapped in a throat already paralyzed with fear, and glanced over my shoulder. Shikoku was coming toward me, head lowered, fangs bared.

I stumbled to my feet, simultaneously backing away, and in that second she lunged.

Chapter 24

Whoever slipped the S into "fast food" was one sneaky little entrepreneurial genius.

—Chrissy, while ingesting a burger the size of her refrigerator

Shikoku snapped at me, missing my arm by a scrawny hair. I twisted away with a screech and careened back down the path. Up ahead, a spiny Joshua tree grew beside the trail. I leapt toward it, planning to scramble up its tortured limbs, but Shikoku was already there, legs spread wide, hackles bristled. I stumbled backward with a rasping gasp.

The barn was light-years away. Still, I had little choice but to race toward it. If I could reach it, perhaps I could slam the door before I was torn to shreds. I torpedoed down the trail, legs pumping, mile after mile, until I felt like my lungs would explode, my heart would burn from my chest. But finally, up ahead... the barn. Just a few more yards.

My foot snagged on a root. I fell, tumbling sideways. Already feeling fangs tearing at me, I rolled onto my back.

"Eleven minutes."

The words were low and steady. I shifted my trembling hand away from my face and scanned the woods through which I had just flown. No killer dog was leaping through the underbrush to tear me limb from limb. I looked right. Hiro Danshov stood not six feet away.

"How did you—" I gasped a shuddering breath as a noise sounded behind me. Twisting toward it, I skittered back on hands and feet as Shikoku loped into view.

"Even with incentive..." The devil dog trotted casually past to settle at her master's feet. A lopsided grin split her canine features. Her silver eyes laughed merrily. Hiro set a long-fingered hand on her head. "You did not break a ten-minute mile."

Grasping a nearby branch in one unsteady hand, I rose to my feet, momentarily forgetting that the dog could still eat my face. "You fu—"

"I am quite certain Daiki could do better."

"And I'm quite certain I can rip your head..." I stopped. "Daiki?"

"You have heard of him?"

I felt sick to my stomach, weak in the knees. "The leader of the Black Flames?"

"The dragon master, yes."

"How do you know about him?"

He didn't deign to answer. "He is twenty-four years of age."

I stood staring at him.

"In peak condition." His gaze slipped over me. "You are not."

My hands were shaking, but I raised my chin, mad enough to tear out his spleen given half a chance. "I'm not dead yet."

"At an eleven-minute mile, I am certain he will help you achieve that goal soon."

"Yeah, well..." I licked my lips, feeling faint. "I plan to shoot him long before we hit a full mile."

"So you are a marksman."

I didn't bother to answer. "What else do you know?"

He raised a half-interested brow.

"About…" It was difficult to say the name. "Daiki. What do you know?"

"Loyalty is of great importance to him."

"So who's his second-in-command?"

I'm not sure what was going through my head. Maybe some really dynamite plan about kidnapping his lieutenant or something. But Hiro's next words disabused me of that fantastic idea.

"Bingo."

"I beg your pardon."

"They called him Bingo, but he is already dead."

I waited for the second shoe to drop, but suddenly I knew. Knew the truth without being told.

"Rivera killed him," I breathed.

"No. Daiki killed him."

"He killed his own gang member?"

"He killed his brother."

Admittedly, I've considered offing my own siblings, but I have not yet done so, and I'm certain I've had more provocation than most. "I thought Daiki was loyal."

"In the world of the Black Flames, loyalty insisted that he perform the execution himself."

"Good God," I breathed.

He nodded. "Perhaps you should pray more often… and when you meet the dragon master, aim for his heart," he said, and turned away.

I wanted something awful to let him go, to see him walk out of my life and never return, but I didn't really want to lose my tongue to an underage goon with a cheesy gang name.

"I don't know how," I said.

He kept walking.

"Damn you!" I snarled, and threw the branch I had just collected. It careened directly toward his head, but at the last moment, he twisted and caught it in his left hand.

"Stay angry. It improves your aim," he advised, and headed toward his cabin.

"What about Harlequin?" Honest to God, I have no idea why I said the words. Perhaps, judging from his relationship with the devil dog, I thought he had some sort of affinity for animals. But more likely it was because I was nuts.

"He's big and slobbery and as dumb as a..." My voice broke. "What'll happen to him if I die?"

His steps petered out. He stopped but didn't face me, and when he spoke it was as if the words were being dragged from him by wild rhinos. "When you run that course in half the time, I shall teach you to use weapons."

I gaped at him. "A six-minute mile? Are you kidding me?" I couldn't do a six-minute mile in a car.

"I see that your math skills are well matched with your physical condition."

"I can't run a mile in five and a half minutes, either," I said.

"Do not worry," he said, and stroked an absent hand over Cujo's silver head. "Shikoku will assist you."

The next two weeks were a cacophony of misery. I ran in the morning, worked like a field slave during the day, and returned to Danshov's cabin in the evening.

"Over here," he said, and never shifting his attention from my eyes, swatted me in the ear.

I swung at him, jabbing madly with my left. He stepped leisurely out of range, then strode in and snapped a fist to my belly. My muscles shrieked at the impact, but he was already out of reach and light-years beyond remorse.

"Here. Right here," he said, and motioned toward his level-set eyes. "Do not watch my hands."

Our daily training—or beat-a-thons, as I began to think of them—were never restricted to one discipline. When the Black Flames agreed to fight by the Queensbury rules of boxing, we would do the same, he said. Until then, it was no holds barred. My hands ached and my muscles shrieked at every movement, but I kept going back for more. Perhaps my persistence had something to do with the fact that I wanted to live to the ripe old age of thirty-seven. But mostly, I think, I just really wanted to knock him on his ass.

While I was fantasizing about that scenario, however, he slapped my face. My left cheek stung. I swung toward him, anger erupting like a volcano. It was like being twelve years old again. A pudgy tween in a family of Troglodyte teens.

He stepped casually backward, as if he were just out for a stroll, and shook his head. "Daiki's grandmother would have seen that coming."

It took me a moment to remember who Daiki was. How far gone do you have to be to forget the name of the man who's trying to kill you? I wondered, and forced my mind back to the reason I was there.

"How do I know you're not lying about everything?" I asked. The question was issued in panting rasps.

He shrugged and sidestepped around me. I held my fists even with my nose, squinting over them. Maybe the squinting was to help me appear badass, but maybe it was because the swelling hadn't completely receded from my right eye. I had checked it in the mirror that morning. The edema had subsided considerably, but the color was still fascinating. When I returned to L.A., I fully intended to buy a blouse in that delectable shade of magenta. After I whipped Daiki's ass, of course, received a commendation from the LAPD, and had some time to enjoy a little retail therapy.

In the meantime, Danshov took a swipe at my nose. His knuckles whizzed past like a rocket, effectively snagging my mind back to the action at hand. I dodged just in time to save my nose from becoming the same entrancing hue as my cheek.

"If you do not wish to have your pretty face injured yet again, you must be present in the here and now."

I almost faltered. Not that I cared if he thought I was pretty, ugly, or built like a duck. But his left-handed compliment caught me off guard. Still, I had learned enough to keep bouncing, to stay on my toes, to hold my knuckles high.

His lips canted up in a shallow grin. I narrowed my eyes even more.

I can honestly say that I have never hated anything more in my entire life. Except maybe Brussels sprouts. Although, seriously, I've never particularly longed to punch a vegetable in the face. "Why should I believe you're not lying about everything?"

Feigning a right, he struck with his left. I bobbed out of reach. His fist breezed past my ear.

It was then that I recognized the devious twinkle in his eyes. I had seen that same damned joy a thousand times on my idiotic brothers' faces.

I stopped dead, breathing hard, and standing flat-footed for the first time in the forty-five minutes we'd been sparring. "Damn you." The words were little more than a feral growl of rage. "Are you lying?"

He grinned, actually grinned. It was the first real expression I'd seen on his face, and it stunned me. A thousand emotions rushed through me. That's when he hit me in the chin.

My head snapped back, but I barely noticed. "Are you?" I demanded.

He danced away, as light as a fairy on his feet.

"God damn it!" I snarled, and lunged at him, anger erupting like a volcano. "Did you make all this up?"

He skipped back, gave me a come-on motion with his left hand, then tapped the side of my head with a right jab.

I kept charging. "You fucking freak!" I snarled, and swung wildly. To my absolute surprise, my right fist plowed into his ear. He danced out of range, but he wobbled a little. I'd like to say that I felt sorry for him, that I took pity on him, but the opposite was true. At the sight of his weakness, something roared up inside me, something feral and ferocious and mean as a drunken Irishman.

I lunged in, swung with my right, then brought a left up from the basement and struck him square in the eye. I was going for his jaw, but in his attempt to escape my right fist, he had bobbed down ... or maybe my swings were as wild as spider monkeys and I had no idea where they were going to land. Regardless, he stumbled backward, blinking blood. I laughed out loud, hooted really, and it was that sound that stopped me in my tracks.

Who was I? What had I become? All the years I had spent learning to be cultured, cool, caring, only to be reduced to this!

"I'm sorry." My voice trembled, and in that moment I remembered who I was ... what I was. An educated individual. A respected therapist. "I'm so sorry," I said, and hurried toward him. He remained where he was, almost against the wall. "I shouldn't have ..." I began, but at that precise moment something went terribly wrong. Maybe it was the insanity that lurks like hungry eels in my gene pool. Maybe it was just the old Chrissy rising up like a demon from hell. Maybe they're the same thing. Whatever the case, I couldn't stop myself. Even as I reached a sympathetic hand toward him, I bent my leg and gave him a front kick to the head. For a moment, surprise shone in his eyes. Then he dropped to the floor. I gazed down at him, amazed. Stunned. Proud. Ashamed.

Then I found myself flat on my back. I'm pretty sure I'll never know how I got there. I'm also pretty sure it wasn't voodoo. Cuz I don't think voodoo leaves the kind of bruises on your backside that I sustained from that fall. All I know is that one second, I was standing there feeling terribly wonderful, and the next, I was down for the count.

He remained exactly where he was, left eye already swelling shut, right eye expressionless. "Four thousand dollars," he said.

I stared at him, tailbone screaming in pain as a dozen other body parts shrieked in synchronized unison. "What?" I could barely manage that single word.

"The bounty."

I shook my head. "What are you talking about? Why the hell don't you speak in full sentences? It's bad enough that you attack an innocent—" I stopped, drew a careful breath, and momentarily forgot about the pain that radiated from every inch of my body. "The Black Flames. They're offering a reward for Rivera."

He didn't answer. I scrambled to my feet, almost able to ignore the agony that shot off in a hundred different directions. "I'm right, aren't I?"

He shook his head, drawing a knife from some orifice I was pretty sure I didn't possess. "They would prefer to have you alive, but they are not so very concerned about your condition."

"The bounty's for me?" I felt blessedly numb suddenly. "How do you know that?"

He raised one brow, giving me time to think.

"Holy crap." The words were barely a breath. "You're an assassin."

"Knives," he said, and lifted the blade in one hopelessly capable hand. "Silent but effective."

I swallowed, mind spinning. "I bet you wish that I was like that."

He stepped toward me, head lowered a little, eyes deadly.

"Silent," I said, stumbling backward, "but... you know... effective."

His face was expressionless again. Fear bubbled in my blood, turning my bowels to pudding, my knees to flan. I was terrified... but apparently not so scared that I had quit thinking in terms of dessert.

"Please," I said, but then he struck.

I shrieked. The knife sizzled toward me, slicing harmlessly between my right arm and its closest boob.

"Weapons tomorrow," he said, and left.

Chapter 25

What doesn't kill me mostly just pisses me off.

—*Vincent Angler, defensive lineman/philosopher*

The following workweek was almost as hard as my workouts. But both were behind me now. Darkness had settled in hours before. I wiped sweat from my half-exposed chest and midriff. Above the makeshift punching bag that hung from the barn's lofty rafter, a single bulb illuminated the hay bales, the wall of tools, and little else.

From the opposite side of the fence that separated the barn from the pasture, Hiro's fantasy horse nickered. Reaching into the pocket of my cargo pants, I pulled out a peppermint candy and let him lip it from my palm.

Josephine flipped gigantic ears at me. I gave her two candies. Turns out, I could more easily relate to an ugly ass than I could to a sexy beast. I wasn't sure what that said about me, but it probably wasn't—

"This all for me?"

I spun to the left. Remus stepped out of the shadows.

"What are you doing here?" My voice sounded a little breathy. Maybe because I'd been taking my frustration out on the punching bag, but could be it was because he was as big as a mountain and I hadn't really gotten a mental bead on him.

"Watchin'," he said. I could feel his gaze settle hot and heavy on my caboose as I turned to collect my sweatshirt from a nearby hay bale.

"Well, don't," I said, and slipping into the outer garment, zipped it to my chin before trying to step around him. He blocked my escape.

"I can't help myself." He grinned, skipping his gaze back to my face. "You're lookin' good enough to spread on toast, love bucket."

I stared at him. My hair was shellacked to my head with sweat. My face, just now losing the last of the blooming bruises, was entirely devoid of makeup, and my ensemble was what one might optimistically call early ugly.

"If I was raspberry jelly I'd be flattered," I said, and tried to slide past him. Again he blocked my path.

"You been workin' awful hard," he said. "Runnin', punchin'..." He nodded toward the bag suspended from above. "Makin' all that fine flesh firm as a spring peach. But ya don't have to try so hard to impress me, sugar button."

"Excellent," I said, and backed away. I was getting stronger every day, and I had learned a shitload about self-defense, but mostly I had figured out that I'm about half as strong as the average man. Remus Hughes was not average. "Because I'm not."

"I know better, dumplin'. You want yourself a little Remus," he said, and reached for me.

My back was against the fence now, but I grabbed a bale hook from the wall beside me. "Listen, numbnuts," I snarled. "I came into this world screaming like a banshee and covered in blood. I got no problem goin' out the same way."

Silence echoed around us. His shoulders drooped. "He ain't no better than me."

"What?" My grip on the hook loosened a little. "Who?"

"Just a stunted little shit."

"Danshov?" I guessed.

"Been nothin' but a pain in the ass since the day we was born."

"Romulus?"

He jerked a nod. "I know he's a charming little crapper, but that ain't everything."

"Is there more than one Romulus?"

"I'm bigger. Better lookin'. Stronger," he said, and flexed a mammoth arm.

I pried my gaze from his bulging biceps with more effort than seemed necessary. "Aren't you ... identical twins?"

"Identical! I'm a quarter inch taller than him. Not to mention Zinger!" he said, and ripped his pants open.

I stumbled backward a pace and froze.

No lie, his penis was as big as a soup can even though it lay against the open teeth of his zipper as quietly as a well-mannered dachshund.

I like to think I'm fairly cosmopolitan, but "Wow" may have slipped from my lips.

"Right? So where you wanna do it?" he asked.

"Listen, Remus ..." I managed to rip my attention back to his face. "I can see you're pretty serious about this whole sibling-rivalry thing. But I'm not going to have sex with you."

"Is it too dark in here? Is that it?"

"What? No, I can see it just fine," I said.

"It's half an inch longer than his and a full—"

"You measured your ... Never mind," I said, and held up a hand to ward off any unwanted images. "This isn't a competition."

"It sure as shit ain't. It'd be like comparing a baby dill to a zucchini squash."

"I mean ... size doesn't matter."

He stared at me dumbfounded for a second, then snorted. "How about in the hayloft?"

My arm was getting tired. I let the hay hook droop. "Not in a box, not with a fox, not in a house, not with a mouse."

"Your room, then?"

"I don't want to have sex with you, Remus."

"Really?"

"Really." It wasn't a lie ... exactly. I mean, this guy was a Neanderthal. On the other hand, he was a Neanderthal with a zucchini squash in his pants. And squash is supposed to be good for you.

"Is it cuz I don't seem as randy as Rom? Cuz I am. I just can't get me enough pussy."

"As charming as that may be, it's not—"

"I'm horny as a two-peckered billy goat."

"A two—"

"When I seen you and Hiro sparrin' a few days ago, Zinger here 'bout went crazy."

But he had just been watching me jiggle around half-naked and he was limp as a dead duck.

Realization dawned slowly; Rom had learned better than to press his sexual advances after my assault with Rivera's club, but Remus persisted despite dire threats and some corporal punishment. Methought the "gentleman" was protesting overmuch. Me also thought I might have been a fairly intuitive therapist once upon a time. I remembered my last session with Jeremy Jones. He and Remus were like night and day. One scrawny, one gigantic. One fiercely defending his heterosexuality, while the other quietly accepted the fact that others thought him gay. But they had both been wounded in the battle of life, and both were hiding something. The trick was to figure out just what that something was and why they felt the need for subterfuge.

"Are you sure it was me you were interested in, Remus?"

"There weren't no other gals there," he said.

"Have a seat," I said, and motioning toward a hay bale, wished like hell I had a couch.

Chapter 26

Hey, Nap, sorry I was such a dick to you when I was a kid.

—Peter McMullen, sleep-deprived father of one

"Why can't I just shoot you in the head?" My question might have sounded kind of childish ... if you didn't consider that I was asking why I couldn't simply put a bullet into my sensei's brainpan.

Hiro scowled at me from the floor. "Do you have a gun?"

"You think if I did you'd still be breathing?" It was two o'clock in the morning. I'd been up since dawn the day before. Generally, I don't awaken at dawn, but if I do make such a heinous miscalculation, I try to counteract it with a morning nap followed by an afternoon siesta. Instead, I'd put in eight hours of backbreaking labor followed by an hour of knife instruction and a millennium of hand-to-hand combat. Hand-to-hand combat, I had decided, is stupid. Maybe that sounds kind of childish, too, but if I don't get enough sleep I can get pretty cranky.

"Are you certain you are intelligent?" he asked.

"Yeah, and I know no self-respecting whack job is going to attack me from a recumbent position."

"What makes you believe this?"

"Because I know a shitload of whack jobs," I said. "And none of them have tried to kill me while napping."

"Then statistics suggest it will happen soon," he said, and curled his hand around my ankle. "What would you do in this situation?" His fingers were long and tapered. His wrist was corded, and his arms, glowing with a soft sheen of sweat, were sculpted with neatly packed muscle that flowed with seamless symmetry into a chest so pretty it would have made me weep...if I hadn't hated him more than Brussels sprouts. Which I did.

"If I had a gun, I'd shoot your ass," I said. Sometimes pain makes me kind of cranky, too.

He held my gaze. It was like being stared down by a cobra. "You would not shoot me, *wuwei hua.*"

"What does that mean?"

"Weakling," he said.

"You're an idiot," I countered cleverly. "And wrong. I'd just as soon shoot you as look at you."

"The gun is the weakling's answer to all things," he said, and tugged at my ankle. I hopped, mood deteriorating from cranky to downright mean. "What will you do now?"

"I'm going to kick you," I said, and tried to jerk away.

"Where?"

"In the balls. As hard and often as possible."

He released my ankle, and with a quick flip of his nubile body, tossed himself to his feet.

"What's going on?" I asked.

"The choice is yours," he said.

"What?" I stared at him. "What choice?"

"If you wish to get yourself killed, it is your right."

"What? What are you—"

"I do not care to waste my time."

"I said I'd kick you in the balls. Lie down." I flapped my hand at the floor. "I'll do it right now."

"How?" Anger traced a furrow between his brows. It was the first time I had seen him look truly irritated. "How... when I am holding your opposite foot?"

"Oh." I scowled. Maybe that was something a cranky self-defense student should have thought of earlier. "Sorry. I guess I'd have to stab you or something instead."

"Stab me?" He sounded incredulous and even angrier. It's impossible to make some people happy.

"What's wrong with stabbing you?"

"Do you plan to walk the streets of Los Angeles carrying a katana?"

"If that's a big-ass knife, yeah, I do."

He snorted, curled his hand around my arm, and tugged me toward the door.

"Fine," I said, bracing my feet against the motion. "What *should* I do?"

"Move to Omaha."

I gritted my teeth and managed to stop our sliding journey across the floor. "No."

He deepened his scowl and opened the door.

"Okay!" I snarled, and turning slightly, managed to kick it shut. "I'll do whatever you say."

The room went silent. We were standing very close. His eyes were dark, insanely intense, and despicably alluring.

My stomach pitched. "You are..." The words stole from my mouth. "Gay, aren't you?"

He snorted.

"Listen, I'm sorry," I said. "I'll do whatever you want."

"Except think, which you must do, for you are far too weak for any other course of action."

"I'm not weak," I growled. Anger rumbled through me, mixing with a buttload of other emotions ... if horniness and pissiness are emotions.

He stepped up closer, bumping me with his chest, nipples erect, skin as smooth and firm as a caramel-coated apple. "I could take you right now." His voice was little more than a whisper. The sound shivered through me.

"T ... take me?" I *think* I said it like a question.

He was staring at my lips again, but in a second he jerked his attention back to my eyes. "Kill you!" he snapped. "You have been trained for weeks, and still I could end your life in an instant."

"Then I guess you're a sucky teacher." I can go from cranky to testy in the blink of an eye.

"Go home," he said.

And testy to irrational just as fast. "I wanna know what to do if someone grabs my ankle."

"Call nine-one-one," he said, and opened the door.

I faced him, heart pounding. "I don't have a phone."

Maybe he noticed the pounding organ, because his gaze dropped to my chest for a second. "Pop another button on your shirt in the morning, Christina, you will have enough in tips to buy one by lunch."

"What if someone grabs my ankle during the breakfast rush?"

He laughed. Actually laughed. The sound was low and exotic, rumbling a little titter of something through my overtaxed system. I ignored it completely.

"Listen, I'm ..." But I couldn't quite finish the sentence. I'd rather devour a live crow than eat it in the more traditional, humiliating manner. But I took a deep breath and plunged. "Sssoo ... ready to do whatever you suggest."

Our gazes met.

His nostrils flared slightly and for a second I thought his suggestions might involve more than ankles, but then he was on the floor again, fingers wrapped around my lower leg.

His grip was firm and warm. I resisted the urge to squirm. "What now?" I asked.

"What do your instincts tell you?"

I didn't answer; my instincts generally don't make socially acceptable suggestions.

"*Wuwai hua*," he taunted, "if you are too frightened to—"

I dropped, elbows pointed down like spikes.

The left one struck his chest, but my right stabbed him directly in the throat. His hand twitched open. I skittered out of reach, but there was no need to be so quick; he was already curling up like a dying salamander. The air wheezed through his damaged windpipe. His face was bright red, his hands like claws against the bare floorboards.

I stood off to the side, watching my handiwork with some satisfaction and waiting for him to draw enough oxygen to congratulate me on my cleverness. But his lips seem to be turning blue. Still, I remained where I was. The seconds droned on, punctuated by his tortured breathing, tattooed by his twitching body.

"Danshov?" I said finally, and moved a scant step closer.

He jerked spasmodically.

"Hiro!" I rasped, falling to my knees beside him. After that, I have no idea what happened. One moment, I was contemplating an actual apology, and the next, I was flat on my back. He was on top of me, hands pinning mine to the floor.

"Again you forget," he said.

"Forget?"

"Never show mercy."

"I thought you were dying." My tone was accusatory.

"Yes?" His knees hugged the slope of my breasts. His chest all but touched my nipples.

"Sometimes the cops frown on murder."

"That has not been my experience." His breath was soft, his body hard.

Frustration, and maybe a little something else, raced through me. I'm pretty sure I wasn't aroused. That would show a certain lack of emotional health on my part.

"Why has your cop not taught you to protect yourself?" he asked.

"He's not mine."

"Whose, then?"

"I think he's the property of the LAPD."

"Whose property are you?"

"Oh…" The word was breathy, my emotions fluttery, but I wasn't brain damaged enough to tell him the eighty-four-failed-relationships story. Or to think he was coming on to me. But for a gay guy, he could really shoot off the hetero pheromones. "I'm kind of a…" No one had questioned *my* sexuality since Father Pat had caught me sucking face with Blair Kase in the rectory. "Kind of an independent contractor."

Fire blazed in his mercurial eyes. His chest touched mine, burning on contact. But in an instant he pushed away, yanking me to my feet.

"Try again," he ordered.

Chapter 27

All I'm sayin', Pork Chop, is a girl like you should probably learn to fight her own damn dragons.

—Glen McMullen, at the top of his diplomatic game while explaining the deplorable lack of available knights

Despite my aching fatigue, I couldn't sleep that night. Bitching muscles kept me restless. I rose early and jogged just enough to give those muscles something to whine about, then headed toward the restaurant.

My bruises were fading, but the limp was new. I considered trying to hide it, but that would have been a waste of energy, a commodity I was sorely lacking, so I braced myself for the inevitable as I entered the kitchen. Rom quit peeling carrots long enough to step back a half pace.

"What the hell happened to you?"

I turned toward him, ready to be haughtily indifferent, but surprise caught me instead.

"What happened to *you*?"

He turned away. "I don't know what you're talkin' about." His right eye was blackened, his lips split, and his nose looked as if it had encountered a blunt object at considerable speed.

"Were you and your brother fighting?"

"Remus?" He huffed a laugh. "I could stomp him like a turd blossom if I had half a mind."

"I thought that's exactly what you had."

He snorted.

"Serves ya right," I said, "for messin' with someone else's wife."

"What? Whose wife?" He glanced around, as if expecting Momma Bess to come charging out of a cupboard. "I don't know what you're talkin' about. I got this... choppin' wood."

"I was there, remember?"

For a second, I thought he might deny his ill-advised affair, but he didn't. "Fuckin' Re can't keep his mouth shut."

"He told the husband?"

"Who do you think?" he asked. "And it was him was hoisting her skirt in the first place."

No, I thought. Remus was batting for the opposition. Thus his oh-so-heartily feigned interest in women and his fairly creative means of setting up his younger brother for a beating. What a tangled web...

"And now he's too chickenshit to show his face," he said, and stabbed the knife toward me.

It took all my self-restraint to refrain from hitting him in the face with a frying pan. Apparently, I was still in flight-or-fight mode, and I was way too tired to fly.

"That's why he left," he said, sotto voce now. "It weren't my fault."

I filled the salt shakers. Wiped down the pseudo tables. "That's why *who* left?"

"Re don't pull his weight. Never did. *That's* why he left."

"Your father?" I deduced, and faced him.

He wiped his nose with the back of his hand.

I thought about that for a second, mind pinwheeling. "Where is he now?"

"Don't know. Don't care."

Sometimes the greatest lies are those we tell ourselves. The fact that I had once read that on a cereal box made it no less true. "How long has it been since you've seen him?"

He shrugged again. If he was going for nonchalant, he should probably quit sniffling. "Fifteen years, maybe..." His gaze skittered away, dragged back. "In May."

"So you were...what? Eight? Nine?"

"Six."

Holy hell, he was more than a decade younger than I was. So maybe his attempted seduction should have made me proud. Instead, I just felt tired. I slumped onto a nearby stool.

"You okay?" he asked.

I rather doubted it. "What happened in May?"

He shuffled his booted feet.

"Rom?"

"Our birthday party."

I felt the sting of rejection as if it were my own.

"You wanna talk about it?"

"No," he said, but if I were a betting girl I could have made a killing.

"Did you have a party?"

"Yeah, presents, a hog roast." He looked away. "One of them piñata thingies."

I said nothing, just waited.

"It was a mule. Bright red. Stuffed to the hooves. Pa hung it from the old sycamore out front, said..." He paused, whipped up some pancake batter, and refused to meet my gaze. "Said whoever was the strongest could have the candy."

It sounded ridiculous, but I had been motivated by less auspicious challenges.

"He liked to have us rassle," he said.

"Rassle?"

"Fight." He made a dodging motion with his big body.

"Oh," I said, and wondered, not for the first time, what was wrong with men.

"I'm tougher than a bear cat. Always have been. But Remus was bigger than me." Silence ticked around us. "And he bit. Real hard sometimes. Don't mean I'm a sissy if I cried a little."

"Siblings can be cruel," I said.

"So can daddies."

I winced, remembering my own sire's form of fatherly love, and dug in.

Fifty minutes later, we were chopping celery in unison.

"And he's never been back?" We were still talking about his father. I had done a lot of that at Hope Counseling. In my opinion, if Mom's not to blame for the kiddie's neuroses, Dad's a pretty fair bet.

"Nah. And I don't care," he hurried to add. "Only..."

I waited.

He clenched his hands. "She used to cry. After he left...we could hear her."

"Your mother?" I probably shouldn't have sounded so shocked, but honest to God, I didn't know wolverines could shed tears.

"Don't know why," he said. "The way they was together, I didn't think she'd care if he up and croaked."

"They argued?"

"Argued." He snorted something between laughter and tears. "If there weren't blood involved it wasn't even a tussle.

Half the time, I thought she'd kill him outright. But she didn't hit him that day."

"The day of your birthday party."

"Just said..." He blew out a breath. "Just said I weren't no sissy and if he couldn't see that he should up and leave."

It almost made my family seem normal. "And he did?"

"Next morning, he was gone. I thought she'd be happy."

"Maybe she was."

"She weren't. She ain't." His Adam's apple bobbed. "Cuz of me."

"Did she say that?"

He didn't answer.

In this case, I suspected, the parents could probably share the blame.

"You were just a kid," I said.

"She stuck up for me and now she's alone."

"Maybe that's best."

"She don't think so."

"Sometimes mothers are wrong."

He thought about it a moment, then shook his head. "If I hadn't been such a pansy-assed weakling—"

"Rom!"

He shifted his watery gaze to mine.

"You were a child. Above reproach. She has no right to make you think otherwise."

His eyes were round, his expression a quixotic blend of hope and despair. "You sure?"

"Yes."

"Damn! You're right!" he said, and slammed the cleaver into the cutting board. "It's Re's fault."

"It's not his fault either, Rom." My tone was steady and sensible... not like me at all. "But if you two don't quit sniping at each other, there'll be more trouble to come. More and worse. I'll promise you that." Pivoting away before I slapped him upside the head, I left the room.

Rom was mostly silent for the remainder of the day, making me think he might actually be considering my words. It was almost like being a therapist. Almost as if the whole psychology thing might make sense.

The entire day went better for it. Despite Hiro's eventual arrival, a million hours of labor, and my own decline back into Hillbilly Hell, I still felt pretty good during the dinner rush.

"What can I get for ya, honey?" I asked, employing my very best southern discomfort.

William Holsten sat at door two. He glanced up from a tattered paperback written by Aimee L. Salter. Concern was a warm balm against my bruised skin. "How are you doing, Ms. O'Tara?"

"I'm just hunky. How about you?" I asked, and nodded toward the novel. *Every Ugly Word* was not exactly a train ride through Happyville.

"Just a little"—he shrugged—"light reading. Are you okay? It almost looked like you were limping."

I didn't glance toward the kitchen, where Danshov was marinating strips of beef, but I felt his gaze on my face. Truth to tell, he didn't look much better than I did. And wasn't that a kicker. Turns out there's nothing like landing a good solid palm strike to a guy's nose to put a little spring in a girl's step.

"Ran into a door," I said.

"Really?" He sounded doubtful.

"Yup. Came out of the kitchen too fast and wham..."

"Most doors aren't so antagonistic."

"If it makes ya feel any better, I smacked it right back," I said, and gave him a cheeky grin. "What'll ya have?"

He ordered a beer and a hot beef sandwich au jus.

Half an hour later, things had wound down considerably. The trio at the car hood had left a pretty decent tip, while Gizzard Manks, true to his miserly nature, had left nothing. But at least he had had the good graces to leave several minutes before closing. Only Professor Holsten remained, nursing his second glass of vino and probably contemplating the mysteries of the universe.

"Anything I can do for you before I take off?" I asked.

He examined my face. I couldn't help but wonder if he could still see the bruises or if he was looking deeper ... into my soul, maybe. "No, I'm good. Thank you."

"No problem," I said, and turned away, but he spoke again.

"Unless you'd let me walk you to your car."

"That's real nice of you," I said, "but I'm just headin' over to the big house."

"Through the dark woods all by yourself?"

I gave him a brave smile. "I'm a big girl."

"With all those nefarious doors between here and there?"

I laughed. At that point in my life, big words made me all but giddy.

He flashed his perfect smile. It was full of intelligence and caring, but maybe there was a sliver of sadness. "What do you say?"

I could feel Danshov's attention on me. There was a considerable amount of evidence to suggest that he didn't give a rat's ass whether I lived a long and fruitful life or was run over by an intoxicated hippo on my way home. But maybe, just maybe, he wasn't quite as cavalier as he seemed. "Well, if you'll promise to fend off all them ill-mannered windows, too..."

"Cross my heart," Holsten said, and rose to his feet.

It was a beautiful night. The moon was nothing more than a golden sickle hung in an ebony sky.

Silence stretched between us, but he spoke finally. "If you're wondering, I'm trying to properly compose the 'what's a nice girl like you' question."

Tempting as it was to show my true PhD nature, I stuck to character. "Ya mean how'd I end up in bumfuck nowhere?"

He laughed. "You do have a way of cutting to the chase, Ms. O'Tara."

"I just needed a change of pace, I guess."

"From where?"

"Ya askin' where I'm from?"

"If it's not too intrusive."

"Ohio, originally," I said, and felt not the least bit of guilt for the lie. "But Vegas more recently."

"Vegas... there must have been a good deal of culture shock."

"Well, there ain't a whole lot of culture in neither place."

He chuckled, halted, and turned toward the lake along which we'd been walking. "That's a lovely sight."

Moonlight glistened on the water, gilding every flowing peak and flirting with the latent intellect in me, but I was playing Scarlet O'Tara, hick girl, for all I was worth. "Probably would be if my dogs wasn't yippin' like malamutes," I said.

"You must be exhausted."

"I used to be the queen of all-nighters. Now I can barely handle all-dayers," I admitted.

"Well, I'm not about to pile more on your plate," he said, and turned back toward the trail. "Come along. I'll see you home."

"More what?" I asked, but he shook his head.

"You've got enough troubles of your own, Scarlet."

And wasn't that the truth?

"I mustn't bother you with mine," he said, but even in the moon-kissed dimness I could see the sadness in his eyes. And ... surprise ... turns out I *wanted* to be bothered. Maybe in the end, no matter how jaded or facetious or harried, we all need to be needed.

"How's your daughter doing?" I asked.

"How did you—" He breathed a soft sigh of surprise. "I've always been a believer in women's intuition, but you take it to new heights."

I laughed, flattered. "Last week you were reading *To Kill a Mockingbird,* a favorite for English Lit teens. Now you're reading a novel usually reserved for angsty girls with acne. It wasn't all that much of a reach."

"I'm just trying to ..." He shrugged.

"Relate to her?"

"Yes. But I don't know the first thing about seventeen-year-old girls."

"Seventeen. It's hard to believe you got a daughter that old."

"I'm going to believe you're surprised because I look too young."

"You do look too young."

"Well ... misspent youth and all that," he said, and glanced over the water again. "I was just hoping"—he sighed again—"Frankie's wouldn't be so ... misspent."

We walked along the water's edge. He was silent. Moonlight danced on the waves. I missed the cushy chair in my office in Eagle Rock. In fact, I missed chairs entirely, but I got the ball rolling. "So her name's Frankie?"

"Francine, yes. It wasn't my idea," he hurried to add. "My wife, ex-wife... Cheryl." His tone of voice suggested that if he was over Cheryl I was the pope's slippers. "Her favorite uncle was named Frank. Perhaps that's where the whole problem began."

I settled onto a good-sized rock that overlooked a little bay. "What problem is that?"

"She moved in with a lad. *Lad*... listen to me," he said, and sank down beside me. "I sound like a right gaffer. He's twenty-three. Frankie was five when I was his age. But he's..." He drew a deep breath, glanced out at the water again. In profile, he looked thoughtful and indescribably sad. "I think he's a stoner. Don't get me wrong; I'm not a prude. I attended university. Smoked my share of the spliff and..." He scanned the dark treetops as if gazing into the past. "It's simply that... she's always had self-esteem issues. She's lovely. I'm not just saying that because she's my daughter. She truly is, but she believes herself to be..."

"Fat," I finished for him.

He jerked. "How did you know that?"

"She's not exactly the first girl who thought she didn't live up to the preset standards."

"Surely you don't believe such tripe," he said.

The surprise and outrage in his tone was so soothing I felt no need to unburden. "Peers can be cruel. Not to mention Barbie."

"Barbie?"

"Mile-long legs, perfect boobs, no visible waist."

"The doll?"

"Spend enough time with that bitch, anybody'd feel inferior," I said.

He laughed, sounding like his troubles were falling away, and making my choice of careers, my whole life, maybe, seem meaningful. "I've never met anybody quite like you, Ms. O'Tara."

"Lucky guy," I said.

"I do feel blessed." His gaze felt as warm as sunlight on my face, making me fidgety.

"Well, Frankie's lucky to have *you*," I said.

"You think so?"

"Pretty sure."

"We're not close." His admission was as guilty as hell. As if there wasn't a bottomless chasm between ninety percent of American fathers and their daughters. "Haven't been since the divorce. Then, when she moved out of her mother's house, we started hanging out again. It's been brilliant. You know, like I got another chance. Not to be ... her father, really. I missed that opportunity. But we've gone to a couple concerts together. Saw Taylor Swift in January."

"You *are* liberated," I said.

"I suppose that sounds rather lame," he said, and tossed a pebble into the lake, "but I don't want to destroy the fragile relationship we've built."

"It's not lame. But she's just a kid."

He was watching me like I had some answers. Like I wasn't just a dumb-ass waitress in a parched little corner of hell.

"And a girl only gets one dad."

"I bet you and your father were close. That's why you're so secure."

The good thing about being a hick was I didn't have to curtail my snorts. I let one rip.

His brows jerked up. "Am I wrong?"

"Mostly, Dad just ignored me." I remembered my relationship with Glen McMullen with a quixotic blend of confusion and unease. But maybe a smidgen of nostalgia too. What the hell was that about? "When he did remember my presence, he had a habit of calling me names better suited for dinner entrées." I thought about the pig in the not-so-distant stable and wondered if *he* was offended by the cognomen we shared. "But he did give me the princess speech."

"Princess speech?"

I shrugged and tossed a stone toward the water. "Said *princesses* might be able to count on Prince Charming to save their asses. But I wasn't no princess, so I'd better learn ta stab a pencil in a boy's eye when the moment called for it."

"And?"

"Tried it out on my brother that very afternoon. Worked like a charm."

He laughed like he thought I was kidding, then sobered slowly and sighed. "What if she turns away from me?"

I shrugged. "What if she gets hooked on meth and looks like Rick Grimes' worst nightmare before the age of twenty?"

"Rick..." he began, but I waved away his question. Obviously, he wasn't a *Walking Dead* aficionado.

"Point is, sometimes, dumb-ass as it may sound, a girl needs a daddy."

He thought about that for a moment. "You're right. Of course you are, but really, what can I do?"

"She's seventeen. Still considered a minor in the state of California," I said. "Your options are practically infinite. You can insist on counseling, get her tested for drugs, put her in rehab. Hell, you can file rape charges against lover boy if he doesn't agree to move on."

He stared at me.

"Or … or so I'm told," I said. "Not that a girl like me'd know nothin' about it. Since I'm just a waitress."

"I know better than that," he said.

"What?" The question was uttered breathlessly, but he smiled.

"You're a wise and wonderful woman."

"Oh, well … yeah … I'm that, too."

He smiled. Moonlight winked off his perfect incisors. "Not to mention beautiful," he said, and set his palm against my cheek.

My heart fluttered like a dying chicken. "Holy fritters," I said, employing my best hick speak. "If I didn't know better I would think you was coming on to me."

He chuckled. "Is that so difficult to believe?"

"Well, no, I mean …" I'm not sure why I was so rattled. "Men come on to me all the time, only …" He leaned in. His lips were warm and firm against mine. "They don't usually have all their teeth."

He laughed as he settled his hands on my waist. "I've been wanting to do that since the first time I saw you."

"Really?" Despite my fatigue, my bruises, and my well-justified phobias, my hormones were beginning to fire off rather lewd suggestions in the general direction of my brain.

"Really," he said, and slid his hands up my sides. His fingers bumped over my newly unearthed ribs. His thumbs brushed my nipples.

I'm not going to lie. It was as stimulating as hell, but despite the slut my body longed to be, my mind was still Catholic, and paranoid, and jumpy as hell. "Thank you," I said, and eased back a little. "I'm flattered, but it's late and I should—"

"You're not going to be standoffish now, are you?"

"If not now, when?" I asked, and tried to rise, but he grabbed my arm.

"Maybe after I've fucked you," he said, and pushed me down. My shirt tore. Buttons sprayed off, but I managed to break away, to gain my feet, to twist toward the path.

He snagged my hair and yanked me up against his chest, and suddenly there was a knife, sharp as death, shoved against my throat.

I froze, afraid to breathe.

"After all the time you've spent coming on to me? I don't think so."

"I haven't been coming on to you." I could barely manage the denial, but he chuckled.

"If you can do those two retards, you can do me."

"I'm not doing anybody. Swear to God."

"You're a liar...just like her," he snarled.

"Who? Frankie? Cheryl?" My mind was spinning, shooting out possibilities. "I know you still have feelings—"

He laughed, low and ugly. "Jesus, you're even dumber than I thought. One little sob story about a daughter and you're ready to spread your legs like a drunken whore."

"It was a lie?" He had lost his accent...and his appeal. "You—" I began, but a twig snapped in the woods. I yanked my gaze in that direction. "Help! Help me!" I begged, but he pressed the blade deeper.

"Shut your mouth or I'll carve you into bite-sized pieces."

I froze. He wrenched at my pants, pulling them down my hips. I could feel his erection against my bare flesh.

"No, please." I was pleading and crying. He laughed and shoved me against a rock, bending me at the waist. His erection felt hard and cruel between my thighs.

"Keep begging, baby," he snarled. "You're going to love this."

I was falling, giving in. And then I saw it...a shadow amid the shadows...watching me in silence. Danshov!

Rage flared through me, torching my instincts, firing my defenses. Knife forgotten, I jabbed my heels into the earth, tossing my weight backward like a battering ram.

We went down together. But I was up first, up and lunging forward. That's when Holsten caught my ankle.

I didn't think, didn't hesitate. I fell on him, elbows like spears.

He howled and contorted. I snatched the blade from his fingers, twisting hard. He writhed in agony. Blood covered his face. He curled his broken fingers against his chest, eyes pleading, but I gripped the knife in both hands, ready to kill.

"You son of a bitch!" My voice was no more than a feral snarl.

"Don't hurt me. Don't." The words were garbled, spoken through bloodied teeth. "Please."

"You've done this before, haven't you?"

"No. I—"

"You're the Carver."

"No!" he said, but I bent low, pushing the tip of the blade beneath his jaw.

"Aren't you?"

"No!"

I twisted the knife. Blood trickled down the blade. He sucked in his breath. "Okay. Yes. It's me. But I'm sorry." He was sobbing now, body heaving. "I'm so sorry. I don't know what's wrong with me. I need help. I know it."

I stared at him, disgusted, but sympathy was crowding in, obscuring my better judgment. I tightened my grip on the knife, trying to mete out the punishment he surely deserved, but my rage had diminished.

"Say you'll never touch another woman again," I gritted out.

"I won't. Never."

"And you'll turn yourself in to the cops."

"I will. I swear it."

"Immediately. You'll go to the authorities and tell them everything."

He drew a shuddering breath and turned toward me, eyes haunted. "I'll tell them," he said.

I straightened, drawing back. "I'll find you if you don't," I said. "I'll find you and I'll kill you."

He nodded spasmodically. I stepped away. My hands were shaking in earnest now. I lurched onto the trail and vomited into the underbrush.

Chapter 28

I'm not saying I hate you, but if you were on fire I'd toast me some s'mores.

—Chrissy, mean but practical

I banged my fist against Danshov's cabin door. It was two o'clock in the morning, but I couldn't sleep. Anger was racing through my veins like hot tequila.

"Open up!" I snarled, and tightened my fist around the knife I had appropriated just hours before.

There was no noise from inside. I pounded again. "Open up, you sorry son of a bitch. You fucking—"

"Ms. McMullen."

I spun around, knife raised.

Hiro stood not five feet away. He skimmed his bored gaze from my face to the knife and back again.

"You bastard!"

He stared at me, expressionless. "Would you like to come in?" he asked, and opening the door, motioned me inside.

"You son of a bitch!" I snarled the words like a junkyard dog.

"You already used that particular expletive," he said, and proceeded inside. I stumbled after him.

"You were there," I said, snapping my head in no particular direction.

He raised a brow, as if questioning my sanity.

"In the woods."

He waited, saying nothing.

"When I was attacked by that ... by that ..." My hand trembled. I tightened my fist around the knife. "Animal."

"Ah, the estimable Professor Holsten. Yes, I was," he said, and turned toward his kitchen. "Tea?"

"You would have let him kill me!"

"Perhaps," he agreed, and lit the burner beneath a copper kettle. "But he was not planning to kill you. Only to rape you ... and to carve out his usual pound of flesh."

"Only!" My voice shook in concert with my hands now, but I managed to raise the knife, to stalk toward him, attention riveted on the back of his head. But he spoke before I could decide where to stab.

"We discussed this, Christina." His tone was a little piqued, a long-suffering tutor correcting his disappointing student one more time. "Your checking hand should always remain in front."

I raised my left arm, shielding. He sighed, checked the water level in the kettle. "And you must keep your chin tucked."

I lowered my jaw, corrected my stance, and eyed the back of his neck.

"I would suggest the soft spot at the base of my skull."

"I don't need help stabbing you."

He glanced over his shoulder at me, curious, perhaps, but not the least bit concerned. "Did I approach you?" he asked.

I tightened my grip, working up my courage. "What the hell are you talking about?"

"You came to me." He turned, settled his loosely garbed hips against the stove with all the casualness of a Sunday brunch. "Asked for my help. Begged me for instruction in the art of self-defense," he said, resting the heels of his hands against the oven door behind him. "If you simply wished for me to teach you to beg for help, you should have stated that at the time. It would have taken far less effort on my part."

"You"—I gritted my teeth at him, incensed—"are a wart. Worse than a wart. You're a mole on a wart."

He shrugged his shoulders. Or maybe just one. My killing rage was not, it seemed, motivating enough to call both into service. "If you wanted a touchy-feely instructor you should have looked elsewhere. One of the twins, perhaps. Or your cop. I am not the sensitive type."

"Sensitive! You're not even human."

"Perhaps not," he admitted. "But I remain curious. *Why* did he not teach you?"

"What?"

"Your lieutenant," he said. "Doesn't *he* care about you either?"

"He wouldn't have stood by while I was attacked."

"Then where was he?" Gliding to the cupboard, he removed two cups...a panther, preparing tea. "If he cares so deeply, why is he not here with you? Protecting you? That is his job, is it not? To serve and protect, I believe you said."

"He does protect me."

"He must love being the hero. Will he be angry that you are no longer helpless, do you think?"

"I was never helpless."

He studied me. "Just dangerous enough to stir his interest, perhaps. Not dangerous enough to frighten him."

"I don't want to frighten him," I said.

He narrowed his eyes a little. "How about him? Does he frighten you?"

"Of course not."

"Nothing but kindly thoughts regarding the good lieutenant, then," he said, and poured tea. It flowed in a fragrant arc into the delicate cups.

I sharpened my glare, though the anger was beginning to simmer down to a soft boil. "My relationship with Rivera has nothing to do with you."

"Rivera." He nodded. "A cool appellation for such a gallant, is it not?"

"It's his name."

"His father calls him Gerald," he argued, and offered me a cup. I stared at it. My right hand was busy with the knife, but my left was free, and it seemed rude not to take it. "His mother, Geraldo."

"How do you know that?"

"The Internet is very informative. Your lieutenant has many commendations. He sounds quite wonderful...lover of dogs, champion of distressed damsels. Most call him Jack. Yet you refer to him as Rivera. Interesting. It makes one wonder if there might be a distance between you and the valiant officer."

"I didn't come here to discuss my relationships with you."

"Why did you come, then, Christina?" he asked, and took a sip.

"To kill you." Now that I said the words out loud, they sounded a little melodramatic, especially with the tea in one hand. Accepting the tea, I realized, had been a mistake.

But he didn't mention it. Instead, he stared at me in silent consideration for several seconds, then, "I appreciate your confidence," he said. "I believe you broke your assailant's nose."

My stomach churned at the thought, but I lifted my chin bravely, then lowered it, protecting my throat when I saw his brows dip disapprovingly. "You deserve worse than I gave him."

"Because I did not come to your rescue."

"Because you're a fucktard."

His lips twitched, and for a moment I thought he might laugh. If so, I was pretty sure I could work up that killing rage again, but he kept his amusement to himself.

"For doing as you requested?" he asked.

"I didn't—" I began, but he stopped me.

"How do you think the encounter would have ended without my training?"

"We're not talking about the training. We're talking about the fact that you sat in the woods and watched me be attacked like it was a fucking three-D movie."

"I give it thirty-seven percent on the Tomatometer," he said, and setting his cup aside, stepped toward me.

"Stay back," I warned, raising my knife, but he didn't. Instead, he took another stride.

"Or what will you do, Christina?"

"I'll..." I paused, unsure about the teacup. "Carve you like a Thanksgiving turkey." Oh crap. Was I really quoting bad movies? Now?

"Do it, then," he said, and stopped not eighteen inches in front of me. Perfect striking distance.

"I will," I breathed.

He nodded. "Focus on the vulnerable areas. Eyes, throat, or just above the clavicle if—"

"I know where to stab you!" I snapped, but I *had* kind of overlooked the clavicle thing.

He canted his head a little. “You were delaying,” he observed, and took another half step toward me. “I thought perhaps you had forgotten.”

“I’m never going to forget how to kill—” But suddenly I was spun about and thrust out the door like a stray cat.

A stray cat holding a teacup.

Chapter 29

> Some folks think success is the best revenge. I prefer anything involving Gorilla Glue and soft tissue.
>
> —*The entire McMullen clan*

"You know anything about this?" Bess asked.

I stopped dead in my tracks. A police officer stood in the middle of the Home's dining area. I turned innocent eyes toward the cop. "About what?"

"I'm Officer Bindsdale," he said. "Can I get your name, ma'am?"

"Scarlet." I tried to keep my gaze from darting about the room like a hunted bunny's. "Scarlet O'Tara," I said, and waited, breath held, for him to call me a liar.

"What happened to your arm, Ms. O'Tara?"

"My arm?" I blinked at the offending limb, surprised such a relatively innocuous bruise was the only one that remained. "I'm taking up boxing," I said. "The punching bag's fighting back."

For a second, I thought he would pursue that thread, but he moved on.

"Do you know this man?" he asked, and held up a five-by-seven snapshot.

I almost made a heartfelt denial, but good sense, or at least lucidity, returned. "Professor Holsten," I said. "He's a customer. I waited on him last night." I glanced toward Big Bess, trying to read her thoughts, but her glare was inscrutable. "Why? Nothin' bad happened to him, I hope."

Silence ticked around me as I waited for the sky to fall.

"His name is actually Matthew Gallager."

"Matthew..." I shook my head.

"State troopers found him beside the interstate at four o'clock this morning."

"The interstate? I don't understand."

"This note was tacked to the dash of his car." He held up a sign. It read: *I am the Carver.*

"He was..." My voice was barely audible. "The rapist?"

"We have yet to ascertain that, ma'am."

"What did he say?"

"He remains unconscious at this time."

"Unconscious?" I steadied my hands against my thighs. He had been fully conscious and blubbering like a talk-show guest when I left him. "From what?"

"Possibly because of the damage to his nose."

Bess's brows jerked upward.

"But it could have been the fact that both arms were broken."

"Both..." I shook my head. Maybe I should have admitted my part in it. Maybe I should have told the officer my real name. But sometimes victims get blamed for the misfortunes of their attackers. You can trust me on this. "Both..." I began again, but I couldn't finish the sentence. Instead, I rushed toward the kitchen, gripped the edges of the sink with both hands, and emptied my stomach into the stainless-steel depths.

When I straightened and turned, Officer Bindsdale was standing behind me. He offered me a towel. "Are you all right, ma'am?"

I wiped my mouth. “I’m not sure.”

He pushed a stool up close to me. “Please, sit down.”

I did so, shakily.

“Was Mr.—” He checked his notes. “The man known as Professor Holsten, was he a friend of yours, Ms. O’Tara?”

“A friend?” I shook my head. “Not really. Just…just an acquaintance.”

Less than five minutes later, Officer Bindsdale was stepping into his cruiser and driving out of my life. I watched him go in absolute bewilderment. Where were the accusations, the endless questions, the thumbscrews?

“Well, what are you waiting for?” Bess asked. “Them salt shakers ain’t gonna fill themselves.”

Chapter 30

> During the day, I know the boogieman is simply a figment of my imagination. But at night, I'm a little more open-minded.
>
> —*Harlequin, better as a lap dog than a guard dog*

"It was you."

Hiro opened his eyes and turned his head slowly toward me, like a man awakening from a dream. It was dark, but the moon had winked on, illuminating his eyes, glowing on his skin, shining like dark magic on his loose hair. He sat cross-legged not fifty feet from where I had been attacked the night before.

"Have you come to meditate, Christina?"

I took a step toward him. "You broke his arms, didn't you?"

"Perhaps," he agreed. "About whose arms do we speak?"

"Gallager's."

He rose to his feet, quiet as a shadow. "I do not believe I know anyone by that name."

"Holsten. You found him. Wrote the note."

"Why would I do such a thing?"

"I don't know. I don't..." I exhaled shakily. "Because you care about me?"

"Is that what you believe?"

"Yes. No." I shook my head, unsure of everything.

"Which is it?" he asked, and took a step toward me.

"I have no idea. Do you?"

"Do I what?"

I hissed my exasperation. "Do you—" I began, but he closed the space between us and kissed me.

My lungs collapsed. My heart exploded.

His lips were volcanic against mine. His right hand, that killer artist's hand, curled around the back of my neck. His breath was warm on my cheek, and when he trilled his thumb across my ear, I'm pretty sure my body went into systemic failure. Still, I managed to speak.

"Don't do that," I said, but my voice was nothing more than a whisper.

"Caring," he said, "makes you vulnerable."

"I'm not vulnerable," I breathed, and tilted my head back, granting him better access to all those sensitive nerve-endings in my neck... and my jugular.

"Are you certain?" he asked, and pressed a thumb to the thundering pulse in my throat.

"Pretty sure," I said, and pulling a blade from the pocket of my camos, pressed it beneath his bottom rib.

His left brow rose half a millimeter. "A fillet knife?" he asked. "Such as the disreputable Dr. Hawkins attacked you with?"

"Paring," I said. "Easier to hide."

His expression remained unchanged, but something blazed in his eyes. I wanted to believe it was fear, but in retrospect it might have been amusement. Although, honest to God, it could have been admiration. It was clear by now that he was one sick puppy... and that I had no idea how to read him. "The blade is not very long," he said.

I snarled a smile and gave the tip a sexy little thrust. "Sometimes size doesn't matter."

"Is that what your lieutenant tells you?" he asked, and skimmed his thumb along my collarbone. I shivered violently but managed to remain conscious. Neither did I burst into orgasmic flames.

"Rivera's got nothing to do with this."

"That is because he has left you to your own defenses."

"Which are pretty sharp," I said, and pressed the knife deeper. His lips twitched the slightest degree.

"Because of me," he said.

"I should kill you."

"I would hurry, then." He spanned my throat with his hand while simultaneously settling his hips gently against mine. "Or you will have difficult things to explain to your cop."

"Don't flatter yourself," I said, and jabbed. I felt the tip pierce his skin.

"*You* flatter me," he said.

"What are you talking about?"

"I could kill you in a matter of seconds," he said, and slipping his hand down my throat, eased it onto my pounding heart. "Yet you look at me like that."

I licked my lips. His gaze settled on them.

"I'm not looking at you like anything." The words made no sense whatsoever, but I didn't care. Feelings, feral as farm cats, were racing through my overheated system. But it wasn't until he opened a button on my shirt that I twisted the blade.

His wince closely resembled a smile. "Do it." His words were a challenge.

"I'm going to," I promised, but he was already opening the next button. I tightened my grip on the knife.

"It is not too late," he said.

"I know."

"Be careful to avoid the ribs." Pushing my shirt aside, he kissed my shoulder with whispering softness. "Or it will be difficult to achieve full penetration," he said, and caressed my collarbone.

I shivered like a palsy victim. "Of course."

"You must push it to the hilt."

"I will." I was breathing hard. My breasts were rising and falling like a motivated porn star's. "I'm going to slice you in two."

He shook his head a little, hair brushing against my bare skin like falling silk. "You do not have a long enough blade for that. But you can damage the internal organs if you strike with enough force." His fingertips followed the down-swept neckline of my shirt.

I valiantly kept my eyeballs from rolling inside my cranium like cue balls. "Will that kill you?"

"It might be slow," he said, and pressed a sizzling kiss to the little dell between my breasts.

"Slow's good," I breathed.

His lips twitched against my skin. I wondered vaguely if he was smiling. "Try to puncture the spleen." He was performing some sort of Asian voodoo on my shoulder with his thumb.

"All right."

"You remember where it is located?" I'm not sure I answered; his hand was already traveling down my midline, circling my waist, sweeping magic up my back. I arched against him. "There." He breathed the word against my lips. "Just below the ribs."

"Uh huh."

"Stab. Remove and stab again."

"And again…" My head dropped back. "And again."

"Do not let the blood scare you."

"Blood?" Somehow I'd not quite considered the blood.

"The human body contains approximately five liters. Several of them could leak out before I go into hypovolemic shock."

I swallowed.

His hand skimmed lower. I felt a little faint, probably due to the talk of blood. "Your cop should have taught you these things."

"He should have taught me how much blood there is in the human body?"

"Yes."

"Are you sure?"

He may have nodded. "And how to pierce a spleen."

His fingers felt scary good beneath my shirt.

"We were…" Somehow, his right thigh had become cradled between mine. "I think we were busy with other things."

"Only a cretin has coitus before teaching his partner how to kill him."

"Holy shit, you're crazy." My knife hand shook, tapping a droplet of blood. Only 4.99 liters to go.

"It is so like a cop to neglect teaching his woman how to protect herself."

"We were thinking of protection of a different kind."

His fingers were pressing a course down my spine, beneath my camos, scaring up another shiver. "But he would have to be able to protect himself first."

"He does fine on that front."

"He does not," he said, and slid his palm over the curve of my ass. "Especially now."

I closed my eyes but managed to contain a moan of pleasure. "You don't know—" I began, then froze. "What do you mean, 'especially now'?"

"It is difficult to protect oneself while unconscious."

"What?" I scrambled away, half fell, found my balance, and braced myself.

He remained exactly as he was, body relaxed, eyes calm. Blood ran down his side to his drawstring pants, screwing with my equilibrium, but he didn't seem to notice.

"What the hell are you talking about?" I tightened my fist on the paring knife.

"He is an officer of the law, Christina. Surely you know the risks inherent to the job."

I stumbled backward a step, oddly disoriented. "Where is he?"

"How would I know that?"

"Where the fuck is he?"

"You are allowing yourself to become agitated."

"Tell me or I'll kill you." I widened my stance, considered a lunge. "I swear I will."

"That would make no logical sense."

I stared at him, then backed away. "Where are your keys?"

"Your hands are shaking," he said, scowling. "I taught you better."

"Where are your damn keys?"

He raised his hand, lifting a chiming cluster of metal out of nowhere.

I snatched it from his fingers.

"You are not ready, Christina," he said.

"Then it's on your head," I said, and turning, raced down the trail toward his rusty Beetle.

CHAPTER 31

Happily ever after only happens to chicks like Cinderella and Sleeping Beauty. Do I look like some lazy-ass white chick to you?

—Lavonn Amelia Blount, destined to drag down happiness by the balls

"Where is he?" My voice sounded scratchy and unused. The drive back to L.A. had depleted my reserves and taken its toll on my already questionable nerves.

Captain Kindred snapped his gaze from his computer screen to me, brows lowering over his long-day face. "What the hell are you doing here?"

"Which hospital?"

"How'd you get in here?" His expression threatened dire consequences and possible dismemberment, but I was too exhausted to care.

I slapped my palms against his desktop. "Where's Rivera?"

He glowered at me, a big black man with a big black attitude. "Dedrich!" he yelled. "What the hell kind of police station is this? Get this woman out of my office."

It was then that someone, probably Dedrich, rushed in behind me. "I'm sorry, sir. I didn't—"

"Just get her out."

"Yes, sir. Ma'am, please come with—"

I had reached the limits of my patience...and possibly my sanity. The paring knife seemed to appear in my hand of its own accord. "Tell me where he is!"

Kindred's gaze dropped to my weapon. His expression was disgusted and maybe a little bit bored. I was getting kind of tired of that. "Are you shitting me right now?"

My confidence disappeared like toilet water. "Please..." My hand shook suddenly, threating to spill the blade onto his desktop. "I need to know."

His brows dropped even lower. His mouth turned down in a menacing snarl. "Cedars-Sinai," he said.

"Thank you. Thank you." I backed away, bumped into Dedrich, ricocheted off the doorframe, and raced for the parking lot.

By the time I reached the hospital, I felt breathless and a little lightheaded.

"Can I help you?" The woman who manned the front desk wore a little plaque on her chest that read *Sonata.* She was pretty, well groomed, and as calm as her name suggested. Even in my current state, I realized we barely shared a species.

"I'm here to see Lieutenant Jack Rivera." My voice sounded bestial.

For a second, she seemed entranced by my hair, but finally she managed to focus on her PC. "I'm sorry. There doesn't seem to be anyone here by that name."

"He's probably in ICU," I said, but she shook her perfectly coiffed head without glancing at her screen again.

"I'm afraid you're mistaken. We—" I reached across the desk, grabbed her by her plastic name tag, plus a good deal of smock, and dragged her up to the counter.

"Tell me where he is, you prissy little—"

"Christina?" The voice behind me was snappy, heavily accented, and familiar. "Is that you?"

I glanced over my shoulder.

Rivera's mother stood not three paces behind me. She was dressed to the nines in a blood-red bodycon and three-inch heels. Her arched brows reached for her blue-black hairline. I felt dusty and kind of extraterrestrial.

"Hello." I cleared my throat, remembering the mind-blowing scene in the restroom not so many weeks before. "Rosita."

"What do you do here?" Her eyes sparked with protective zeal, like a sleek mother bear protecting her only cub.

"I, um ... I came to see ... Jack."

She narrowed cool jalapeno eyes. "Why?"

I felt shaky and winded. "Is he okay? Tell me he's okay."

She studied me in silence. Seconds ticked madly away. "So you *do* love him."

A thousand denials raced through my mind, but I couldn't quite voice them. "I try not to." My voice was little more than a whisper.

"Such is the way with men who are difficult but worthy, no?" Her smile was oddly melancholy, strangely proud. "Ah, well ... perhaps you should release the pretty receptionist, then."

"Oh ..." I blinked and set Sonata free. She stumbled backward with a little huff of relief mixed with outrage, but I barely noticed her indignation; she wasn't even armed. "How is he?"

Rosita stared at me.

"Jack." The name hurt my throat. "He's here?"

"*Si*. He is here."

I nodded, knowing nothing. "Is he ... conscious?"

She was silent for what seemed an eternity, then, "Follow me," she said, and turned briskly away. The hallway was a labyrinth of white on white.

We stopped in front of room 320. "I will leave you alone," she said, and turning on her murderous heels, marched away.

I took a deep breath, prepared for the worst, and stepped inside.

Rivera, scruffy faced and handsome as hell, was sitting up in bed. His guest, fat chested and flirty, was perched on the mattress beside him.

I could do nothing but stare.

Then she leaned toward him and giggled.

Maybe that's what set me off. But maybe it was the bone-wearying fatigue. Or the aching muscles. Or the fact that I am, beneath it all, no more than a wild-ass wolverine.

Whatever the reason, I crossed the floor in three stiff strides.

"McMullen!" I could just see Rivera's shocked expression past the woman's left shoulder.

"What the hell's going on?" Maybe it was my snarl that had her slipping from his bed to face me.

"What are you doing here?" Rivera asked.

"What's *she* doing here?"

She drew herself up like a snotty choir conductor. "I'm his therapist, and you shouldn't—"

"His *therapist*?" My tone may have lost its honeyed quality of just a few moments before, but at least I didn't pull out the cutlery.

She raised her chin, imprudently game. "Senator Rivera hired me to massage his leg, so—"

"Get out."

"I haven't even given—"

"Get the hell out," I growled, and she got, skittering past me with a wiggle and an accusatory backward glance.

I shifted my attention to Rivera.

"You weren't supposed to return until I contacted you," he said.

"Was it all a ruse?"

"What?"

It hurt to say the words, but I managed to push them out. "Is this Kurt Hudson all over again?"

"What the hell are you talking about?"

I shook away thoughts of my ex's alleged death. "Are the Black Flames even real?"

"Have you been smoking something? Let me see your pupils," he said, and reached for me.

I swatted his hand away. "My damn pupils are fine! Tell me the truth. Were you just trying to get rid of me?"

The room fell into silence. He seared me with his deep-water gaze.

"Look at you." His voice was gravelly, thick with emotion.

I winced, touched my spider-web hair. "I haven't had a lot of time to—"

"You think I'm crazy?"

"Well, maybe—"

"Any man in his right mind would want you."

I stopped my fidgeting, stared at him. "In your opinion, are you in your right—"

"Come here," he rumbled, and pulled me onto the bed.

His chest felt as hard as granite against mine, his hand strong when he cradled the back of my head.

"Jesus, McMullen! Jesus!" He sounded scared and desperate and relieved all at once. "You weren't supposed to come back until I told you it was safe."

"But..." It felt sinfully good in his arms, traitorously comforting. "How were you going to do that? You didn't know where I was."

"I would have found you." He drew back, just far enough to meet my gaze with piercing eyes. "I would have found you anywhere."

Something warm and wonderful exploded inside me. And then I was crying.

"Hey, hey." He cuddled me against his body, stroking my hair. "It's all right. It's okay now."

"You're wounded." I wasn't entirely sure if that's why I was crying. I mean, geez, take your pick.

"It's just my leg. I've got an extra."

I snuffled a sob.

"I'll be all right," he promised.

"What about the Black Flames?"

"Daiki's dead. He got his licks in." He shifted his wounded leg gingerly. "I was lucky, though; his bullet went through muscle. No bone. No major blood vessels."

"You were unconscious?"

He shook his head, eyes never leaving mine. "Moments. Just a matter of seconds. I'll be discharged tomorrow. Next day at the latest."

"But your beautiful muscle..."

He grinned crookedly, sobered quickly. "It's over." His inhalation was long and slow, making his chest rise dramatically beneath me. "Most of Daiki's underlings are incarcerated." I felt the tension in his body tighten and ease. "We have a strong case against them."

I closed my eyes and slid into the welcome warmth of his embrace. "I should have been here for you."

"No, you shouldn't have."

"You were in danger. You could have died and I would have..." I stopped myself before hysteria grabbed me, and lifted my watery gaze to his. "I don't know what I'd..." I touched his cheek. It felt rough and solid beneath my trembling fingers. "What would I do without you?"

"Grieve for the rest of your life," he said. "Never have sex again."

Tears leaked from my eyes.

He chuckled and, wiping the tears away with careful tenderness, took my hand in his. "I'm fine," he said.

"You're not. You're..."

"You're safe. In my arms. In my bed. Life's perfect. Or it would be..." He trailed his thumb across the palm of my hand. "If you'd close that door."

His meaning sunk into my brain like hot buttered rum. "What about..." A hundred potential problems. "Your mother?"

"If I remember correctly, she's pretty good at standing guard." His voice was low and suggestive, firing up a thousand sexy possibilities.

But I shook my head. "That would be..." He kissed my knuckles. The sensation flittered like fireflies up my arm. "Wrong," I breathed.

"Are you sure?" he asked, and kissed my wrist.

Sometimes lust is sneaky, but sometimes it hits you like a mallet. I struggled under the blow. "I'll get the door," I said, and turned, but he still held my hand. And suddenly, his expression wasn't so amiable.

"What happened to your arm?" he asked.

Chapter 32

Guilt, a little gift from mothers and Catholics everywhere.

—*Christina McMullen*

"What?" I glanced at my arm. I'm not sure how I had forgotten about the fights, the bruises, the wounds. But for a short time they had entirely slipped my mind. "Oh, it's nothing."

"Nothing?" He pushed the flannel sleeve toward my elbow, saw the discoloration, and speared me with his gladiator eyes. "What the hell happened?"

I have no idea why I felt guilty. I'm just going to go ahead and blame it on Catholicism. "I don't think it's good for you to get upset."

"Upset?" He already sounded like he might bust a blood vessel. I wasn't sure if I should be flattered or punch him in the face.

"I'm fine," I said. "Really."

"Tell me what happened."

"I just... had a little trouble." If a little trouble was a pair of oversexed twins, grueling combat training, and attempted rape/dismemberment thrown in for good measure.

"With who?"

I shook my head. "Just... a customer."

His eyes bored into mine.

"I left here with nothing, Rivera," I reminded him. "No cash, no credit cards, no phone. Barely enough gas in my…*your* car to make it a hundred miles. I had to make some money." I thought back, realizing suddenly that I needed time, probably a lot of time, to think things through. I forced a shrug. It was about as casual as a land mine. "I got a job as a waitress."

"Let's skip to the part where some asshole touched you," he snarled.

"If you promise not to become distraught I'll—"

"Who did this to you?"

"Hey, Lieutenant…" I turned at the chipper voice. A too-pretty nurse in lavender scrubs and a ponytail was peeking past the curtain. "It's time for your sponge—"she began, but he didn't even glance up.

"Get out," he said.

She jerked, froze, then scooted out of sight.

Something warm and fuzzy purred inside me.

"Tell me," he said.

I shook my head. "It was nothing, really. Just—"

"Nothing?" His fingers had formed a fist. His knuckles were scathed. I picked up his hand and kissed them.

"Just a scuffle," I said, and stroked his wrist. "He didn't hurt me. Not really."

His fingers eased open a little. "How'd he look?"

"What difference does it make?" I asked, and felt suddenly that it made none. It was over. Past. I was ready to forget. To move on. To make love. I kissed his wrist. His fingers unfurled a bit more, but his expression was as kick-ass as ever.

"Tell me," he said.

I swallowed and lowered my gaze to his hand. It was easier to speak with his fingers in mine. "He was just a..." I shook my head, shoving the ugly memories behind me. "A man at the restaurant where I worked. Where I stayed."

"I'll kill him!" His voice was low and brutish. I managed not to smile.

"You can't kill him," I said.

"Is that what *he* told you? That he's so fucking tough he's untouchable?"

I almost laughed at his vengeful tone, his possessive protectiveness. Life seemed right suddenly, easy.

He watched me, eyes scalding. "Give me a physical description."

"It doesn't matter, because—"

"Doesn't matter? I send you away to keep you safe. Worry every fucking day that you might be dead in a ditch somewhere. And now you're battered like a..." He ran out of words, clenched his teeth. "Tell me how he looked."

"It doesn't matter, because he's already in jail." I wasn't ready to tell him about Hiro. There were too many uncertainties, too many tangled emotions.

His brows dropped lower. "In jail?"

"Yes. I..." Didn't know how much to tell him. He'd obviously been through enough himself. "He...grabbed me. Said some vile things. So I told the authorities."

"You told the cops that he grabbed you."

"And...said mean things."

"And they took him into custody."

"It's not L.A. There's not much going on." It's possible I had never told a bigger lie.

He inhaled carefully, exhaled slowly. "Describe him for me," he said, tightening his hand around mine.

I stifled a sigh, bumped a shrug. "Medium height, I guess."

"Be specific."

"Five ten, maybe. Medium—"

He started to speak, but I corrected myself before he could. "A hundred and sixty pounds."

"Ethnicity?"

"British."

"British?"

"Caucasian. Caucasian, I guess."

He scowled but continued. "Hair color?"

"Light brown, worn kind of long." I felt a little sick thinking about the Carver, but I pushed on.

"Any distinguishable scars?"

"Not that I noticed."

"Tattoos?"

"Don't think so."

"Teeth?"

"Yeah," I said, and reveled for a moment in the fact that Rivera was there, that he was safe. That I wasn't alone. Gratitude swelled in me, leaving ashy terror in its wake.

"*Yeah*?" he questioned.

"He had teeth," I said, and linked my fingers in his. "How about I close the door now?"

Fire stoked in his eyes, but he kept it banked. "You were in danger. Because of me. Because of..." He gritted his teeth, squeezed my fingers.

"It wasn't your fault."

"Whose, then?"

I opened my mouth to object, but he spoke first.

"Whose, Chrissy? When you're around, I can't keep my head on straight. Can't concentrate. Can barely function.

I'm an officer of the law, for God's sake, and all I can think about is how you feel. How you look."

I liked the way this was going. "How do I feel, Rivera? How do I look?"

"Perfect," he said, and kissed me.

"Screw the door," I whispered. He chuckled and tilted his forehead against mine.

"God, I was so worried about you. Not knowing if you were alive or dead."

"You told me not to call." I pulled back a little. Our faces were inches apart.

His gaze was hot with the tail end of tension, the beginning of relief. "You did the right thing."

"I was worried, too."

"Were you?"

"Harley gets colicky if he doesn't get his meals on time."

He snorted.

I squeezed his fingers, all kidding aside. "He's okay, right?"

"He's ecstatic. Probably chasing Rocky around the dog park right now."

Sloppy relief sloshed through me, then disappeared like a double-stuffed Oreo. "With Rocky... and Tricia?"

"Don't get all riled up."

"He's with your ex?" Tricia Vandercourt was cute as a button and sweet as a candy cane. I was neither of those things. Generally, the most flattering expletive used to describe me is *prickly*.

But he slipped his arm around my back and pulled me closer, apparently unconcerned about the barbs. "She's good with dogs."

"So is Eddie. Why couldn't *he* keep him? Or Micky or... hell, for all I know, Jack the Ripper's swell with—"

He laughed. "Mama delivered Harley. I never even talked to Trish. But it would have been worth it just to see the jealousy in your eyes." He kissed me again.

"This isn't jealousy."

"No?" His fingers were scaring up a buttload of twittery feelings and he hadn't even reached the good stuff yet.

"It's killer rage."

"Yeah?" he said, and skimmed his hand beneath my waistband.

My hormones, unattended for far too long, threatened to send me spiraling into spontaneous orgasm. Which would have been embarrassing as hell, but possibly worth it.

"Better watch out," I rasped, trying to stay lucid. Orgasmically lucid. "I've learned some new moves."

"Moves!" He froze, scowl replacing his more congenial expression with strike-force speed. "Did he try to get you in bed? *Did* he get you in—"

"I meant defense moves," I said, deftly defusing him even though I kind of enjoyed firing him up.

"Oh," he said, and slipped his hand onto my abs ... which I had ... actual abs. I had barely noticed my new musculature until that moment. Funny how all that trying-to-stay-alive stuff will distract you from something you've been trying to achieve since the day you were spanked into the world. "You've been working out."

"Some." I was becoming a master of understatement.

"So that you can protect yourself." He drew his hand away. His expression was self-incrimination at its finest. "Because no one helped you. No one took care of you."

"I can take care of myself, Rivera," I said. "I don't need you."

His eyes bored into mine.

"But that doesn't mean I don't *need* you," I whispered, and fisting my fingers in his hair, kissed him with everything I had.

"Jesus!" he said, and rolled me to my side. His hands were everywhere.

He tore at my pants. I ripped at his stupid-ass hospital gown.

"Jack!" someone gasped.

I jerked around. A woman stood in the doorway. She was dark-haired, buxom, and beautiful. She was also pregnant.

I rose slowly. A growl rolled up from below decks, but she didn't cower, didn't back away.

Either very brave or very stupid.

"Mac..." Her voice was a throaty rasp.

I stumbled, mind tripping over itself as facts and fears tumbled around in my head. "Who...?"

"Mac!" she cried, and ripped off her wig. Strawberry-blond hair rippled to her shoulders.

"Laney?"

She staggered toward me. I ran to meet her. We fell into each other's arms.

"You're okay? You're..." Her fingers trembled against my cheek.

"I'm fine. I'm good," I said, but she was crying. Weeping like a child, tearing me apart.

"I'm sorry, Laney." I gripped her hands. They were cold and shaky. "I couldn't call. Couldn't—"

"Where were you? Rivera wouldn't tell me. All he said was that you were safe, but—"

"I *was* safe. Completely safe."

"Then why couldn't you call? I was half-crazy with worry."

"I'm sorry." I shook my head, guilty yet again. That I'd barely spared a moment to realize how terrified she would be for me. "It was just…" What was it? I had no words to explain, and maybe no real desire. Not now, anyway. "Really busy." Okay, maybe that was a bit of a stretch, but seeing her so shaken rocked me to the core.

"Mac…" She squeezed my fingers, held my gaze, reading me like no one else could.

"I'm okay," I said, and took a deep breath as my world settled cautiously. "Really."

She inhaled audibly, exhaled long and slow. "You scared the life out of me," she said, and winced as if in physical pain. "Almost."

"You shouldn't have come all this way," I said, remembering her delicate condition. "You know—"

"Chrissy…" Rivera said, but I ignored him.

"Where's Solberg?"

Laney grimaced, and I froze.

"What's wrong? He didn't let you drive alone, did he? Holy crap! He's such a moron. I'm going to rip him a—"

"Chrissy…" Rivera said again.

"Don't you defend him!" I snarled. "Look at her, she's practically falling off her feet. How could he—"

"Lie down," he said.

"What?" I turned toward him with a start.

"She's in labor," he said.

Chapter 33

Bitchiness: still cheaper than the pill.

—*Shirley Templeton, mother of many and a firm believer that teenagers' tater tots should be laced with birth control*

Laney gave birth in Rivera's hospital room. One perky nurse and two snotty ones tried to convince her to mosey along to the delivery ward, but by then she was entrenched on his bed.

A doctor—female, of course—later insisted that she relocate to the birthing center, but Rivera was adamant that she do whatever she wished, and she wished to remain where she was. And to...God help us all...give birth naturally. I held her hand and tried not to pee in my pants until her husband arrived wild eyed and wiry haired.

"Angel!" He burst into the room like a disheveled little tornado and fell to his knees beside the bed. "Sweetie, what are you doing here?"

"Having a baby." There was some gravel in her voice by now. Apparently, pushing a watermelon out of an orifice more accustomed to a cucumber is not as pleasant as it sounds. "Been preparing for some time. I thought"—she paused to pant like a Labrador—"you knew."

"But this isn't how we planned it." His voice was squeaky, his Adam's apple bobbed wildly. "We were supposed to deliver at Del Mar, with our doula and our midwife and our doctor and our footed bathtub with the—"

"We're doing it here," she growled. "And we're doing it now."

Across the bed from me, I saw Solberg's face pale to cocaine whiteness. He and I had some history. Most of it consisted of him calling me a hundred versions of the word *babe* and trying to cop a feel, but since meeting Laney, he'd forgotten there were other women on the planet. His adoration was all-consuming, and because of that, I could forgive him for the fact that I had once risked my life to save his. In fact, I could *almost* forgive him for having once inadvertently touched my boob.

"Rivera," she said, face contorting, "promised she was safe. But he wasn't answering his phone anymore. And I had to find out..." Another pause as she blew out hot, gusty breaths of air. "Find out about Mac."

Remorse swamped me. I squeezed her hand tighter, though honest to God, I thought if I tried to pull my hand away my fingers might remain in her fist. "I'm okay, Laney. I'm okay now. Let's just worry about you."

She caught my gaze, emerald eyes solemn. "And the baby."

"Yeah," I agreed, and she smiled.

Then she screamed, convulsed, and tried to yank my arm out at the shoulder. After that, there was a lot of gasping and sweating and crying. But they let Solberg stay anyway, until Rivera had to pick him up off the floor and drag him, paddling pathetically with one limp foot, into the hallway.

"Almost there. One more push," the doctor said.

Cheeks red, brow scrunched, Laney pushed, and in that second she was almost... not the most beautiful woman in the world.

But in the end, she was presented with a baby. It was wrinkled, purple, and ugly as an ogre. But that wasn't the only surprise. It was also a boy.

She cried when she saw him...for obvious reasons, I thought, until she was able to speak.

"He's beautiful. Oh, he's so beautiful." She touched his goopy face, hugged his little ogreish body. "Isn't he the most beautiful thing in the world?"

At this point in my life, I had elevated lying to an art form, but I hesitated a moment, maybe to make sure she wasn't pulling my leg.

"Mac?" She looked up at me, eyes swimming with baffling adoration.

"Yeah, he's...He..." I winced, cocked my head a little. "Sure is."

"We'll name him Wesley."

"Like Buttercup's Westley?"

"Like my father, Wesley."

"Oh, right," I said, and it wasn't as if I was disappointed. I didn't need some slimy little ogre that she loved more than life named after me, even if I *had* shared my ice cream with her in grade school...kinda. I mean...

"Wesley Macaulay Butterfield Solberg."

"It's that kind of mean? The name's longer than—"

"But we'll call him Mac."

"Holy sh...moly!" I breathed, as a dose of Laney's mommy hormones struck me. "Mac? Really?"

She laughed. "If it's okay with you."

"Yeah," I said, and felt dumb-ass tears swim in my eyes. "I guess that'd be all right."

Chapter 34

Kids, just say no.

—Chrissy's mom, who forgot to do so on at least four occasions

I wandered hazily through the Maze Runner corridors of Cedars-Sinai in search of an exit, mind whirring fuzzily. No, little Wesley Mac wasn't much to look at, except maybe to lower primates...and, apparently, mothers just recovering from the throes of torture, aka labor. But little buck-toothed Laney hadn't exactly been a beauty, either, for the first decade or so, and look at her now.

High on hormones and lack of sleep, I found a door and wandered into the parking lot. Danshov's ugly Beetle winked its lights at me when I managed to press its fob. I stumbled to the driver's door.

"Hey."

I turned, startled. The man in front of me looked plump and pleasantly innocuous. Or he would have if it had been fully light and I hadn't recently been attacked by every passing Tom, Dick, and Hiro.

"Who are you?" Not very convivial, maybe, but sometimes murder attempts make me kind of snippy.

"Oh, I'm sorry, I'm Jeff. Jeff Halloway. Get inside, will you?"

"What?"

He smiled a little. "Get inside," he said, and lifted his hand. Hiro's key fob dangled from his fingers. I gasped, glanced at my empty fingers, and jerked back a step.

"How did you—?"

"Never mind that," he said.

"But I do mind. I do. Why are you..." I was babbling already. "Just take the car. You can have it."

He gave the rusted Beetle a dubious glance and smiled. "Believe me, honey, I don't want your car."

"What *do* you want?"

"Just a little conversation."

I shook my head and backed away, ready to punch or kick or scream, but suddenly I couldn't speak, could barely move.

"Don't worry," he said, tone oddly dramatic as he reached past me to open the driver's door. "You can't talk right now, but it will only last a short time."

I gawked at him, but he was already pushing me inside. I seemed unable to resist. My hands felt strangely disembodied against the steering wheel.

"That's right. Just relax. Everything'll be—"

"Stay right where you are!"

I shifted my gaze groggily to the left.

Rivera was hobbling toward us. A kindly breeze kicked up his hospital gown, giving me a momentary glance of a few of the goodies I had been bereft of for so long. But Jeff seemed unimpressed.

"Ah, shit!" he moaned. Abandoning his staged drama, he raced around the car and jammed himself into the passenger seat. "Go. Go. Go!"

The Beetle seemed to start of its own accord. We were already zipping forward before I could get my bearings.

"Holy cow, lady," Jeff said, and twisted his head to look behind him. "Another one?"

I yanked my gaze to the rearview mirror. Hiro Danshov seemed to be racing after us, running flat out, overtaking Rivera as if he were standing still.

"Eyes on the road! On the road!" Jeff yipped, and grabbing the wheel, turned us onto Beverly. "Geez, you wanna get us killed?"

I shook my head, emphatic.

"Good! Excellent. You got any others?"

"Any other what?" My voice was scratchy but functional.

"Knights. Heroes. Cavalrymen just dying to come to your..." He glanced behind him. "Holy crapola, what is he, part cheetah? Step on it."

I did, though to this day I don't know why.

"Take a left. Here!" he ordered.

I squealed onto Third.

"Why are you doing this?" My voice was raspy, my hands shaky, as if I were coming out from under anesthesia.

"I just wanted to get to know you a little."

"You wanted to..." I glanced sideways. "Oh God." The earth fell out from beneath me. "You're the guy from the parking lot. From the gym." Memories, half forgotten over the traumatic weeks, stormed in. "And from my house. You're—"

"Watch the road!" he squawked, and steered us back on track.

"Are you a Black Flame?"

"A..." He glanced to the right. "Pull in here."

"What?"

"Take a right!"

Trader Joe's parking lot was packed to the gills.

"Pull in there, between those two vans."

I did as ordered, though I was certain he was going to shove me into one of those vehicles. I'd never be seen alive again. I knew it, but I was unable to rebel.

"Damned SUVs. You can't throw a dove in the air without it crapping on one of them. Get about, what? Go ahead and turn off the car. They must get, like, two miles to the gallon? Climate change on wheels, that's what I call them. And folks wonder why their kids are yakking up their lungs with asthma and stuff. Do you want kids, Christina?"

I felt like my head had cracked open. "Who are you?"

"My brother," someone said.

We cranked our heads to the rear in tandem surprise.

Tony Amato, Sunrise Coffee's barista, sat in the tiny back seat, as cool as a Slurpee, surfer-dude hair attractively tousled, pretty eyes irritated.

"Hey, Chrissy," he said, and slumped a little against the cracked vinyl.

"I … I …" I tried to clear my head, but it seemed perpetually foggy. "How did you … ? Where did you … ?"

"What the hell, Cosmos?" my abductor asked. He sounded more miffed than surprised.

"Cosmos?" My mind was stumbling with fear, stuttering with questions. "What happened to Tony? You said your name was Tony. I like the name …" I stopped rambling with a gasp. "You said if family determined … Holy shit! You're a hit man! You're a family of hit … people."

"What? No! I wish it was something that … normal."

"Tony?" My captor snorted. "Jesus, Cosmos, you might as well call yourself Eugene or Ralph or—"

"This is Zephyr Zovello," Tony said, sounding disgusted. "He's a magician."

"Conjurer! God damn it, Cosmos, what's wrong with you? Ulysses said you sold us out, but I wouldn't believe it. I suppose you've told her everything?"

"Everything?" My voice was misty.

"The levitating alligator. The disappearing head."

"Disappearing—"

"Nobody cares how you levitate an alligator, Zeph."

"*The Middleton News* called it bitingly brilliant."

"Middleton, Ohio, population: fifteen."

"It was standing-room only." The volume was rising.

"In the little boys' room?"

"At the renowned Middleton Lyric—"

"I told you my family was crazy," Tony said.

"Why are you here?" I sounded fuzzy and kind of faint.

"Crazy!" Jeff/Zephyr cried. "We're magic geniuses."

Tony rolled his eyes, then settled his gaze on me. "You have to have a rudimentary understanding of physics, of course. But most of the work is done with pulleys and magnets—"

"What the... Well, that's just great!" Zephyr huffed. "Now we'll have to disappear her."

"Disappear—"

"We're not going to make her disappear," Tony said. If his tone were any more bored he'd have fallen into a coma. I wasn't quite so insouciant.

"He's right. You're right," I agreed, twisting vaguely from one brother to the other. "You don't have to—"

"She's just using you to gain the sacred secrets of the amazing Zovellos."

"There are no secrets of the Zovellos. Sacred or otherwise. And we're not amazing."

"She's in cahoots with Menkaura," Zephyr hissed, and snapped his accusatory gaze on mine. "Aren't you?"

"What?"

"Menkaura! The Mystical Menkaura."

"The ... the ... Las Vegas guy?" I asked, remembering vaguely, again, that, some time ago, I had met a magician while searching for Laney's missing husband.

"You actually know him?" Tony asked.

"No. Well, kind of. I talked to him once."

"Hah!" Zephyr barked. "She admits it. She's Menkaura's spy."

"*Really?*" Tony asked.

"What?" I shook my head, sure I had stumbled into some kind of alternate universe. "No. I was looking for ... for ..." I was momentarily at a loss, but the memories swarmed. "Solberg. J.D. Solberg. He'd disappeared in Vegas. And my best friend ... she was in love with him. I know ..." I shook my head. Reality was slipping away. "Inconceivable. She's beautiful and funny and kind and smart and he's ... Well, he's none of those things. Except smart, I guess. Though you wouldn't know it to look at him. Or to talk to him. Or ..." I sighed, feeling foggy. "Sometimes when two people meet, there's an exchange of qualities, a quid pro quo, sort of. Good looks for bushels of cash ... that sort of thing. That wasn't the case here. She has everything. He has nothing, except an amazing ability to make me want to barf on my shoes. I've considered hiring someone to get rid of him, of course, but ... Hey." I blinked. "Do the amazing ... what's your last name again?"

Tony stared at me in silence for a second, then, "She's not Menkaura's spy."

"Seriously?" Zephyr said, in dumbfounded disbelief. "I came all the way from Boston to protect our sacred secrets and ..." He shook his head. "No. I don't believe it. *Everyone's* heard of the amazing Zovellos."

"She's not a spy," Tony said. "She's a psychologist."

My abductor snorted. "Like you're a *barista*?" He shook his head. "And Mom thought you were the one with talent."

"What's wrong with being a barista?" Tony asked.

"It's lame, that's what. Just wait till I tell Mom you're a traitor."

"I'm not a traitor."

"Are too, a traitor and—"

Suddenly, they were scrambling over the seat, trying to get at each other like rabid dogs. Somehow, the passenger door popped open. They tumbled outside, wrestling, rolling.

It took me a moment to realize I was alone in the car. I reached for the key, but the ignition was empty. I have no idea how that happened. But it was hardly the first mystery of the day. And not one I was willing to hang around to figure out.

Wrenching open the driver's door, I stumbled to the asphalt just in time to see two men racing around the corner. Rivera and Hiro! They were dodging cars, scrambling past pedestrians.

On the far side of the Beetle, the two combatants paused, rose. Zephyr hissed something. Tony scowled, then raised a dramatic arm. There was a moment of breathlessness, a puff of smoke, and then Zephyr was gone.

Tony sighed as he turned toward me. "What else could I do? He's my damned brother."

I blinked, at the dissipating smoke, at Tony's disgusted expression.

"He ... he kidnapped me."

"He wouldn't have hurt you," he assured me. "The Zovellos are weirder than shit, but we have a catch-and-release program for *spiders*."

"Yeah, well, I'm not a spider. And he..." I felt a little breathless. "He belongs in a cell."

"LAPD!" Rivera yelled. He was still forty feet away and limping nearer, but I could see by the overhead lights that he had somehow located his badge. The amazing Zovellos weren't the only crazies in this crowd. As for Hiro, he was nowhere to be seen which was disconcerting but not all that surprising.

"Holy fuck." Tony scowled at Rivera. "Is that your ex? The guy from the restaurant?"

I winced, remembering how I had abandoned Tony for ten minutes of heavy breathing in a high-class restroom.

"Maybe."

"Maybe?"

"Promise your brother wouldn't have harmed me?"

"Swear to God, he's as odd as a two-headed bunny, but he'd give you the cape off his back."

"Step away from her!" Rivera yelled.

"It's okay. It's all right," I said. "He didn't hurt me. Nobody hurt me."

"Get down on the damn ground! Hands behind your back."

"Oh, for God's sake, he doesn't have to get down on the ground," I said. "This is Tony. The guy from The Blvd. Remember? My date."

Rivera snarled something, making me think perhaps I could be handling things better.

"He saved me," I added.

"From what?" Rivera growled.

"From his..."

Tony cleared his throat.

I shot my gaze to him. His summer blue eyes were troubled, his young brow creased. I scowled, sighed, then lifted the back of my hand to my forehead and faked a swoon.

Chapter 35

I'd rather be crazy than boring.

—*Chrissy McMullen, age fourteen, who, that said, should be pretty damned satisfied with her current state of affairs*

Being home felt surreal. I cried when Harlequin was returned to me. Bawled like a Kardashian. He slobbered on my ear, knocked me over, then lay across my prone form and whimpered with happiness.

Rivera watched, looking tired but amused.

Harley allowed me to sit up after a while, as long as I continued to cuddle. "Shirley said you told her I was going to be gone for a month, so she should reschedule my appointments," I said.

He shrugged. "I figured if they're crazy now, they'll be even crazier later. It's a win-win."

"I'm surprised you didn't take up psychology yourself," I said. "Sensitive soul that you are."

"Like a saint," he said, and pinned me with his hard-ass gaze. "So your assailant insisted that you park in the lot at Trader Joe's?"

I dragged my attention from Harlequin, who had rolled onto his back, jowls drooping. I stroked his chest. "Yeah." After my masterful faux swoon, Rivera had pretty much forgotten about Tony...and Hiro...and Zephyr. He had concentrated solely on me. And I'd enjoyed it, until he'd insisted on calling an ambulance. Then I'd felt it necessary to fake coming to. I wouldn't have minded a little R and R, but I wasn't about to pay for a gurney ride to the nearest hospital. Instead, I had moaned and sniffled and begged him to carry me. In retrospect, it had been kind of mean considering he was still recovering from a leg wound and had just done about a seven-minute mile. And since Tony was the only one with an available car, Rivera had dutifully hobbled to it.

Hiro reappeared just as the lieutenant was tucking me carefully into the back seat. Our gazes caught for a second before he shook his head in amused disgust and turned toward his Beetle. I hadn't seen him since. Not that I cared. I was just lucky Rivera hadn't felt it necessary to question me about the fleet-footed Zen master.

"Where Mr. Amato just happened to be shopping," Rivera added.

I exhaled, going for breezy. "I guess."

"That doesn't seem a little strange to you?"

"Life *is* strange," I said, and rose to my feet. "I thought you would have noticed that by now."

He watched me go to the cupboard where I keep the doggy treats. Harley scrambled to his king-sized feet and pattered noisily after me.

"*Yours* is," Rivera acknowledged. He was watching me a little more closely than I thought necessary. I was entirely unsure how I wanted to handle the situation with Tony/Cosmos and his weird-ass brother, Jeff/Zephyr. But I was safe. I was home. And I didn't want to think too hard. "It's not usually quite *that* weird, though."

I shrugged, fed Harley a heart-shaped biscuit.

"How did he get in the car?"

"Tony?"

"Yeah, Tony." He was sounding more tired by the minute.

"I don't know."

"Weren't the doors locked?"

"I think so."

"You think so, or you know—"

"He must have had the wrong girl."

"What?"

"Z... My abductor," I said, remembering I had somehow neglected to tell Rivera Jeff's real name. "I believe it was a case of mistaken identity."

He watched me, eyes narrowed. Don't ask me why I was protecting the creepy little magician. Maybe it was because he was Tony's brother, and I kind of owed Tony a favor. Maybe it was because I have brothers of my own who I didn't want to see get hurt because of some lame-ass stunt that... Nope, that wasn't it. I was sure of that much, if nothing else.

"You're not worried?" Rivera asked. "Not concerned that he'll come for you again?"

"Well, you know..." I shrugged, showed Harley another treat. "With Tony around to protect me..."

Someone growled. It might have been Harlequin, but I didn't think so.

I couldn't help but laugh. "I'm kidding," I said. "Tony just happened to be shopping at Joe's."

"And he recognized you."

"Yeah."

"In a dimly lit parking lot, in an unknown car."

"I guess."

"So he just popped into the back seat and wrestled this Jeff guy outside."

"I can't help it if he's young and strong and—" I began, but I was interrupted by the doorbell.

Rivera scowled toward the front of my little house as if it were being deliberately obstinate, but I was happy to escape the current conversation. This wasn't the first time my dialogue with Rivera had felt like an interrogation. Also not my first experience with being an irritating smartass.

I glanced through the peephole, felt my heart rate bump up a notch, and opened the door.

Hiro Danshov stood on my stoop. Shikoku was beside him.

Harlequin pattered up and snaked his neck around my legs, gaining a front-seat view without risking his bulk. I put a hand on his boxy head.

"What are you doing here?" It was Rivera who spoke. I turned toward him slightly—surprised, probably foolishly, by the abrupt animosity in his tone. Danshov took that opportunity to step inside.

He ignored Rivera completely. "I came to say goodbye."

There was something about the intensity in his gaze that made me feel a little hypoxic. "Oh, well ... goodbye."

He nodded, held my gaze. "So this is your Dane."

"Yes ..." I cleared my throat. I could feel Rivera's presence like a disapproving solar flare behind me. "Harlequin. He's a little shy."

"He is not a little anything," Hiro said.

I laughed.

"Shikoku," he said, and motioned almost imperceptibly toward the wolf/dog.

The animal strolled into the kitchen, eased onto the rug, and laid her muzzle on her paws.

"Ummm ..." I said.

"What the hell's going on?" Rivera asked, and stepped into Hiro's personal space.

Their gazes met, mercury on mocha.

"The dog will stay," Hiro said.

Rivera narrowed his mocha. "The hell she will."

Hiro stared at him. "The hell she will not."

"Ummm..." I said again, pretty sure that *this* time it would clear up any misunderstandings.

"If you did not wish for interference, you should have kept her safe," Hiro said.

"I *have* kept her safe."

Hiro huffed his disbelief. "She did not even know of the saphenous artery."

"Not this again," Rivera said.

"*Again?* Not *what*—" I began, but Hiro spoke over me.

"If you had educated her properly, she would not have been compromised."

"If you had done your fucking job, she wouldn't have been battered like a damned cod."

"You expected me to trust you?" Hiro huffed his disbelief. "To assume you were not setting me up for—"

"Jesus! Have you forgotten you owe me? That I—"

"How?" I asked.

"Don't," Rivera began, but I had rounded on him with a growl that made both dogs cock their ears.

"You knew where I was!" I snarled. "Knew all the time."

He scowled. Hiro was silent.

I took a cleansing breath. "I would like you to tell me how."

"Listen, McMullen..." But I stopped Rivera with a slice of my hand that had Shikoku rising to her feet and Harlequin hiding behind her.

"I want to know how!"

"The Black Flames were raising hell. Shit! They offered a reward for you! Do you realize—"

"There was a tracking device in his Jeep," Hiro said.

Rivera's glare sharpened, but I pulled myself off the barb and turned toward Hiro.

"So you've known the lieutenant for..." My voice was breathy. I took a step toward Danshov. "For years?"

Hiro held himself perfectly straight. "We worked together some time ago."

"And you're a..." I shook my head. "A cop?"

"Not while there is breath in my body," he said.

Behind me, Rivera snorted. I didn't bother to kill him.

"What, then?" I asked.

Hiro held my gaze. "It does not matter."

"I told you to protect her, not beat the crap out of her," Rivera growled.

"And I could have done so," Hiro agreed. "But in this world there are many Things."

"What the hell are you talking about?"

"He told you to..." I remembered the grueling workouts, the gnawing fear... the kiss. I also remembered, rather hazily, that Hiro had told me about Rivera's injury, causing me to skitter back to L.A., *before* I jumped his bones. But at that precise moment, I wasn't sure if that made me grateful or increasingly angry. "To take care of me?"

Hiro lowered his head a fraction of an inch. "Any woman whose amour has faked his own death must learn to care for—" he began, but in that instant I tackled him.

We went down together, me on top. I jerked my knee toward his privates. He blocked the blow with his thigh. "You son of a bitch!" I snarled, and slammed my forehead into his nose.

That's when Rivera stepped in, plucking me off Hiro like an angry blueberry. I came up swinging.

"Easy. Easy now. I'll handle—" he began, but I wasn't foolish enough to let him finish. Instead, I twisted out of his arms and thumped him in the chest with both hands.

"Were we under attack?"

"*What?*" he asked, and took a step toward me.

I'm not sure, but I think I might have been frothing at the mouth. "At your place ... after the incident at the gym ... when I went to you for help ... were we or we were not under attack by the Black Flames?"

"Listen, McMullen, the Flames are nothing to fool with. They're killers. Without morals. Without—"

"But they hadn't come to your house, had they?"

A muscle twitched in his jaw. "I was worried about you. Couldn't take a chance—"

"Who was it?"

"What?"

"Your kitchen window. I heard it break."

He held my gaze. Seconds ticked away. "Sometimes the neighbor kids get a little carried away playing ball," he said.

I stared at him, mind whirring. "Are you serious?"

"Yeah. It's a problem. Damn teenagers—"

A pulse thundered in my temple. There was a pretty fair chance my head might explode. "I was marooned with a bunch of cannibalistic ..." I paused, exhaled, caught my breath. "Shots were fired," I said, certain of that much.

Rivera managed to hold my gaze, but his lips twitched, just a little.

"*Weren't* they?" Okay, maybe I wasn't *absolutely* certain about anything.

"Davey Kipling's been having some trouble with his air-to-fuel ratio."

I shook my head, slowly, so my world wouldn't swing out of orbit.

"A car backfired," Hiro said, interpreting for me.

I took my time ingesting that. "And the vehicle that followed me?"

"Guess you about ran over one of the Jorgenson kids." Rivera shoved his hands in the front pockets of his jeans. "Took me a full week to convince Tad to drop the charges."

I inhaled leisurely, still thinking. "I thought I heard gunshots from your kitchen."

Rivera watched me in silence, foolishly allowing me time to consider the possibilities.

"You fired your weapon," I said. "To make me believe we were under attack. To make me believe—"

"Just—" Rivera said, but I threw back my head back and laughed, guffawing at the ceiling like a wild hyena.

When I was done, Rivera was staring at me. Hiro had narrowed his eyes. Only Harlequin was wise enough to take cover. "I bet I scared the bejesus out of those kids when I came ripping through your garage door, huh?"

"I know you're mad," Rivera said, and peaceably raising a hand, took a step toward me. That's when I spun, dipped, and kicked him in the chest. He stumbled backward, struck his injured leg on the couch, and dropped to the carpet.

I prepared for the kill, but a voice from the doorway stopped me. "Mac?"

"He knew!" I snarled.

"What's going on, honey?" Laney's voice was soft, placating.

"Maybe this is a bad time." Solberg's voice was as timid as a kitten's when he stepped in behind her.

"He knew where I was, Laney. Knew all the time. I was so..." I wiped my nose on the back of my hand, turned shakily toward her and the baby-sized bundle she carried. "I didn't know if he was alive or dead. And it was all a lie."

She glanced toward Rivera, just wrestling himself to his feet. "Is that true?" she asked.

"The Black Flames—" he began, but she nailed him with her never-lie eyes.

"Is it true?"

"I sent the coordinates to Danshov. Told him to look after her."

She nodded once, turned toward the other dumbass in the room. "You're Danshov, I assume."

I'll say this for Hiro, he could look at Elaine without falling to his knees. It was more than could be said for most men with a full pair of testicles. "And you are the friend she would die to protect."

Her eyes filled with tears. She narrowed them, studying him. "What about you?"

He watched her, filled his lungs, let his head fall back half a degree. Something not quite human passed between them. "Everyone dies... even *wuwei hua*," he said, and speared me with his haunting eyes.

"What the fuck does that mean?" Rivera asked, and took a limping step forward. Elaine held up a hand, stopping him, addressing Hiro.

"Why didn't you tell her the truth if you were there to keep her safe?"

"The truth is a dangerous machine driven by few, manipulated by many."

"Oh for fuck—" Rivera began.

Hiro twisted toward him. "You do not deserve her!"

Rivera snorted a laugh. "And you think you do?"

"How many attempts must be made on her life before you—"

"I wasn't the one who let her—"

"Leave." Laney's directive was soft but incontestable.

We all faced her.

"You should go now," she added quietly.

"Listen—" Rivera began.

"I do not—" Hiro said.

"I'll wait in the car," Solberg promised.

"I didn't mean you," she said, and reached for his hand.

He nodded and clasped her fingers in a terrified but brave manner that a less enlightened women might find endearing. As for the other two asshats, they were still faced off like ... asshats.

She raised her perfect brows at them. "We'll let you know," she said.

"Elaine ..." Rivera began, but Laney spoke first.

"She's had enough, Jack," she said.

He caught my gaze, held it steady, then glared at Hiro for a second before turning toward the door.

"You too," Laney said, and nodded at Hiro.

He shifted his hot mercury gaze to mine. "The Things will not bother you, though they are here."

"What?"

"It is said that they plan to open a restaurant in the city."

"What city? *This* city? The twins?"

"Neither will the one called Jeff harm you."

I almost stumbled back as the truth struck me: While Rivera had been rushing me into the backseat of Tony's car, Hiro had been hotfooting it after my abductor. "What did you do?"

He raised a brow.

I took a threatening step toward him.

"We spoke," he said, though, as usual, he seemed more amused than terrified.

"Is that some dumb-ass euphemism?"

He laughed. Actually laughed. The sound was soft and low and disturbingly erotic. "He is hale, *wuwei hua*," he said. "But he is ... enlightened where you are concerned."

"You found Halloway? Where is he?" Rivera asked. "What's his real name?"

Hiro shifted his attention to the lieutenant.

Their gazes clashed, then they stepped toward each other, heads lowered.

"Quit it!" I snapped. They stopped. I inhaled, flexed my fingers, softened my tone. "I'm tired," I said, "but I swear to God if you two don't get out of my sight I'll rip off your heads and feed them to the dogs."

They looked mad enough to eat bullets, but finally they turned and shuffled out the door in tandem ill-content.

The house fell silent. Harlequin scooted across the floor on his belly toward Shikoku.

"*Wuwei hua?*" Laney asked.

"It means 'weakling' in ... some dumb-ass language," I said, and dropping onto the couch, covered my face with my hands. "You'll let them know about what?"

"Which one you choose."

"Which one ..." I huffed my outrage. "I'd rather be shackled to a freight train. I'd rather be buried alive. I'd—" I was just getting started, but she had already moved on.

"You okay?"

"No." I closed my eyes. "Maybe. Probably. Why do men hate me?"

"Are you serious?"

"Rivera didn't even bother to let me know he was ..." I lost my breath for a moment. "I was actually *worried* about that ..." I glanced at baby Mac. It's hard to swear around an infant who bears your name. "Dummy," I finished lamely. "And Hiro..."

"What about Hiro?" She was silent for a second, then, "Has he always called you 'fearless flower'?"

"What?" I straightened, concerned that labor had driven her mad.

"*Wuwei hua,* loosely translated, means 'fearless flower.'"

I shook my head, but I never actually doubted her accuracy; Laney was born speaking languages I've never even heard of. "He was complimenting me?"

She shrugged.

"After the hell he put me through, he..." I paused, trying to catch my breath. "He has a crush on me?"

"At least," Laney said.

"Men suck!" I said the words with a fair amount of feeling.

Little Mac whimpered. Laney rocked him with that age-old rhythm women who aren't me seem to instinctively understand. "Honey," she said, glancing at Solberg, "could you run out to the car and get—"

"Absolutely. Coming right up. Be right back," he wheezed, and shot out the door.

I raised my brows at his hasty exodus.

She gave a minimalistic shrug. "I gave him the miracle of Mac," she explained.

"So he has to act like a rabbit on speed?"

"So he has to spend the rest of his life trying to repay me."

"Holy... moly," I said, voice fizzling. Not swearing was almost worse than men.

"Are you okay, Mac?" she asked.

I inhaled, filling my lungs with the feeling of stability and home and friends of varying species. Harlequin gave Shikoku's left ear a tentative lap with his velvety tongue.

"It's been kind of a bad month," I admitted.

She shook her head. "You're the toughest person I know."

I thought about that for a moment, then, "I *am* a pretty kick-ass chick."

"And the best," she added.

"Still kind of high on the mommy hormones, aren't ou?"

She laughed, watched my eyes for a second longer to make certain I wasn't going to implode, then lowered her loving attention to the baby in her arms.

I stepped up close, sharing in the moment.

"Isn't he beautiful, Mac?"

Wesley Mac Butterfield Solberg squinted up at me from a face that looked alarmingly like a constipated Shar-Pei's. I winced and tried to lie, but as practiced as I was, I couldn't pull it off. Not with Laney. "No, honey, he's not," I said. "He's really not."

"Are you sure?" She glanced up, surprised and oddly unoffended.

"He doesn't even have hair," I said.

She stroked his bald pate as if it were a Golden Globe.

"And he's…" I gazed into his wizened little face. "He's kind of blotchy."

She kissed his cheek.

"In fact…" I tilted my head, searching for the human in him. "He looks kind of like Solberg."

"He does, doesn't he?" she said, and sighed happily.

"Only smaller and wrinklier."

She smiled, glowing like Madonna on an estrogen high. "Yeah, but you still want one, don't you?"

"Y—" I began, then snapped my gaze to her face, fear folding over confusion in my battered system. "What? No!

Are you kidding? Can you imagine me with a—" I huffed a breath. "I have the maternal instincts of a ... McMullen."

"You want one," she said.

"No, I don't. Of course, I don't, and even if I did, who would father ..." I flapped a hand toward the door through which Danshov and Rivera had exited. "I mean, okay, they're mildly attractive, and Hiro's pretty cerebral in that hotter-than-hell, Zen ..." I was beginning to sweat like a mule. "But Rivera ..." I remembered the thrum of his heartbeat as he cradled me against his rock-hard chest in the backseat of Tony's car. Remembered a dozen wild instances when he had come charging to my rescue in the nick of time.

My gaze met Laney's. The universe stood still to the count of ten.

"Holy ... macaroni," I breathed, and felt the truth strike me like a bullet to the brainpan. "What am I going to do?"

"That's the question, isn't it?" she said, and laughed as if all was right with the world.

Discover More by Lois Greiman

Chrissy McMullen Mystery Series:

Not One Clue

One Hot Mess

Unmanned

Unscrewed

Unplugged

Unzipped

Uncorked

Hope Springs Series

Finding Home

Home Fires

Finally Home

Home in the Hills Series

Hearth Stone

Hearth Song

American Historical Romance:

Surrender My Heart

The Gambler

European Historical Romance:

Highland Wolf
Highland Flame
Highland Jewel
Highland Heroes Box Set
Highland Hawk
Highland Enchantment
Highland Scoundrel
The Lady and the Knight
Bewitching the Highlander
Tempting the Wolf
Taming the Barbarian
Seducing a Princess
The Princess Masquerade
The Princess and Her Pirate

Paranormal Romance:

Charming the Devil
Seduced By Your Spell
Under Your Spell

About the Author

Lois Greiman was born on a cattle ranch in central North Dakota where she learned to ride and spit with the best of them. After graduating from high school, she moved to Minnesota to train and show Arabian horses. But eventually she fell in love, became an aerobics instructor and gave birth to three of her best friends.

She sold her first novel in 1992 and has published more than thirty titles since then, including romantic comedy, historical romance, children's stories, and her fun-loving Christina McMullen mysteries. A two-time Rita finalist, she has won such prestigious honors as Romantic Times Storyteller Of The Year, MFW's Rising Star, RT's Love and Laughter, the Toby Bromberg for most humorous mystery, and the LaVyrle Spencer Award. Her heroes have received K.I.S.S. recognition numerous times and her books have been seen regularly among the industry's Top Picks!

With more than two million books printed worldwide, Ms. Greiman currently lives on the Minnesota tundra with her family, some of whom are human. In her spare time she likes to ride some of her more hirsute companions in high speed events such as barrel racing and long distance endurance rides.

http:/www.loisgreiman.com
http://www.facebook.com/lois.greiman
http://www.facebook.com/ChrissyMcMullenMysteries
Blog with Lois at ridingwiththetopdown.blogspot.com
Follow Lois on Twitter @loisgreiman

Made in the USA
Middletown, DE
07 April 2017